The
GIRL
ACROSS
the
WIRE
FENCE

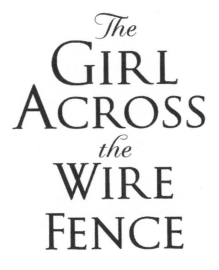

The GIRL ACROSS the WIRE FENCE

IMOGEN MATTHEWS

Bookouture

Published by Bookouture in 2021

An imprint of Storyfire Ltd.
Carmelite House
50 Victoria Embankment
London EC4Y 0DZ

www.bookouture.com

ISBN: 978-1-80019-716-9
eBook ISBN: 978-1-80019-715-2

Prologue

Kamp Amersfoort, Holland

Late summer, 1944

The sun beats down but still they make him stand there, his flimsy uniform offering little protection against the scorching heat. His skin is on fire and his tongue now sticks to the top of his mouth. *How much longer?* he wonders.

A clock chimes out the hour, informing him it is midday, when the privileged few will be lining up at the canteen for lunch. He can only imagine what it's like. The food he knows tastes foul, a ladle of something lukewarm and stinking, but food all the same. His stomach gurgles and the bored guard stops his walk up and down outside the twisted wire, and sniggers.

Another hour passes and he squints skywards to see how far the sun needs to inch before it edges behind the watchtower to his left. He glances at the jagged wire, its coiled tendrils ready to ensnare him. All it will take is one small stumble – he's seen it happen. He inhales sharply as he pulls himself upright.

Why call it the rose garden? There are no sweet-smelling roses or spiky thorn bushes to wander through and enjoy. Just bare concrete, barbed wire and misery surround him.

His left knee begins to tremble but he's determined not to let his exhaustion show. Any excuse for the guard to scream abuse and beat him with his hard wooden bat. He's seen it – any prisoner dropping to the floor will be dragged away and dealt with.

He stares hard at the beech tree over the perimeter wall, the soft green leaves fluttering in a breath of air. For one mad moment, he envisages grabbing hold of one of the branches that dangles tantalisingly close and catapulting himself out to freedom. Instead, he closes his eyes, remembering the avenue of beech trees he used to walk down, arm in arm with his sweetheart. It was their shortcut through the woods and they liked to sit on the bench halfway along. That bench was where he never quite had the courage to make the promises he wished he had now.

The distraction seems to have worked. He doesn't know when it happened but he is now half in shadow. It can't be much longer.

A commotion from outside the gates brings him to his senses. A horse whinnies, then a clatter of hooves, and a boy's voice calls out, 'Whoa!' The guard runs over to see what all the commotion is about, allowing him to crane his neck a little so he can take a look himself.

New prisoners stream in through the gates, some dressed smartly, each carrying a suitcase he knows they'll never see again. If only he could warn them, but what good would it do? Soon, they will line up for their first inspection, not knowing what's about to hit them. And then their initiation will take place: standing stock-still for several hours in the rose garden, testing which of them are strong enough to endure the punishments in store.

He catches another glimpse of the boy, now standing beside the horse, and sees him push his face into its mane. He knows he must be scared. As the guard marches back to dismiss him and release him from his torment, the boy turns to look straight at him. From within his wire prison, he gives the boy a slight nod, then drops his gaze to his sun-blistered feet.

Chapter One

Amersfoort, Holland

Spring, 1944

Frans

A lone figure stood bent over in concentration, thrusting a spade into the thick clods of earth in readiness for planting the seed potatoes at his feet. His dark shape was silhouetted against the golden line of the horizon, blurred by the early morning mist beginning to disperse against a lightening sky. Just visible was the fold of his dark brown jacket over baggy trousers hanging loosely around muddy clogs anchored in the soil.

It was a timeless Dutch scene – a vast flat field disappearing into the mist – it could easily have been lifted straight from an early Van Gogh painting depicting Dutch peasants tilling the soil. A scene played out by many generations of farm workers, unchanging in more than a hundred years. Yet the young man at the centre of this setting had other concerns. For four long years his country had been at war, the Nazis had infiltrated every part of people's lives, and it was only getting worse. Shops in the centre of town were closing due to shortages of food, household goods and clothing, which many suspected the Nazis were diverting to Germany for their own people. No one dared leave their houses after dark because of the strict curfew; even then people in town were petrified of the prospect of an unwelcome raid from German soldiers demanding to hand over their wireless sets, their one link to the outside world. Worst of all were the rumours of what took place behind the high wire fence just down the road. Who were these people who kept arriving on foot and in lorries at all times of the day and night? Could they really all be criminals? Often it was all he could think about. A world away from the simple farming life and everything he had ever known.

Frans straightened up, stretched his neck and rolled his shoulders. He lifted his hand to shield his eyes against the sun as it inched above the horizon and bathed the field in a soft orange glow. It was going to be a warm day and he was grateful he'd made an early start. But time was pressing on. Glancing at his watch, he knew his father would be back any minute. He was never in a good mood first thing and expected his son to be in the yard waiting to meet him and take over. Leaving his spade thrust deep into the soil, Frans slowly made his way across the uneven ground, his wooden clogs sinking into the heavy clay with every step.

Back in the yard he stamped his feet to get rid of the worst of the muck and looked up as the horse-drawn cart came clattering noisily through the gate.

'Hello Pa!' he called out and raised a hand in greeting.

His father grunted a reply and Frans noted the line of his mouth was set firmer than usual. He watched his father clamber down to unhitch the horse and hand him the reins. Nuzzling his face up close and whispering softly, Frans led the horse across to the barn and fastened the reins to the rusty old ring set high on the wall.

'Hurry up and get the bins down,' said his father impatiently. He was drawing back the bolts that secured the side of the cart, letting it drop down with a thud.

Standing side by side, the similarities between father and son were striking. Both were powerfully built and on the short side, both had piercing blue eyes and wore their short hair in a side parting. Frans was the fairer of the two; the strands of his father's thinning hair were sandy grey and his face wore the marks of a hard life outdoors tilling the land. On the rare occasions when he smiled, the corners of his eyes folded into creases, lighting up his face. It always gave Frans a warm feeling and made him smile too. Such a small thing, but when it happened Frans felt all was right with the world. But at other times, Frans was wary of being at the end of his father's tongue. Of course, he knew his words were only bluster and that he'd never lift a finger to him or his brother and sisters, but the sound of his booming voice alone was still enough to make him quake.

Between the two of them, they hoisted the metal containers onto the cobbles. Frans wheeled them into the scullery, where he tipped the potato peelings into an enormous pan ready for boiling up into a steaming mush for the cattle. He'd helped his father with this daily task ever since he was strong enough to heave the pan up onto the stove. Back then, the place where his father went twice a day to collect potato peelings to feed their cattle had been a prison. He still had an agreement to go there even now, though it had changed hands and was no longer a prison; these days everyone called it 'the camp'. Frans had heard rumours about what took place behind the high wire fence, but didn't want to believe they were true.

Frans was finishing up when Pa appeared in the doorway. 'There's something I want to talk to you about.'

Frans turned to him with a frown. What could it be now? Only last week, an acquaintance of theirs had disappeared suddenly after receiving the order to go and work for the Germans. It worried him that no one knew what had happened to the man. Frans hoped that Pa hadn't got himself into some kind of trouble, too.

'Let's get breakfast out of the way first,' said Pa, before striding over to the house. Sighing, Frans followed him in. There was no time to dwell on what may or may not be about to happen and he wasn't going to let it spoil his enjoyment of breakfast. He walked through the scullery and into the warm fug of the kitchen, where he was mobbed by the girls. First came Lien, barely more than a toddler, followed by five-year-old twins Mieke and Elsje, all squabbling for their older brother's attention. Frans's mother was at the stove, leaning over a large steaming pot of porridge while the children tugged at Frans's hands and begged to sit next to him. His ten-year-old brother Cas was already seated, swinging his legs in anticipation of a hot breakfast.

'Whoa, let off,' said Frans, laughing, and ruffled each of the girls' curly heads before going over to his mother to plant a kiss on one of her rosy cheeks. 'This smells good.' He sniffed loudly.

'Get away,' his mother said good-naturedly. 'Go and wash your hands, boy, you're filthy. Then you can give the girls their porridge and make sure they behave.'

'Yes, Ma,' he said, pulling a face at Cas, who was trying to suppress a snigger.

'That's enough, now settle down, else we'll all be late,' said Pa, catching hold of Lien, the smallest, as she chased her older sisters round the table. He swung her up in the air amid shrieks of laughter. Down she went onto her chair with a plump cushion to lift her up, so she could sit right next to her beloved papa.

Finally, the family were all seated, each with a bowl of porridge and large tumbler of milk. Frans loved it when they were crammed around the kitchen table, chatting, laughing and bickering. It was a time when Pa seemed to forget his worries, and joined in with anecdotes about what went on around the farm. Today, he was telling them about the time when he was a boy and… it was a story he'd told time and again, but the children always listened eagerly and he had to remind them to finish their breakfast so they wouldn't be late for school.

Frans watched as, one by one, the children hurriedly swallowed down their last spoonfuls of porridge and drained their mugs before noisily getting down from the table. Their mother fussed over them, making sure they were properly dressed and that the twins were wearing their own shoes the right way round. Lien was whining as she tried to get her mother's attention by tugging on the hem of her skirt. Cas waited patiently, the way Frans used to. Now it was his turn to walk his sisters to school on time, while Frans stayed behind to work on the farm. Frans couldn't help but give his brother a sympathetic look.

Finally, the children were ready to leave and their mother shooed them out into the yard, still nagging till she was sure they were absolutely ready for school. Frans was glad all that was behind him.

A quietness descended on the two left in the kitchen, the only sounds the kettle hissing gently on the stove and, from the hallway, the tick-tock of the antique wall clock.

Frans waited for Pa to speak.

He sat staring down at the table for so long that Frans wondered if he'd forgotten what he wanted to say. Finally, he let out a long sigh and gripped the table edge with his large hands. 'This war isn't going to end any time soon. I'm going to need all the help I can get to see us through the coming months.'

'Of course, Pa. You know you can rely on me,' said Frans, trying to ignore the sense of foreboding creeping over him. He knew things were bad, but his father had never spoken to him this way before.

'It's been bothering me for some time. The longer this war goes on, the harder it is to make ends meet. So far we've been lucky they haven't come stealing from us, but it won't be long until they do. I've been hearing terrible stories about the farmers over in the West, forced to hand over produce and left barely enough to feed themselves. And now we're weeks away from bringing in the harvest and I don't see how I can get my quota of workers. Anyone who's working age is disappearing over the border to work in German factories and it's almost impossible to get an exemption. At least you're not old enough to be called up.' He gazed at Frans and the creases around his eyes seemed to deepen, adding to the seriousness of his words.

'I'll do everything I can to help. You know I will, Pa,' said Frans, trying to keep the anxiety out of his voice.

'I've been thinking. I can't afford the time to go to the camp twice a day as there's too much farm business for me to organise. The harvest is coming and I need to go round the villages and visit all our regulars to make sure they can come and work for us this year. It won't be easy, as the Germans are taking more of our lads to work for them, but I'm confident we'll get by. So I'd like you to go every so often to pick up the potato peelings. The commandant won't give you any trouble and he's given me his word he'll inform the guards you're my son. He trusts me because I've been doing the job for years, even before he arrived, when it was still just a prison.'

Now the words were out Pa seemed to relax, but Frans wasn't reassured. If anything, he felt scared. He'd tried to ignore the stories Pa had started telling him from time to time, how the prisoners inside the camp were beaten, how little they received in the way of food or anything else and the cruelty of the guards. Pa had said he was sure that they delighted in making the prisoners' lives a misery.

Frans had always avoided going near Kamp Amersfoort and now his father just expected him to take over. Was it even safe for him to go there?

'Pa,' said Frans in a determined voice. 'Those guards will look at me like any other prisoner. How can you be sure that they won't take against me?'

'I've thought of that,' his father replied. 'You're only sixteen and if you take Cas with you too, no one will take any notice. You'll just be a couple of children on an errand for their father. It's what children do.'

'So, that's how you still see me? A child?' said Frans. He felt disappointed, even though he knew his father was right. Since he'd started working on the farm, Frans had been quietly pleased that his father seemed to have noted his maturity. Now he was sixteen, he felt more like a man and was pleased to take some of the weight of responsibility from his father. But as much as he felt like an adult, he could see that appearing younger would actually be to his advantage.

Pa didn't react. He spoke wearily. 'No, that's not how I see you. You're proving to be invaluable around the farm and I know you'll do a good job.'

Frans opened his mouth to speak but thought better of it. The persistent tick-tock of the clock filled the space between them as Frans processed the weight of his father's words.

Chapter Two

Frans tried to block out the sound of his brother's steady breathing in the bed next to his. It never usually bothered him how closely pressed together their beds were in the narrow space under the eaves, but now that he was unable to fall asleep, it was all he could hear. And the thought of his three little sisters sound asleep on the other side of the thin wall made him even more restless.

He threw back his bedclothes and went over to look out of the skylight. In the distance, he watched a beam of light swoop across the dark sky, sometimes disappearing entirely before soaring upwards like a huge golden bird in flight. He knew it came from inside the camp from the top of the large watchtower where a guard was on night duty. They were searching, Frans had heard, for anyone trying to escape. Jews, gypsies, people picked up in raids because they had failed to report for work in Germany, political prisoners and petty criminals dealing in black market goods – it seemed the Germans were looking for any reason to lock people up. He so wished it weren't true and feared for all the people he and his family knew, ordinary decent people who no longer felt they could venture safely outside their own homes in case they themselves ended up behind that forbidding wire fence. What made it worse were the snatched conversations people were hearing among the guards when they went drinking in town, leaving no one in any doubt that they thought the prisoners inside the camp deserved the harsh treatment they received. Frans simply did not believe such cruel behaviour could in any way be justified.

Tonight, it was perfectly quiet. There was no sound of distant barking from the guard dogs or the wailing sirens that sometimes started up for no reason to wake him from a deep sleep. He'd often feel tense as he lay in bed, as if he was waiting for something dreadful to happen – he wasn't sure what – but by morning everything would be back to normal. The familiar clatter of crockery as his mother prepared breakfast and the soothing sound of his father whistling as he strapped the horse to the cart would make him thankful that his family were still all together.

Behind him, Cas mumbled incoherently and rolled onto his side. Frans gazed down at his sleeping brother and smiled. 'I'll look after you,' he whispered, before climbing back into bed. For a long while, he lay thinking and staring up into the darkness, before eventually falling into a fretful sleep.

'I'll harness the horse to leave by six thirty. Make sure you're up and ready to leave. If all goes well, you'll be back within the hour,' Pa had told Frans and Cas earlier that evening.

'Won't I have to go to school?' piped up Cas, fizzing with excitement ever since he found out he'd be helping his big brother.

'Of course you'll be back in time for school, but you mustn't go telling your friends where you've been.' Pa leaned forward and lifted his son's chin. 'It's really important that you don't say anything to anyone.'

Cas nodded his head vigorously. 'I promise.'

'At the gates there'll be a guard and he may demand to search the cart. I always let him look inside the containers to see they're empty. Then he usually doesn't bother me on the way out. I expect he'll do an inspection your first time as they're a suspicious lot,' he told Frans as Cas stood nervously beside him.

'What are they looking for?' said Cas, screwing up his forehead.

'They search for anything they think will help the prisoners escape. I once left a couple of spades and wire cutters in the cart, which the guard tried to confiscate. I told him if he took them I wouldn't be able to work on my land, so he agreed to let me leave them at the gate. Now I always make sure there's nothing left on the cart that might give them any reason to think I'm helping the prisoners.'

Cas seemed to think about this. 'But do you want to?'

Frans's eyes flickered over to his brother, remembering he'd once asked this same question of his father.

His father smiled sadly. 'Of course I do. The people inside that camp that don't deserve to be there. Everyone knows that. If the opportunity arose, I would do all I could to help.'

Pa looked awkward and Frans suspected he didn't want to tell Cas about the rumours circulating about the ill-treatment of prisoners – there was no need to cause him unnecessary worry. But the truth was he and Cas were at risk too and shouldn't do anything to bring attention to themselves. Frans knew his father had their best interests at heart and wanted to protect them.

'My job is to go in every day and pick up the peelings so that our cattle get fed. I never forget that being allowed this valuable food waste is a privilege. None of us should take it for granted. We mustn't forget how lucky we are to be able to keep the farm going, even if the guards are a bit awkward from time to time. Now, all you have to do is sit quietly next to your brother. If you do that, no harm will come to you.'

Cas sucked at his bottom lip, something he always did whenever he wasn't sure what to say.

'Pa's right,' said Frans, determined to not to show his brother that he too was nervous about taking the horse and cart through those front gates. 'There's nothing to worry about. And you're going to love it up on the cart. If you're good I might even let you take hold of the reins.'

Cas's eyes shone brightly as his gaze darted between Frans and his father. 'Can I really?' he said.

'Really.' Frans smiled. He was warming to the idea. Knowing he'd be in charge with his brother next to him made him feel more positive about what lay ahead.

'Come on, you need to get to bed,' said his father, pulling himself up to standing and ruffling Cas's mop of sandy hair. 'We don't want you oversleeping your first time out.'

Frans began to relax once they were under way. As long as he didn't think too closely about what lay ahead, he was able to control his nerves. His father had said little about what to expect inside the camp, so he forced himself to believe that everything would be fine. Besides, Cas was proving to be a good companion, distracting him by chatting animatedly about nothing in particular. He was eager to show he could be useful by taking the reins, but he didn't really need to do much as the horse knew the way, its hooves clopping over the ruts, causing the cart to judder and jolt along the track. The fields on either side were beginning to turn green with the spring crop. A cluster of birds were busy scavenging for worms and they flapped skywards amid loud squawking as the cart clattered past. Cas burst out laughing and clapped his hands. At the crossroads, Frans took over and slowed the horse to walking pace before turning onto the avenue, lined with tall beech trees that stretched up above them, the tops of their branches meeting overhead to form an arch like the nave of an enormous church. Now and then, a shaft of sunlight pierced the canopy to catch giddy insects swirling manically in the bright beam.

Frans found himself tensing up when they approached the high wire fence that stretched away towards the front entrance to the camp. At the outer corner stood a tall wooden watchtower, the one whose swooping beam Frans often followed from his bedroom window at night. Apprehensively, he stared up at it. Up close, it was far more fearsome, more real.

'Are we nearly there?' said Cas, who was trying to catch one of the elusive insects.

'See that tree in front of us?' said Frans, pointing to an enormous beech tree that towered over their path, with a trunk as thick as four trees stuck together, their spreading branches swaying gently in the breeze. 'That tree's seen a lot of things in its lifetime, more than you or I will ever want to. Did you know that tree is more than two hundred years old?' he went on, recalling the same words his father had once said to him. He stared up between the leaves and saw a blackbird perched up high, its beak trembling as it repeated the rippling notes of its song. For a moment, he forgot his nerves.

They drew level with the huge wrought iron gates, firmly shut against anyone foolish enough to want to go in or leave. Square in the middle stood an SS guard, dressed smartly in a belted coat, shiny leather boots and peaked cap, his chiselled features betraying no emotion as he stared straight ahead with no indication he'd seen them.

'Hold the reins and wait here till I tell you what to do,' Frans told Cas, who had looked scared as soon as he spotted the guard. Frans gave him an encouraging pat on the hand, and swallowed nervously. He climbed down and walked towards the guard, who turned his stony stare onto Frans while moving his hand to the gun-shaped holder at his waist. All at once he seemed to spring to life and his hand flew to his cap in a salute, barking out, '*Heil* Hitler!', accompanied by a sharp click of the heels.

For a moment Frans hesitated, unsure of how to respond. He'd seen guards around town before, but had managed to avoid meeting any as he spent most of his time on the farm. He'd heard of people being arrested for refusing to repeat this greeting. His own father was proud that he would never show deference to Hitler, but he wasn't his father and didn't believe this was the best way of speaking to unpredictable, menacing-looking people such as the man standing before him. He decided he would simply pretend to comply and hope for the best.

So he muttered a response without enthusiasm. 'I'm Frans Koopmans, from the farm.' He concentrated on keeping his voice from wavering. 'My father usually comes to collect the potato peelings, but I've come today.'

The guard continued to hold Frans with an icy stare as he shifted his position and let his hand drop to his side. His lack of emotion was unnerving and Frans wondered if he'd been trained to behave that way.

'I can't let you in with that.' The guard flicked his hand dismissively towards the horse and cart.

Frans took a deep breath, determined to keep calm. 'My family has always picked up the food waste for our cattle. It's been agreed with the commandant.'

The guard sniffed deeply before replying. 'That may be so, but I will first need to make a search.'

Even though it was to be expected, Frans found himself tensing up. *Keep calm*, he told himself, *you've nothing to hide*. 'Please go ahead,' he said in a level voice, though his heart was pounding.

Behind him, Cas sat bolt upright in his seat. His knuckles were white from gripping the reins – it was as if he thought that any small movement would cause the horse to rear up and bolt past the guard and down the avenue.

'He wants to take a look in the cart, so you'd better hop down.' Frans spoke calmly to Cas as if his request were routine.

'And who is this?' said the guard, ambling over. He wore his peaked cap low over his forehead, almost hiding his eyes. He began circling the cart and peered at Cas, who looked terrified.

'My brother. He's here to help with the bins.'

'Is that so?' said the guard, coming up close. Cas closed his eyes tightly as if he could make him go away.

'Turn out your pockets!' The suddenness of the command made Cas jump and he let out a sob.

Something in Frans snapped.

'Leave off, will you? He's a child, not a criminal.' What Frans didn't have in height, he made up for in build; he knew he could easily pass for eighteen. He drew himself up, determined to stick up for his defenceless younger brother, even though his heart was pounding with fear.

But the guard didn't seem to notice and stood, arms folded, an unpleasant smirk curling his lip. 'Anyone unknown to us who tries to come in must be questioned and, if I think fit, must be searched. Didn't your *father* tell you that?'

Before Frans could answer, they were interrupted by the arrival of another man in uniform, who Frans recognised by his peaked cap and the insignia on his lapel. It was the commandant his father had told him about. The man stepped between the two of them and shook Frans by the hand. 'You must be Evert's son,' he said. 'Such a likeness. He told me you'd be coming in his place. And this must be?'

'My brother, Cas,' said Frans, turning to give Cas an encouraging smile. Cas raised his downturned eyes warily. 'I already told the guard we're here for the potato peelings,' Frans went on.

The commandant frowned briefly. 'Of course. There'll be no need for an inspection. You will let them through,' he addressed the guard, whose expression was back to one of cold blankness.

Frans climbed back onto the cart and waited for the officials to stand aside. He remembered to touch his cap as he guided the horse through the gates, the clatter of hooves echoing as they struck the hard ground. To their left rose a high fence topped with vicious-looking wire spikes. Briefly, Frans thought he could see the outline of two men standing behind it, but he might have been mistaken. To their right was another wire fence, separating the prisoner compound from Kamp SS, the camp's headquarters for the Nazi guards.

Frans concentrated on steering the cart past a line of low brick buildings and through a concrete arch into the vast courtyard beyond. Apart from a couple of guards in long, belted overcoats striding around the perimeter, the place was empty. Frans glanced to the far corner of the compound, noticing the shadows of dozens of prisoners behind another wire fence, some moving about, others staring outwards. It was eerily quiet.

'Where are we going?' asked Cas anxiously, following Frans's gaze.

'Shh. No questions in here. See those people over there?' he said, nodding at a group of men straight ahead. 'They're peeling the potatoes. I'll see to the horse and you can unload the containers.'

The kitchen block was a long, low building with several trestle tables and benches out front, where eight or nine prisoners sat peeling potatoes from a large mound piled up in the middle. They sat in silence with their heads bowed as Frans and Cas approached. Frans found it unsettling that none of them even looked up and how small and listless they seemed, but what unnerved him even more was that they were all so young, not much older than himself.

He watched for a moment as the men chucked the peeled potatoes into a large black cooking pot and dropped the peels into bins between them. Once full, the smallest prisoner, who looked to be the youngest, took the peels over to the cart and waited for Frans to hand down the bin.

'Shall I tip them in or do you want to?' he said, turning to Cas.

Cas looked up in surprise at being addressed. He stared at the prisoner's thin face and the grey shadows angled below his jutting cheekbones.

'In there, that's where we put them.' The man pointed at the container next to Frans.

'Cas, take the bin, will you?' Frans asked him. Cas reddened, then made things worse by dropping a load of peels as he tried to tip them in.

'I'll pick them up,' Frans heard the man say quietly. When he turned he saw him slip a few into his pocket in a panic. Cas saw it too and turned to Frans with a confused expression.

'Thank you,' whispered the young man to Frans and patted his pocket. 'See you again.'

Cas scarpered back onto the cart, where he waited for Frans to finish off. At last Frans was ready, and they rode back through the arch into the yard, which was filling up with prisoners filing into rows. A thickset guard was pacing up and down and barking out instructions in German.

As they rattled past, Frans glanced across and one or two prisoners stared back. Halfway back in a row of about ten prisoners, he caught sight of an older man who stood out with his white hair. All at once, he was reminded of his favourite uncle Geert, who had white hair and dancing blue eyes and entertained the family with his nautical stories on his rare visits. Frans looked down briefly, yet again unnerved by what he had seen. Ordinary men, who could be his friends and family, locked up and punished. He realised that some had a yellow star on their jacket, singling them out from the others for being Jewish, but others wore many emblems of different colours. His father had once told him about this discrimination, but he could no longer remember what they stood for.

The guard at the entrance had reverted to his previous stony posture and barely acknowledged them as the horse trotted through the gates; they creaked shut behind them with a decisive clang.

'Are you all right?' Frans asked Cas, when they were well away from the perimeter fence.

'I think so,' said Cas in a faltering voice. 'That prisoner, why is he so thin?'

'I can't be sure, maybe there's something wrong with him,' Frans replied. He hated himself for lying, thinking it was too early to voice what he believed to be the truth. But Cas's questions kept coming and Frans realised it would be better to be honest than pretend what they'd seen was normal.

'Surely he's not going to eat those scraps. What do you think he's going to do with them?' Cas looked across at Frans expectantly.

'I don't know, but I've heard the food in there isn't up to much. Watery soup and porridge, that kind of thing.'

'But what about all those potatoes? When Mama serves up *stamppot*, I always eat so much I get a pain in my tummy,' said Cas, his face brightening.

'They won't be getting any *stamppot*. Those potatoes are for the men who run the camp,' said Frans, wishing it weren't so. He remembered he'd had the same reaction when his father had told him how little food the prisoners were receiving.

'Why? That's not fair,' Cas kept on. 'I think we should take some food in for that prisoner. He looks as if he could do with it. We've got plenty to spare, haven't we?'

Frans sighed. He had the same desire to help, but what if it put their family in danger? 'I wish it were as simple as that, but we shouldn't interfere in things we don't understand.'

Cas fell silent. The rhythmic clip-clop of the horse's hooves and rattle of the cart were the only sounds as they made their way back home. Frans pondered on their conversation. Maybe there was a way to help, but for now he had no idea what that could be.

Chapter Three

Saskia

Saskia had always been proud of her father's drapers' shop in the centre of Amersfoort. She loved staring up at the sign bearing his name, P. Dekker, in gold lettering embossed above the door. The shop had been in the family for three generations and handed down from father to son; as an only child, she was expected to take over when she was old enough.

When she was little, Saskia was sometimes allowed to spend the afternoon in the shop with her father. He would sit her on a stool next to the counter and hand her a wooden box of buttons to sort into different colours or sizes. When the little bell above the door tinkled to announce the arrival of a customer, Saskia would swivel her head and give a coy smile at whoever had come in. She got to know all her father's best customers and they were charmed by her, sometimes slipping her a sweet when her father's back was turned. How she loved it when they asked to see the silk scarves or gloves, which he kept in shiny wooden pull-out drawers that gave a quiet sigh every time they were closed. Naturally, she was forbidden to touch the merchandise, so could only imagine how soft the butter-coloured chamois leather gloves must feel when slipped onto the perfectly manicured hands of a wealthy customer, or the gossamer touch of a turquoise silk scarf against a rouged cheek.

Paul Dekker's window displays were the talk of the town and he always made sure they showed off the latest fashions, which he faithfully updated and maintained in immaculate condition. His eye for detail, learned from his father, and pleasant manner had earned him a reputation that kept customers coming back time and again. As best he could, he kept the business going during the early part of the war, until shortages began to impact heavily on trade and the number of customers fell. Saskia remembered the shock she'd felt on visiting her father at the shop as a young teenager and discovering how much his supply of garments and accessories had dwindled. He'd explained he'd been forced to reduce his stock and concentrate on selling the bare basics needed to repair, darn and generally keep people's clothes from falling apart. But it was the only time he'd ever spoken about business matters and she'd been unaware of the seriousness of her father's situation. It never occurred to her to question him.

Besides, her mind was taken up with other things as she became older and spent less time in the shop, such as when the next Humphrey Bogart film was showing at the local cinema. Often, on Saturday mornings, she and her best friend Corrie cycled into town to catch the matinee performance. They must have seen *Casablanca* at least six times, swooning over Bogart's handsome good looks and imagining themselves as Ingrid Bergman in his arms. On Saturday mornings, the movie reels kept running and no one seemed to notice the two girls sitting at the back watching the main film through more than once. Afterwards, they would cycle home side by side, giddy with the scenes they had just seen and loudly reciting their favourite lines in fake American accents that set the other off into peals of laughter. It was the best of times.

Since she'd turned sixteen her parents had allowed her to go out one evening a week, as long as she was back before dark and, more importantly, curfew. It was a time to catch up properly with her friends Aart and Frans, whom she'd known since primary school, meeting at a local café in town. Recently, the conversation had turned to what they would all do when they left school. Frans had already left to spend more time learning about running the farm from his father. He was becoming more self-assured and different to the quiet boy she'd known at school. Sometimes she caught herself admiring him, the kind way he talked about his four little siblings and his willingness to turn his hand to any task his father gave him. Aart, too, seemed to have his life mapped out and was planning to study Law at university.

Saskia wished she could be so sure about her own life. She was dismissive about working in a shop, even the high-class one belonging to her father. Aart said she should apply to go to university and that it would open up all kinds of opportunities as a teacher, a lecturer or a mathematician, but she couldn't see herself devoting herself to years of dry academia. She'd ridiculed the idea, harbouring thoughts of something much more thrilling, thoughts she kept to herself for fear her friends might laugh at her. The secret she harboured was of going to New York and leading an exciting life as an actress or singer. She had an aunt who lived in the city who would send Saskia's mother letters about her glamorous life going with friends to shows on Broadway and eating in swanky restaurants. It seemed a world away from the deprivations of occupied Holland and provincial Amersfoort. The truth was, Saskia hadn't yet worked out what she wanted to do or how she would set about achieving it.

One evening, the family had just sat down to supper when her father announced he had some bad news. Saskia noticed, for the first time, that the angles and hollows of his face gave him a haunted look, and it made her nervous. She had never seen her kindly father look so serious. She glanced quickly at her mother, but her face revealed nothing as she spooned fried potatoes, onions and an egg onto each of their plates. Saskia wondered if she knew what he was about to say.

'I'm unable to keep the shop open any longer,' he said. 'Just for the time being, until the situation improves.' He managed a thin smile, but Saskia suspected he was covering up his deep sadness at being compelled to take such a step.

'But why? What will happen to all the customers? Where will they go for their sewing materials?' she asked, shocked at what it would mean to her family if her father was unable to provide for them.

'People will have to make do with what they've got. There's been no demand for the finer things in life for some time. We can't make ends meet on the sale of darning needles and a few spools of thread.' He gave her a tired smile.

Saskia watched his face and tried to read what was really going on behind his strained expression.

'There's another reason,' he said, accepting his plate. 'I've had several visits from the Gestapo, who are determined to make life difficult for me. They accuse me of being a Jew, even though I have the ID to show I'm not. But it seems it's not enough. They say I fit their description of someone who is Jewish.' He shook his head sadly.

Saskia had a vague recollection of her *oma*, who had died when she was only three. She remembered how she had loved being lifted onto her soft squishy lap and staring up at her *oma*'s kindly creased face. She had been too young to notice the size of her nose, but she knew about it because her father had so often joked that this was where he'd got his from. But it was no joke now. Everyone had a story about someone they knew who had been challenged by the Nazis because they did not fit their rigid view of an Aryan 'master race' of blond-haired, blue-eyed people. Saskia wondered about her own thick dark curly hair... Should she be nervous, too?

'The only way I can think of avoiding all this is by closing the shop,' her father said with a sigh. 'I saw it coming, so I've approached an acquaintance in the trade who is willing to buy up the stock and the cabinets. I've accumulated enough savings and for the time being we'll be fine. I'm sure it won't be too bad...' he finished, his voice trailing off.

Saskia felt her chest constrict as she cast her mind back to those beautiful mahogany display cabinets that her grandfather had had specially crafted for the shop. How could her father even contemplate parting with them?

'The acquaintance was very understanding and says he'll return the cabinets when this is all over,' said her father, as if guessing her thoughts.

'What's going to happen to us, Papa?' She hadn't called him that in years, not since she'd been the little girl on her stool helping her father sort out the button box. It felt right to call him Papa now. Tears pricked at her eyes and she caught sight of her mother hiding her face behind the pale pink linen handkerchief that she used to blow her nose.

'I see it as a temporary measure because I have no choice. I've seen how the Germans will stop at nothing in their desire to persecute innocent people. We have to survive,' he said sadly. 'Now, let's put it aside for now and eat up our food before it gets cold.'

Saskia stared down at her plate, at a loss as to what she could do. Her strong capable father seemed crushed by his loss and her mother was stoical in her acceptance of what was to come. It was the first time she'd seen them so vulnerable and her heart swelled with the realisation that she must find a way to help them get through this terrible, uncertain time. She simply couldn't stand by and watch her parents suffer so.

Chapter Four

Theo

The owner of the café was counting up the takings behind the bar when he called over to Theo, who was gathering the last of the glasses and wiping down the tables. *Not tonight*, thought Theo, keen to get away as he'd promised to spend the evening with Annelies. She'd only recently moved into a room in a large house round the corner from the café after starting a new job at the local primary school. The attic room was hidden away under the eaves at the top of the house with barely enough space for the narrow bed positioned under a skylight and the chest of drawers that, incredibly, contained all her possessions. It was the safest place for them to be together.

He'd promised he'd be along as soon as he'd finished work, and was looking forward to seeing her. But he knew she would be wondering why he'd been held up. It wasn't the first time, but when he'd told her he was only staying on for a drink with Piet who lived on his own and liked a bit of company, she'd said, what about her, didn't she count? But the real reason was she didn't trust Piet and his talk of anti-Nazi propaganda and she didn't want Theo getting mixed up in it. Theo had no intention of doing so, but was fascinated by Piet's anecdotes about the underground group and their activities, such as distributing pamphlets across town challenging Nazi propaganda. He made his activities sound so daring and exciting that Theo was intrigued to find out more. He resolved to have just one drink with Piet, then get away to Annelies before she started to worry.

'There's something you might be interested in,' said Piet, as he reached for a jenever bottle from a selection on the shelf behind him. Theo's heart began to beat a little faster as he watched Piet pick out his favourite, a *zeer oude* Bols, presented in a traditional brown stone bottle. Filling two tiny glasses to the brim, he held one out to Theo. 'Come and sit down,' he said, bringing the bottle to the table.

'*Proost!*' they said in unison and chinked their glasses together.

As the liquid burned a fiery trail down his chest, Theo felt any resistance he might have had ebb away. *One can't do any harm*, he told himself.

Piet leaned in and began to talk excitedly about the Resistance leader who was new to the group. He paused to fill their glasses once more. Theo smiled across at him, eager for him to continue. He was captivated by what Piet told him about the man who was part of a movement to drive the Nazis out of Holland and restore peace. It was clear that Piet was enamoured by what he'd heard and could hardly wait to hear the new leader speak later that evening, so when Piet suggested that Theo accompany him to the meeting, he did not hesitate in accepting.

A door painted bottle green stood to the left of them as they arrived outside a darkened café. Piet looked all about him before rapping out a series of knocks that Theo recognised as the first beats of Beethoven's Fifth Symphony. After some seconds came the sound of muffled footsteps descending a staircase. Two men dressed in black overcoats and hats pulled low over their foreheads appeared at the door. They nodded a greeting to Piet, but took no notice of Theo right beside him. Theo was slightly unnerved by the ease with which he'd been allowed in, but assumed Piet's authority must be enough. He followed them up the steep narrow staircase which led to a densely packed smoky room lit by a single bulb in the centre.

Men stood around in groups, lit cigarettes in hand and conversing in animated voices. The room was full of excitement, crackling with anticipation, as if something momentous was about to happen.

'We'll get a good view over there. He's about to start,' called Piet over his shoulder. He jostled his way through the crowd to a spot close to a stack of wooden boxes resembling a makeshift stage. They didn't have long to wait. From a door at the back of the room strode a man, who looked to be in his thirties, wearing a brown suit and matching trilby. Theo watched spellbound as the man Piet had described took his place on the stage and surveyed the room, waiting for a hush. Then he announced himself as leader of the underground group for the area, and a massive cheer went up from the crowd. He proceeded to whip them up with story after story about the appalling treatment meted out to ordinary innocent people, friends and neighbours, all in the name of the so-called Fatherland.

'Do you want to keep living in fear at the sound of hobnailed boots marching outside your house, the dread of thumping on your door and a load of thugs forcing their way in?' he roared. 'Turning your house upside down, all because it's forbidden to own a wireless set? Or because someone, some Nazi sympathiser, has betrayed you because you've helped people *in hiding*? Do you want to live in fear like that?'

The crowd erupted into chanting: 'Out with the *moffen*! Out with the *moffen*!'

The speaker waited for the noise to die down, before speaking again, more quietly. 'How many of you know someone who's been arrested by the Nazis and simply disappeared?'

Another roar erupted and almost every man, including Piet, thrust their fist into the air. 'Come on!' cried Piet, raising his voice above the din. Theo needed little encouragement to join in with the chants and found himself swept along on a tide of fervour. He was exhilarated. He had never before experienced anything like it. But as he gazed around at the intense upturned faces, he was unable to ignore his own growing unease.

The noise was so deafening that it was over before anyone had any idea what was happening. The first Theo knew of anything was when the speaker leapt down from the stage and disappeared through the door at the back of the room. That was when at least half a dozen men in heavy black overcoats came thundering up the staircase and lashed out with batons in all directions. Some of the men present tried to fight back with their fists, but were quickly overcome with a strike to the back of the head.

Theo was unable to move and could only watch in horror, rooted to the spot. His heart beat wildly. An image of Annelies flashed across his mind, worry furrowing her brow and warning him to be careful. What had he done? Why did he even agree to come?

All at once, Piet was at his side, yanking his arm hard till he came to his senses. 'We've got to get out!' he shouted and made for the exit.

Everyone had the same idea.

In their panic, they shouted, shoved and elbowed anyone in their path, causing some to stumble and slowing down their escape.

Theo lost sight of Piet as he was caught up in the surge. At one point the crowd parted and he found himself being carried down the staircase. Right in front of him, he could see the open door. He just needed to reach it.

At the foot of the stairs, he could see a dozen or so men spilling out onto the street and beginning to run. He was almost at the bottom, almost there, almost free.

The last thing he remembered was a strong hand gripping his shoulder like a vice, and a fist knocking him to the floor.

Some time later, he came round in the back of a van, sardined in a row between at least half a dozen others. He had no idea where he was or where he was being taken.

Chapter Five

Frans

The unassuming café was tucked between a row of town houses down a side street, with two large picture windows inscribed with the words *De Singel Café-bar*. Anyone passing might have thought it shut were it not for the two lanterns flickering faintly above the door.

The church clock struck six in the nearby square as Frans pushed open the door to step inside the dimly lit interior. He was greeted by a rush of warm air and the aroma of cigar smoke. The cigar smoker, sitting at the bar, looked up briefly to see who had come in.

Only a couple of tables were occupied. No one sat at the large table, which was covered with a faded blue and red Persian rug and a few dog-eared magazines. Dark wood panelling lined the walls and soft light from overhead lamps pooled onto the long bar. At the back, light bounced off the glasses and bottles of spirits were stacked up to the ceiling. At the counter, the bartender was polishing a glass to a high shine. He nodded a greeting at Frans. All in all, a typical Dutch 'brown cafe', where friends gathered undisturbed to share a drink and talk in low voices about the things that mattered to them.

For a moment, Frans stood blinking in the doorway as his eyes adjusted to the low light, before spotting his friends, lost in conversation, at a table in one corner. Removing his cap, he quickly ran his fingers through his hair and went across the room to take a seat opposite them.

'Sorry I'm late,' he said, shrugging off his jacket and hooking it on the back of his chair.

The girl shook back her dark curls and half got up so she could lean across the table to kiss Frans once, twice and three times on the cheeks. 'We thought you'd forgotten to come. I hope you don't mind but we already ordered.' Saskia glanced briefly at the two half-full beer glasses on the table. 'Were you held up?'

'My father needed help with one of the cows. She went into labour this afternoon and got into difficulties. It took two of us to get the calf out. Oh, it was nothing,' Frans said quickly, as he caught sight of her faintly disgusted expression and wished he'd spared her the details. The truth was, when she turned her beautiful dark eyes on him, he'd wanted to impress her, but the words had come out all wrong.

'You look as if you could do with a beer. Let me fetch you one,' said Aart, getting to his feet and patting his friend on the shoulder with a look of sympathy.

Saskia smiled up at Aart as he went off to the bar. He was a good head and shoulders taller than Frans and cut an imposing figure in his navy blue shirt that matched his eyes. Frans had always been a little envious of his taller, more confident friend, who had been cleverer than him at school and was popular with the girls. But it was different with Saskia, who had been the other member of their group for as long as Frans could remember. She had always had time for Frans, helping him when he struggled with his schoolwork and smiling sweetly when he managed it, but now that Frans had left school, he was beginning to feel left out. No wonder she's enamoured of him, thought Frans enviously, as he watched her follow Aart with her eyes. Not wanting to be caught staring, he dropped his gaze and began twisting his cap in his lap, conscious of the awkward silence that had fallen between them.

'Well, this is nice…' said Saskia just as Frans opened his mouth to speak. They caught each other's eye and Saskia giggled. Frans shook his head and tried to ignore the heat rising in his cheeks.

'Tell me Frans, how have you been?' she said earnestly, leaning in closer. 'We miss not seeing you in class.'

He missed them too. But it was Saskia he missed the most, more than he was prepared to admit. He couldn't remember a time when they hadn't been together, their easy friendship and willingness to look out for one another. His departure from school at Easter had been sudden, but not unexpected. Since the beginning of the year, his father had struggled to keep things going on the farm, relying heavily on his eldest son to help out when his usual workers stopped coming, even before asking him to help collect the potato peelings. At first Frans had been relieved to have an excuse to be free of the daily grind of sitting in class. He never did see the point of learning algebra or reading the Dutch classic novel *Max Havelaar* when he knew he could be doing something practical out in the open air. But after he'd left for good he hadn't reckoned on the hollow feeling whenever he thought of his friends in each other's company every day. Especially Saskia.

He was saved from replying by Aart returning and handing Frans a tall glass, two-thirds filled with golden beer and finished off with a thick layer of white foam. It was exactly what he needed.

'*Proost!*' he said. They all laughed and chinked glasses. Tipping back his head, he swallowed a large mouthful of the cool, slightly bitter *pils*. 'Hah,' he breathed out. 'That's good.' Feeling more mellow, he smiled indulgently, thinking it had been worth making the effort to come out for a drink. These Friday evenings were special. More so because they were becoming less and less frequent as each of them worried about how much they and their families were at risk.

It was so quiet in the bar that, when the door clicked open, they all looked round. Two Germans in uniform entered, surveyed the room and let their gaze settle briefly on the trio in the corner. One of the men whispered something to the other that made him snigger.

Frans turned back to his friends and frowned. He wasn't going to let on that he thought he recognised one of the officers, a tall arrogant German he was sure he'd seen in the camp. But then, they all looked the same, the men in uniform parading around the yard carrying swagger sticks, which they so seemed to enjoy slapping against their legs when shouting at prisoners. Frans had no desire to become engaged in conversation with the man.

'Since when have the Gestapo been coming here?' Frans said in a low voice, not really expecting an answer.

Aart shrugged, frowning with concern. 'There's a lot more of them in town and we should be careful. I don't suppose you've heard what's going on at school?' he asked Frans in a whisper.

Frans shook his head.

'We've been lucky they haven't forced us to close. But it's got really overcrowded with pupils coming from other schools shut by the Nazis. They've taken them over to run their own operations. And it's not just that – several teachers have left and gone to work in munitions factories over the border.' He let out a lengthy sigh.

'Come on, Aart, it's not that bad,' said Saskia, linking her arm through his and giving it a squeeze. 'He does like to exaggerate,' she told Frans. 'Two teachers left after Easter and one of them has moved back to Belgium to his family.'

Aart pulled his arm free. 'Well, I don't think you realise quite how serious the situation is…'

'Shh,' said Frans as quietly as he dared. But it was too late. Chairs scraped over the tiled floor as the two Gestapo officers stood up and made their way over to their table.

'Good evening,' they said in unison, speaking in heavily accented Dutch.

Frans forced himself to look up, hoping he'd been mistaken about recognising the officer from the camp. But he was right. It was him.

'Show me your personal identity cards,' ordered the officer, a faint smirk lifting the corners of his mouth.

Inwardly, Frans groaned. He'd heard about these spot checks for underage drinkers and was confident he had nothing to hide.

He'd had it drummed into him to keep his ID on him at all times. But he didn't want any of this attention in case it impacted on him or his family. He handed over the slightly worn card that bore his photo, date of birth and address.

'Hmm. I thought I recognised you,' the officer said, opening it to the photo. 'Aren't you the one who collects potato peelings from the camp?'

Frans gave a brief nod, unwilling to offer any further information in case it caused trouble next time he went into the camp.

'Well. Commandant Berg speaks highly of you, so that's good enough. *Alles in Ordnung!*' he barked in that horrible voice of his, and handed him back the card. 'Next!'

Aart affected a bored expression, as if he had better things to do than prove his age. But Saskia's hand shook as she passed hers over for inspection and Frans's heart went out to her. He felt himself hating the man even more.

They took their time over Saskia's ID, staring first at her, then at her photo, while passing it from one to the other. They murmured something Frans couldn't understand – his knowledge of German was sketchy. What could they possibly take exception to? Her ID was no different to his and she was even a few months older than Frans and Aart. Or maybe it's because she's an attractive girl, he thought in disgust.

The bartender, who'd been watching this episode unfold, came over to ask if anything was the matter. 'These young people are regular customers of mine and never cause me any trouble,' he told the Germans nervously.

'You have nothing to concern yourself with,' said the other officer, whose insignia on his lapel suggested he was the superior of the two. 'We are merely undertaking routine checks.' He slapped Saskia's ID card shut and handed it back to her with an amused look. Turning to the barman, he said, 'We'll be seeing you next time.'

The three friends watched as the German officers headed for the door, their steel-capped boots clicking as they marched across the floor.

'Are you all right?' Frans asked Saskia, who had gone very pale.

'That was horrible. Why did they make such a fuss over mine?'

Aart pulled Saskia into a hug, saying she shouldn't let them upset her. 'They like to come in here and throw their weight around. There's nothing more to it,' he said. She nodded and let her curls fall across her face, hiding her expression. 'She'll be fine,' Aart mouthed at Frans.

The bartender approached their table, holding a tray with three small beers. 'On the house', he said, placing a glass in front of each of them.

'That's kind of you.' Frans lifted his glass in gratitude.

'I thought I should warn you to be careful,' the barman answered softly. 'Those two have been coming in every evening this week. They sit at the same table and drink schnapps while discussing official matters. I overheard something you should know.' He leaned in closer. 'There aren't enough young men reporting for work in Germany and the authorities aren't happy about it. They're unable to trace all those who have slipped through the net. So there's talk of lowering the call-up age to sixteen to make up the numbers. You might want to avoid coming in here for now.' He began to wipe his cloth across the table and paused to say, 'Underage drinkers aren't the only people they're after.'

Chapter Six

It was a grey morning with the whisper of drizzle in the air. In the distance, the clouds were already thinning with the promise of a fine warm day ahead. Frans sighed, knowing that today marked the beginning of the harvest that would last a good two weeks. Two weeks when the whole family and extra men would be working every day from dawn till after dusk to gather in the crop for stacking up in the barns and hayloft above the cowshed. He heaved another sigh, this time out of frustration, because he wouldn't have an opportunity to find out how Saskia was dealing with the increasing menace posed by the presence of German soldiers on the streets. Since their encounter with the Germans in the café, he'd endlessly turned over the words of the bartender in his head, worrying about the threat to himself, his family and, not least, Saskia. Why did those men spend so much time examining her papers when she, out of the three of them, had the least to hide? From her reaction, he could tell she was worried too. Was there something she wasn't telling him?

Frans's thoughts were interrupted by the sound of voices drifting from the track running to the farm. The sun broke through and shone into his eyes as he tried to focus on the men walking through the gate. There were only three. Maybe the others were following on behind, he thought. He had been told by his father to expect at least five men from the village.

Frans was to take them into the fields to instruct them how to build hayricks that didn't fall over or get so hot they'd burst into flames. Soon, the fields would come alive with activity, the rumble of the tractor trundling up and down and carving a way through as it cut the tall stems of wheat, and the swishing sound the men made as they pitchforked them into sheaves. For as long as he could remember, Frans had loved the rare occasions the hayricks caught fire, the delight in seeing a sudden whoosh of flame shoot up to the sky and the crackle of sparks flying off in all directions. It was a serious business, though, and everyone was always roped into a frantic dash to douse the flames with buckets of water.

'*Goedemorgen*,' said one of the young men, holding his hand out to introduce himself. The others did likewise. Frans recognised them; they had helped with the harvest the year before, and he remembered that they were brothers.

'Frans Koopmans,' he introduced himself. 'I'm glad to see you. The conditions are perfect and we should be able to get the crop in before the rain.' He looked out at the field, which stretched away like a golden carpet as far as the eye could see. The long pale stems swayed and rippled in the breeze. 'We were out yesterday evening and Pa told me the seeds have hardened up, so are ready. Here, test them for yourselves.' He held out his hand so they could each bite on the seeds. Since he was twelve, Pa had drummed into him everything there was to know about the preparation of the soil, when to sow the seeds, the importance of keeping a close eye on the crops for blight or pests that could devastate a whole year's work, and the optimum time to get started on the harvest.

The men nodded their approval and trooped inside the farmhouse after Frans for breakfast. Each removed his cap before Frans's mother, who greeted them with a warm handshake and asked how they had been.

'Oh, you know, trying to keep out of sight of the *moffen*,' said the eldest of the three, whose name was Jeroen. 'Though probably not for much longer – I got my letter yesterday calling me up for factory work in Germany. It didn't say what, but I bet it's ammunition.' He looked quite pleased at the prospect. Frans frowned, at a loss to understand why this was such a good idea.

His mother was silent as she placed a bowl of porridge in front of each of the young men. 'Will you go?' she said to Jeroen.

'I don't have much choice, do I?' he said. 'But it'll make a change from all this, that's for sure.'

No one spoke as they concentrated on eating breakfast. Frans mused on what Jeroen had said, wondering if the threat of enforced conscription was nearer than he'd imagined. But Frans was far too young and was sure the war would long be over by the time he reached eighteen.

Eventually another of the young men, Dirk, spoke. 'Well, I don't intend to go when it's my turn.'

'Nor me,' said the third, Maarten, letting his spoon drop into his bowl with a clatter. 'Why should we do their dirty work when our own country needs us? When my time comes, I'll make sure I disappear.' He shot a challenging look at his older brother, who snorted.

Frans slipped out of the kitchen to check on Cas, who was milking the cows. He found him trying to catch one of the chickens, which was flapping and squawking across the yard.

'It's all right, the cows are happy,' he said, giggling, as he dived down and missed again.

Frans wasn't listening. He peered along the track, but still there was no sign of any other men arriving for work. He supposed he'd better fetch the men who had turned up and take them up to the field.

'Wait here for Papa and tell him we've made a start,' he instructed his brother. When Cas ignored him, still rushing after the chickens, Frans lost patience and told him to stop mucking about and make himself useful. But his mind was elsewhere, worrying about how they'd be able to finish the harvest with so few hands.

The three men knew what was expected of them and had completed two rows when Frans's father appeared at the top of the field.

'All good?' he shouted as he clumped towards them in his wooden clogs.

'All good,' the three men chorused.

Frans straightened up, chewing on a stem of wheat. 'We're doing pretty well, as you can see. We're a good team.' He felt he owed it to his father to be upbeat. But his father wasn't listening.

'So, only three of you?' he said to Jeroen.

'Barend and Gerrit said they were coming, but they disappeared a few days ago, leaving no word. Everyone knows it's because they got their call-up papers. There's no one left now. And if the *moffen* are still in charge next year, I won't be here either. After this job, I'm off too. To work in a factory over the border,' said Jeroen with a broad smile.

'Hmm. I suppose you'll all go?' Father said, his gaze moving to the other two.

'What Jeroen does is his business, but Dirk and I have no intention of working for the *moffen*. We're applying for exemption,' said Maarten.

'Do you honestly think you'll get it?' scoffed Jeroen. 'What happens when they refuse? I wouldn't fancy being locked up in *that* place.' He glanced over the fields in the direction of the camp.

Frans followed his gaze, uncomfortable about what he knew since he and Cas had been driving the horse-drawn cart inside the gates. He'd managed to have a few words with one or two prisoners peeling potatoes and discovered they received so little food that they would steal scraps when the guards weren't looking and chew on them for sustenance. But every small transgression was punishable and they were all in fear of a place called the 'rose garden', though Frans hadn't found out why.

Maarten was still engaged in an intense argument with his brothers. Frans stepped in, anxious to keep the peace. 'I'm sure it'll all be over soon and we'll be back to normal.'

Pa snorted. 'I've seen enough things to suggest that the *moffen* are in it for the long haul.'

'What have you seen?' said Jeroen, prodding his pitchfork into the soil so he could lean on it.

Frans held his breath as they all waited for Pa's reply. After all the times Pa had told him to stay silent, never to talk about their job inside the forbidding wire fence, surely he wasn't going to tell them now?

Pa spoke in a low voice. 'Prisoners are coming in faster than they're leaving. Last week, I was in town when a group of several dozen men came marching through accompanied by a bunch of vicious-looking guards. They'd come from the station. A sorry sight they were – they didn't look in good shape at all. All along the streets, people stopped and stared. And no one lifted a finger to do anything to help. Too scared, I reckon, in case someone locks them up too.' He stopped to spit on the ground. 'More prisoners mean more guards. From Dachau, I've heard. You should see them, nasty pieces of work, throwing their weight about and beating the prisoners for no reason.' He fell abruptly silent, as if he'd said more than he'd meant to.

The words sent a chill down Frans's spine. His father had come out with the truth that none of them wanted to hear. Jeroen retrieved his pitchfork and began prodding the soil, his earlier bravado forgotten. He glanced at his brothers, who were exchanging worried looks.

'That's enough talk for now,' said Pa, with a wave of his hand. 'I have business to attend to and you have a job to do.' He started off back towards the house, then turned round abruptly, as if he'd forgotten something. 'Whatever you do, be careful. I've seen lads your age inside, arrested for being in the wrong place at the wrong time. You really don't want to end up in there.' He walked away without another word.

'Come on, let's forget about it,' said Frans, with a nervous shake of the head. 'Pa's been under a lot of pressure to get the harvest started and I'm sure he doesn't mean half of what he says. Jeroen you can work the machine, can't you? Maarten, Dirk, you can help me sort out the chaff.'

Twice, Evert Koopman walked to neighbouring villages in search of any man under forty capable of farm work. But each time he returned empty-handed with confirmation that more young men had been recruited to work in German bomb factories. Families were fearful of their sons staying behind, believing they would all be in danger of reprisals if they did.

Fortunately, the weather held, along with tempers. Once they put their backs into hard physical work, the three brothers seemed to forget their differences of opinion about whether it would be better to work for the Germans or defy them by going into hiding. All that mattered was getting the job done, however long they toiled, from early till late, when the light had leached from the sky. The best time of day was when Mama came up into the field with all the children for a picnic at sunset. Everyone gathered round exhausted, but content to rest against the hay bales and wolf down fresh bread, lumps of sausage and cheese, washed down with sharp juice made from the apples from the orchard. This, and the spectacle of the sky transforming from burnt orange to a fiery red, made no words necessary.

On the last evening, Frans sat back against a hay bale, gazing at the dying embers of the sunset, tired and happy it was over. Tomorrow, Sunday, he had the day off and he made up his mind to cycle over to see Saskia. It was nearly three weeks since he'd last seen her and he'd been unable to get her look of worry out of his head. With more guards on the streets and a sense that things were about to take a turn for the worse, he knew he had to go and see her.

Chapter Seven

Saskia

The road up ahead shimmered in the heat as Saskia pedalled wearily back home after visiting her friend Corrie. She'd hoped it would be easier going if she set out later, but the sweat pooled in the small of her back as much as it had at midday. Out of the mirage came a distorted figure and she squinted to see more clearly, but it wasn't until the cyclist was quite close that she saw it was Frans. They both stood on their brakes and came to a halt side by side.

'Saskia! I didn't expect to see you out in this heat. Where are you going?'

He looked as hot as she felt and she watched as he pulled out an enormous handkerchief to mop his forehead and run over his hair. She couldn't stop herself from giggling as she stared at Frans, who was quite unaware he'd pushed his hair into a strange quiff. It suited him, she thought, making him look handsome and older than his sixteen years. Briefly, her breath caught in her throat.

'I was actually coming back from visiting a friend. And you?' She glanced down at the bulging saddlebag attached to the side of his bike.

'I finished work early and am dropping off a few provisions to an elderly neighbour who can't get out in all this heat.' He tipped his head in the direction of a row of unassuming cottages lining the next field. 'Then I thought I'd see if you were in, but now you're here.'

Saskia smiled. Her hair felt heavy and damp as she lifted it away from the nape of her neck with one hand. 'I suppose the harvest must be over now.'

'Yeah.' Frans sighed. 'Thank goodness.' He wiped fresh sweat off his brow. 'I'm sorry I haven't been around to meet up, but you know how it is. Have you and Aart been going to our café?'

Saskia shook her head in a quick movement. 'Let's walk along a bit. I'm not expected home yet.'

They wheeled their bikes along the hot road in silence, then stopped under the shade of a large tree with broad overhanging branches. Saskia kicked her bike stand into place and stretched her arms above her head so she could luxuriate in the relative coolness of the shade. Frans leaned his bike against the tree and gestured for her to sit next to him on a log facing stubbled fields. He looked at her expectantly and she realised she hadn't answered his question.

'We haven't been back since those two German officers came in demanding to see our IDs. Who'd want to with all those Nazis swarming around the centre of town? I'm avoiding town, though I do miss going to the cinema with Corrie. And us meeting up,' she added, biting her lower lip.

'And there was me thinking you were seeing Aart in the café while I was stuck out on the farm. It's funny how you can get things wrong.' Frans stared straight ahead, while fiddling with a stick he'd picked up off the ground.

For some reason, his comment made her think about her father and how he'd been mistaken for a Jew. She felt a rush of warmth towards Frans, who seemed so solid and reliable, and decided to confide in him.

'I'm scared, Frans. My father's had to shut the shop. He's sold the stock and even sold off the cabinets that have been there since my grandfather's time. I still can't believe it. It's heartbreaking to see all his efforts gone to waste.'

'I had no idea things were so bad. Why didn't you tell me?' Frans gazed at her, his clear blue eyes reflecting her pain. Saskia began to sniff and he put an arm round her shoulder. She leaned in, grateful for his concern. 'It wasn't something I wanted to talk about.'

Frans nodded. 'I understand. It must be a great shock to you all. But it seems to be happening all over the place these days. The centre of Amersfoort no longer looks the same.'

'I know,' she murmured, only half listening. 'But it's not only that. Did you know the Germans are arresting people for no apparent reason? Twice, German soldiers came into the shop demanding to see Father's ID. They accused him of being Jewish, though they had no grounds. My father thinks it's because of his looks. Now every time he leaves the house I fear for him. The whole thing has made me worried, too. Every time a Nazi passes me in the street and gives me a cold stare, I imagine I'm under suspicion. You remember when those officers kept staring at my ID in the bar? It wasn't long after Father told us what had happened to him. All I could think of was that they must think I'm Jewish too and how badly that would turn out for me and my family. Frans, you don't think I look Jewish, do you?' She stared at him with big worried eyes and pushed her springy hair away from her face as if she could hide its thick bushiness. When he didn't immediately answer, she took it as a sign that it must be true. 'I knew it. And those horrible Germans must have thought so too.' She reached into the small leather bag she always had strapped to her waist and pulled out her ID card for Frans to examine. 'Here, tell me truthfully. Do I look Jewish?'

Frans gazed at her photo for a long moment. He didn't want to worry her. 'All I see is someone with dark hair and beautiful big eyes.'

Saskia searched Frans's face for any signs he might be mocking her but there were none. He gave her a warm smile and squeezed her hand. His felt surprisingly cool for all the heat, and she became self-conscious at how hot and damp her own must feel, but he didn't give any indication that he minded. They continued to sit hand in hand with their arms touching.

'Feeling better?' he asked after a while, holding her gaze with trusting eyes.

Reassured, she gave a tentative nod. 'Thanks for listening, Frans. And for being such a good friend.' She gazed back, conscious that she wanted him to be so much more than just a friend – she'd felt this way for some time. But did he? On impulse, she leaned in and kissed his cheek, before quickly drawing back, worried she'd mistaken his concern for something more. But Frans put his hands on either side of her face and kissed her on the lips, leaving her in no doubt as to what his feelings were towards her. She let herself relax in his arms and, for now, let her worries slip away.

Chapter Eight

Theo

The train station was densely packed, more and more people descending onto the platform, all clutching their possessions tightly to their chests. Every one of them had a look of pure terror on their face. No one dared speak in case they attracted the attention of one of the uniformed Germans in steel-capped boots who yelled and lashed out at anyone who was not moving along. The sight of grown men being humiliated and struck for no apparent reason was enough to silence them all.

At the far end of the platform a whistle sounded, long and shrill. They were to march two abreast, no more, there was to be no conversing and anyone who did not keep up would be beaten. Nothing about where they were heading or even why they were here, though all had a strong sense of foreboding that it would not end well.

Theo gripped his small bag to him with both hands. He was cursing himself for not packing more than the few meagre possessions it contained, when he was jostled from behind. His irritation turned to surprise when he saw Piet at his elbow. Piet was the last person he'd expected to see, but this was no time for explanations. His grey face was drawn, but he managed a pinched smile as he moved closer to whisper how sorry he was that he'd got Theo into this mess. Theo was about to open his mouth in reply when the crowd lurched forward. He grabbed Piet's arm, grateful to have someone he knew beside him. He let his gaze dart about him, recognising a few other faces from the evening before. They no longer looked buoyed up and defiant in the face of the Nazis, but seemed as shocked as he was to be arrested in this brutal manner and at finding themselves here. And all because they had wanted to resist the Nazis for the chance of getting back their liberty, snatched so cruelly away from them. Theo finally understood what they were fighting against and regretted not acting sooner.

The past twenty-four hours had been bewildering, from the moment he'd come round in the van to the interrogation at the police station, resulting in an overnight stay in a cell. In his opinion, he'd done nothing wrong, but he'd been given precisely one hour to return to his lodgings and pick up his belongings before reporting back at the police station at noon. He'd tried to argue on what grounds he needed to return, but was met with blank stares and a wall of stony silence. There was nothing to be done. He'd had the sense to realise that if he didn't comply with orders the consequences would be severe.

With only half an hour to pack a bag, he spent twenty minutes of this precious time trying to compose a note to Annelies to apologise for his disappearance. He didn't want to worry her unduly, but thought anything he said would make her even more anxious. In the end, he decided to lie. He wrote that he'd run into an old friend who needed his help tending to a sick relative who lived in Groningen and would be away for a few days. He promised to write again very soon and asked her to have faith in him. It was the best he could do, but not enough to push away the mounting sense of dread that threatened to overwhelm him. He knew that something bad was about to happen. He knew he might never return. And how would Annelies cope if he vanished?

On approaching the town centre, Theo became aware that people were stopping to stare at the spectacle of hundreds of men marching through. Children looked on wide-eyed as they clung to their mothers' hands, shopkeepers appeared in doorways and a grocer's boy got off his bicycle to take a good look. Theo stared at his feet, ashamed to be part of this ragtag column of men, screamed at by smug Nazis parading alongside. He lifted his gaze above the heads of the gathering crowd to avoid the judging stares and noticed yet more people watching from their windows. It was too much. The sense of injustice he felt seemed to engulf him. All he wanted was to shout out that there'd been a mistake and he shouldn't be there. But instead, he thrust his chin up and stared back. It was enough for several figures to melt back from their windows. It took him a moment to dampen down his anger and focus on putting one foot in front of the other.

'Are you all right?' came Piet's quiet voice. He must have noticed Theo trembling beside him.

Theo couldn't bring himself to speak.

The march went on and on. Theo had forgotten to put on his father's watch so had no idea how long it was taking, but he guessed they must have been marching for the better part of an hour, maybe even two. Not that he wanted it to end. Marching was preferable to facing the unknown.

They turned into an avenue, long and straight, and lined with tall leafy beech trees that cast welcome shade onto their hot weary bodies. Theo tried to push away the memory of another avenue of beech trees, where he and Annelies once walked, talking about anything and everything. The wooden bench, carved to fit around the base of the massive beech tree, was where they always stopped to sit and hold hands while listening to the birdsong high up in the branches. It was all so innocent. Theo had been in awe of this girl's beauty and self-composure, wondering how on earth she would be interested in him, a mere boy six months younger than her, so he'd never made clear his intentions. They left school, Annelies moved to Utrecht to become a primary school teacher and Theo deeply regretted he hadn't told her how he felt. It wasn't until a friend offered him a job as a waiter in Utrecht that he allowed himself to believe they might meet again. It didn't take him long to find out where she was working, but somewhat longer to pluck up courage to go and find her. One afternoon, he went to the school entrance and waited for her to come out, feigning surprise when she came walking towards him. Her delight in seeing him confirmed that he hadn't been wrong after all. It was fate, he'd told her, and soon they started seeing one another again.

Theo forced his mind back to the present and fixed his attention on an enormous tree up ahead, its trunk so thick it must have been centuries old. But before he could allow his attention to wander further, the column came to a sudden halt. Several of the uniformed guards came striding down the line, shouting out orders for everyone to stand back. Those who didn't respond quickly enough were shoved harshly aside.

Up ahead Theo could hear the clip-clop of a horse and clatter of a cart piled up with metal containers that clanged as they bumped against each other. Everyone stopped to look. The road was narrow and the driver reined the horse to a slow walk in order to ease a way through.

'Move back!' roared a guard, whacking several men across the shins. One of them was Theo, who cried out in pain and was rewarded with another blow. The horse took fright at the noise and rose up with a terrified whinnying sound. Several men tried to back away but were manhandled roughly back into position. Theo found himself caught in a painful grip. His face twisted in pain and he opened his eyes to see the driver looking straight at him with a look of such sympathy that it was all Theo could do not to cry out to him for help.

The moment passed. The driver managed to regain control of his horse and disappeared down the road.

Chapter Nine

Frans

Frans was up early in readiness for the trip over to the camp. He glanced over at the horse, which was munching contentedly from its bucket of oats and didn't seem any the worse for wear from the upset the day before. Frans blamed himself for what happened. He'd allowed himself to be distracted by Cas talking beside him on the way out of the camp, and when he'd turned the cart onto the avenue, he'd almost rammed into a group of men being marched in their direction. The horse had taken fright, rearing up and causing the cart to shake violently. Frans held on with all his might to stop it from overturning and shed the potato peelings all over the road.

But he'd been more shocked by the sight of those men, some wearing long overcoats over polished shoes, others in buttoned-up jacket and trousers, and all carrying either a suitcase or a bag. Helmeted German soldiers in greatcoats marched alongside them, keeping them in order. Frans had only managed a brief glance at them in his efforts to bring the horse under control, but had seen how exhausted and fearful the men looked. He was still struggling with the reins when he'd noticed a young man, not much older than himself, being restrained in an armlock. Frans was horrified to see the man twist round and stare at him with a look of such distress that it was all he could do not to jump down and assist him. It was over so quickly, but Frans had been unable to push the scene from his mind.

*

Cas came careering out of the back door as Frans was hitching the horse to the cart. The buttons on his shirt were done up all wrong, his long socks were already round his ankles, and his shoes were on the wrong feet. Frans raised an eyebrow as Cas stumbled to a halt beside him. Late again, but Frans didn't remind him of the fact. He was prepared to forgive his little brother, knowing how hard it was to get out of bed so early and put in a full shift before school.

'Hop on board and sort out your shoes.' Frans smiled, pointing at Cas's feet. 'Then we'll be off.' Cas gave an apologetic grin and scrambled into his seat.

A word from Frans and the horse set off out of the yard, the clop of its hooves hollow against the cobblestones. The track took them along the edge of the big field till they were parallel to the water channel Pa was clearing. Frans called out a greeting and Pa acknowledged them with a tilt of his head before returning to his work. Frans let out a long breath, relieved he'd avoided the usual lecture. Pa repeated the same old stuff every day – make sure there's nothing on the cart to arouse any suspicions, stand your ground and don't put up with any nonsense from the guards, make sure you look after Cas, and so on. Pa also expected Frans to tell him every detail of what happened each time they went into the camp. Today he was glad to be on his way.

'Can I ask you something?' asked Cas in a querulous voice, once they'd turned onto the long avenue that led to the camp. 'What happened to the prisoner that took the scraps? Where do you think he's gone?'

Frans frowned as he recalled the incident from their first trip into the camp. He couldn't honestly remember if he'd seen the prisoner since, for they all looked the same with their shaven heads and ill-fitting mismatched uniforms. Prisoners came and went all the time, moved around on the whim of the camp authorities. But Cas claimed he had disappeared.

'You don't think something horrible has happened to him?' Cas bit his lip. 'Like he's died?'

'No, you mustn't think that,' said Frans, concerned that his brother had been worrying all this time. 'More likely he's been transferred to work in another part of the camp.' Frans hoped it to be true. He remembered now how emaciated the prisoner had looked.

Cas cheered up when Frans handed him the reins and he seemed to forget about the fate of the gaunt prisoner who'd been troubling him only moments before. But Frans knew he must watch out for any signs that Cas was upset and do a better job of looking after him.

The guard on the gate waved them through with a disinterested expression. The cart clattered across the empty yard under the concrete arch and over to the kitchen block, where the prisoners were already at work peeling potatoes. Frans exchanged a look with Cas and gave an encouraging smile. They jumped down and approached the nearest prisoner, dressed in a loose-fitting shirt and trousers that hung off his frame. He didn't look at all well and had dark smudges under his dull grey eyes.

'Hello. We're here to pick up the potato peelings,' Frans said with forced cheeriness. 'Can you fetch the bins?'

The prisoner glanced nervously towards the arch as if expecting someone to turn up.

'I take over from my friend Sergei,' he said in a thick accent Frans couldn't place. Could it be Polish, or Russian? 'He's back in there, where I just come from,' he said sadly. He gestured over his shoulder towards Block IV, the medical centre, housing the sick prisoners. 'I don't think he last long.'

Frans inclined his head and gave him a sympathetic look. His father had told him that many of the prisoners peeling potatoes had been deemed unfit for more physical tasks, such as felling trees in the forest and heaving concrete blocks for the new accommodation building. Peeling potatoes was easier work, but the guards saw it as a soft option and had no tolerance for anyone slacking. They watched these prisoners for the slightest infraction, handing out punishments frequently just because they could.

Cas was waiting up on the cart while Frans finished loading the last of the bins when he heard footsteps behind him. He turned, to come face to face with the man he'd seen so roughly pummelled when the new arrivals were being herded through the gates of the camp. Hot shame shot through him; he knew he should have stopped, said something, done anything, but instead he'd turned away and left him to suffer. He knew he must make amends.

'It was me who was driving the horse and cart when you arrived. I didn't like what those guards were doing, but I'm sorry, I should've stopped. Are you all right?' He peered at the man, who didn't seem to be listening and was breathing quickly. The man, now shorn of his thick fair hair, looked wary and let his eyes dart all around him, before thrusting his hand in the pocket of his loose trousers.

'Please, will you take this?' he whispered with a despairing look and shoved a scrap of folded paper at Frans.

'What is it?' Frans hurriedly crumpled it into his own trouser pocket.

The man's desperate look softened. 'My girlfriend, Annelies… can you let her know where I am? And tell her not to worry.' He tried to smile, but looked close to tears.

'Yes, of course I will,' said Frans, except he was nervous at what he might be taking on. But he knew he had do something. 'My name's Frans,' he said. 'I'll make sure she gets it.'

'I'm Theo,' said the prisoner. 'And thank you.'

Frans watched as he hurried back into position among the other prisoners peeling potatoes. He didn't look round.

'Can we go now?' came Cas's impatient voice from the cart.

Frans reluctantly dragged his attention away from the prisoner, conscious of the scrap of paper weighing heavy in his pocket.

Chapter Ten

Shielding his eyes, Frans squinted through the darkened shop window. A light came on and he was relieved to see Saskia come over.

'Come in quickly and make sure you shut the door. We don't want to be seen,' she said, pulling him inside. Frans nodded, aware that a chance meeting with a German could lead to unpleasant questions. Not that they had anything to hide, but he didn't want to put Saskia in unnecessary danger.

He closed the door shut with a click and looked about him. He'd last been in here several months ago on an errand for his mother, when it was still a functioning shop with a large counter and display cabinets lining the walls. Now, there was a sad air about the place and all that remained were one or two chairs and several boxes scattered across the floor. It had been Saskia's idea to come to the empty shop, where they could talk undisturbed. She'd been given a key to the premises by her father, so she could sort the remaining stock for safekeeping in the storeroom at the back of the shop. In one corner, she'd made a pile of useful items – darning wool, sewing thread, needles, scraps of material, that kind of thing – stuff she knew her mother could use.

'Let's sit away from the window and you can tell me what's going on,' Saskia said, looping a strand of her wavy hair behind her ear as she scraped the chairs over the bare floorboards so they could sit next to each other.

'Something happened in the camp this morning. I came straight over as I couldn't think who else to talk to.' Frans took hold of her hands for reassurance and she was silent as he told her about the prisoner he'd seen manhandled outside the camp, meeting him in the yard and the note the man had pushed into his hands. 'It happened so quickly that I didn't have time to think. He looked so panicked, so upset… He must have recognised me and thought I could help. Then he gave me this.' Frans fished it out of his pocket. Unfolded, it was no more than a scrap of lined paper that looked as if it had been hurriedly ripped out of an exercise book. Frans and Saskia both looked at the handwriting, almost indecipherable, so obviously written in a panic. Not much was written there, just a name, address and an urgent message. 'Please tell her not to worry,' it said, written in a scrawl.

Saskia stared up at Frans, her large dark eyes bright with tears. 'The poor man. He must be desperate ending up in a place like that. Who knows what he's done… but you have to help. And this Annelies too – she must be sick with worry. You have to get a message to her, tell her where he's ended up, even if it's not the news she wants to hear. I can write to her if you like?' Saskia gazed at him.

'Would you?' said Frans in relief. 'I wouldn't know what to say.'

Saskia nodded sadly. 'He can't be the only one. There must be others in there desperate to get messages to their loved ones. I don't suppose the *moffen* allow them to communicate outside of the wire fence, from what you've told me.'

'No. I don't think so. I've only ever seen guards treating them with disrespect. It's horrible seeing them being shouted at and pushed around. I've often thought there must be something I can do to help, but I could get caught myself.'

Saskia was listening intently and her face took on a more purposeful expression. 'It can't be difficult to smuggle the occasional letter out, can it? Not if you're careful.'

'But how? All it would take is for one of the guards to spot me doing it.'

'They didn't, so it must be possible. Surely it's worth trying, if we can bring a little happiness to those poor people?'

Frans's heart lifted when she said 'we'. She wasn't suggesting that he should do this alone, but that they'd manage it together, somehow. 'Let's take it slowly,' he said. 'If you write to Annelies and ask for a reply, I'll make sure Theo gets it.'

'Theo.' Saskia smiled. 'So that's his name.'

Chapter Eleven

A week passed before Frans was able to go to the camp again. The turnips were ready for lifting and Pa needed the job doing quickly. He hadn't forgotten the time he'd been caught out by German soldiers who'd turned up just as the last of the turnips had been brought in. They came in trucks and loaded them up while Pa stood by, with their guns pointed at him. If he'd protested he would have received a bullet to the head, so was forced to watch silently as all his hard work disappeared down the track. He was determined for it not to happen again, so had Frans work long days and evenings to bring the crop in. Frans was a fast worker and time was of the essence. The quicker they could harvest the vegetables and distribute them to people in the neighbouring villages, the less chance there would be of the Germans arriving with their trucks and taking the lot across the border to feed their own people.

Frans didn't complain – he wanted to get the better of the Germans as much as his father did – but he was anxious to see Theo again. Saskia had written to Annelies and received a reply back almost immediately, thanking her profusely for taking the trouble to tell her what had happened to Theo. She'd enclosed a note for Theo and begged Saskia to stay in touch with any news, good or bad.

The work was done and, the following day, Frans offered to take over the run to the camp. He tucked Annelies's letter into the waistband of his trousers, the safest place he could think of should the guards decide to ask him to turn out his pockets. With any luck, they'd wave him through as normal. But when he pulled up at the gates, a different entrance guard stepped forward, his hand raised in a stiff salute. Frans felt himself tense up. He must be new, thought Frans warily, noticing he looked even more fearsome than the last one.

Frans copied his salute and mouthed *Heil* Hitler while his mind went, *please don't stop us*. The cart edged forward.

'*Halt*! I have instructions to make a search.' The guard had deep grooves etched from his nose to his mouth, which was set firm in a grimace. Frans had come to expect random searches, although this was the first time he'd had anything to hide. If the guard concentrated on the cart, he reasoned, he'd have nothing to fear.

'Open up!' snarled the guard, banging on the side.

Frans spoke calmly in a low voice, telling Cas to wait up in the cart. Cas stared straight ahead, keeping rigidly still while Frans lifted down the empty bins. The guard climbed up and began to prod around under the tarpaulin.

'Boy! Get down so I can look under your seat.'

Frans widened his eyes at Cas, who stepped down. He looked terrified.

Frans held Cas's hand as they watched the guard poke his swagger stick under the seats. He grunted twice, clearly disappointed not to find anything. When he straightened up, the lines by the side of his mouth seemed to have grown deeper.

'Can we go through now?' asked Frans impatiently.

'Yes. But I will search again when you leave.' Frowning, the guard gave Cas a hard stare. 'What is your name, boy?'

'Cas,' he stammered, looking petrified.

'And what are you doing here?'

Frans put a reassuring hand on Cas's arm. 'He's my brother and we pick up the food waste together. Didn't Herr Commandant tell you?'

'No. I had instructions to allow the local farmer in, but no one else.'

'We're his sons and it's been agreed that we come in his place from time to time.'

The guard placed himself between Frans and Cas and spoke in a low gruff voice. 'This morning, a prisoner tried to escape in a delivery van. He made it as far as the gates, but fortunately Herr Berg was able to intercept him. Foolish man. For his troubles he was shot. Now do you understand?' He spoke these last words with a nasty smile.

Frans turned cold and responded with a curt nod. 'Come on, Cas. We have a job to do.' He spoke through gritted teeth.

They returned to the cart. Frans willed the guard to hurry up and let them through before he changed his mind. He sauntered to the gate and took his time unlocking it. Finally, he stood aside and gave an exaggerated salute. '*Heil* Hitler! Remember, I shall be waiting for you.'

Frans lost no time driving over to where the prisoners were hard at work. Straight away, he spotted Theo – he was taller than many of the other prisoners and was recognisable by the blond stubble that covered his scalp. He wasn't as thin as the other prisoners, although his baggy shirt and trousers hung off him in folds. He looked up and, with the flicker of a smile, caught Frans's eye.

Frans glanced about him, taking note of a couple of guards at the far end of the compound. Drawing in a breath, he gestured to Theo to come over to the cart.

'Can you help unload the bins?' he whispered. And to Cas he said, 'Climb down and keep a watch out for those guards.'

Cas did as he was told and positioned himself where he had a good view of the yard. Frans handed down one of the bins and Theo wheeled it to the side of a building where the large metal containers were kept inside a wooden fence. Frans followed with the second bin.

Once they were out of sight, Theo spoke quickly. 'Why didn't you come? I nearly gave up hope of getting a message to Annelies. The man who came... was he your father?'

'Yes. We take it in turns to come, but I was needed on the farm to dig the turnips. There's only me left to do the heavy work since the casual workers left after the main grain harvest. But listen, I have good news.' Frans gave Theo a brief smile and pulled the creased letter from the depths of his jacket pocket. He could see Theo's hand shaking as he grabbed it from him and quickly concealed it in the waistband of his trousers under his loose jacket. Theo's eyes were shining. He seemed lost for words.

Frans sniffed, pushing down the emotion that threatened to overwhelm him too. He'd never imagined that such a small gesture could mean so much. But there was no time to lose. If he stayed round here close to Theo for any longer they'd arouse suspicion.

'Help me load the bins, will you?' Frans said, more gruffly than he'd intended. He glanced over at Cas, who gave him a thumbs-up.

They worked quickly and quietly, speaking in low voices to avoid attracting the guards' attention.

'How is it they allow you in to do this?' Theo asked.

'We've been collecting feed for the cattle for years. My father started when it used to be a prison. And when the Nazis took over, my Pa just carried on. It means they get rid of the food waste and our cattle get fed.'

Theo told Frans that he was interested in the running of the farm. He knew a bit about farming as he used to spend summers working on his uncle's farm in Westland near the Dutch coast.

'Is that where you're from?' asked Frans.

'No, Rotterdam. We lost everything after they bombed the place to smithereens. Me and my parents, we ran for our lives. Our house went up in flames and there wasn't time to grab anything, not even our shoes. We had to walk in bare feet all the way to Delft. There were hundreds like us and they us put up in a draughty old school hall. We couldn't go back – no one could, so my family ended up in Utrecht at a cousin of my father's.'

They both looked up, alarmed, at the crunch of heavy boots approaching.

'Watch out,' said Theo, immediately trundling his full bin out and nodding to Cas to help him lift it onto the cart.

Frans was shocked by what Theo had recounted and wanted to hear how he came to be in the camp, but his heart lurched when he saw it was the guard from earlier approaching. He was accompanied by a ferocious-looking dog that he was having difficulty restraining.

'*Heil* Hitler!' barked the guard, trying to execute a salute while tugging on the leash.

'*Heil* Hitler,' said Theo in a quiet voice.

Frans placed himself in front of a trembling Cas. The guard loosened his grip, letting the dog edge nearer, growling and sniffing its way towards the cart. With a loud bark, it scrabbled with its claws against the side.

'*Ach so.* I think we should take a look inside.' The guard lapsed into heavily accented Dutch as a nasty smile spread across his face.

'Really, there's no need. We've only just finished piling in the waste,' said Theo.

Cas hid behind Frans and held onto the hem of his jacket for safety. Frans held his breath. Didn't Theo know that prisoners shouldn't speak to the guards unless instructed to? He knew how badly it ended if a prisoner stepped out of line: the slaps across the face, the kicks to the crotch, the crack of a whip across the back, and now this slavering beast of a dog that looked as if it wanted nothing more than to sink its teeth into Theo's leg. What could Theo be thinking and had he forgotten about the letter hidden in his trousers?

'*Mund dicht! Es ist verboten zu sprechen!*' The guard raised his voice even more, which set the dog off barking. 'Get it down so I can do a proper search.' The guard yanked on the dog's leash, making it bark more ferociously.

'You won't find anything but potato peelings in those bins. I can vouch for it,' said Frans, with a boldness that belied the pounding in his chest and a determination to stick up for Theo.

'You can vouch for it, can you?' said the guard, in a cruel imitation of his voice. 'Then it won't matter if the prisoner tips them out to show me. And shovels the lot back in again.' He pointed to a spot on the ground and, with a sound halfway between choking and coughing, spat. The dog let out a long low growl, but Theo didn't move.

'Empty the bins!' roared the guard and the dog emitted a series of menacing barks.

'Is this really necessary?' said Frans. 'I need to get this lot back to feed the cattle.'

'Stay out of this, *farmer's boy*.' The guard's face turned a strange purple colour.

'Perhaps it would be best if we leave?' said Frans, trying to be reasonable, though his heart was pumping with fear. But instead of defusing the situation, the guard turned his fury onto him.

'Not until I discover what's hidden in those bins!' he roared, breathing fast as if he'd just been running a race. 'Empty them!' He turned to Theo with a look of pure hatred.

It was chaos. Theo upturned one of the bins and a mountain of peels came tumbling out and spilled across the yard. Some landed on the guard's shiny black boots and he stepped back in surprise, bumping against his dog, which turned on him, snapping and growling. While he was distracted by the dog, Theo, Frans and Cas scrabbled on the ground sweeping the potato peelings back in and were joined by several prisoners who had been standing by watching. It was obvious the guard had lost control of the situation, which made him even madder.

Of course, there was nothing hidden among the rotting potato peelings, which enraged the guard even more. And all Frans could think as he left the camp was that Theo was going to be punished for it. And that hidden on him was Annelies's letter.

Chapter Twelve

'The rose garden,' the prisoner whispered. He was a balding man of about thirty, wearing a shabby uniform several sizes too big. 'The guard sent him there after you left and he's still there now.'

Frans was puzzled. That was more than eight hours ago. Why would Theo have been sent to sit all day in a garden? He'd heard the prisoners mention the rose garden from time to time and naively imagined it to be the one refuge where prisoners were allowed to go for some respite. A place full of sweet-smelling roses. But the defeated expression clouding the prisoner's face made him realise it wasn't like that at all.

'What's it like in there?' Frans asked in trepidation.

The prisoner shrugged his bony shoulders, but couldn't meet Frans's eye. 'They make you stand there for hours on end till you fall against the wire spikes.' He pulled up one frayed sleeve to reveal a mesh of thin angry red streaks against white skin.

Frans caught his breath. He couldn't believe what he was hearing.

'We all get sent there at some point,' said the prisoner, staring at his wounds.

'I'm sorry,' said Frans, not knowing what else to say. His mind was already on Theo and whether there was anything he could do to help him. He'd been shaken to the core by those few words Theo had told him about losing his home. What could possibly have led him to end up inside here? Whatever had happened must have been terrible, but he refused to believe Theo had done anything wrong. Besides, nobody deserved such a punishment. The more Frans learned about what went on inside this brutal place, the more shocked he was that any person, let alone the guards, could carry out such inhumane acts. But he'd seen a spark in Theo that the brutes hadn't yet managed to extinguish. He knew he couldn't allow them to break him now.

'Come with me, Cas.' He turned to his brother, pale-faced and uncomprehending beside him. Frans took his hand firmly in his own and set off through the arch, to be faced with dozens of prisoners filling the yard, forming row after row, ten to a row. Evening roll call was just beginning. Two hefty guards stood by wielding truncheons and were shouting out commands in German at the prisoners, who were expected to answer back. The ones at the front were forced to count loudly, '*eins, zwei, drei, vier,*' and so on. The guards' beady eyes scanned the men, looking for any transgression. Not giving the correct answer, not speaking loud enough, not meeting their eye when addressed, all of these were punishable.

Every other time Frans had witnessed this humiliation they'd been up on the cart heading swiftly for the exit. Not wanting to draw attention to themselves, Frans skirted close to the buildings and tugged on Cas's hand to hurry him up, just as one of the guards roared at a boy, surely no more than fifteen, to step out of line and face the others. He was slightly built with short fiery red hair that reminded Frans of a boy who was always getting into trouble at school. Whatever this prisoner had done wrong must have been bad judging by his punishment, thought Frans. First, he was pushed hard from behind, making him lose his balance and fall to the ground. A kick to his back followed by the command to get up, and each time he groaned he was ordered to drop down again.

They edged by quietly, as the abuse continued: up, down, up, down. Frans winced at the boy's obvious distress and watched as the rest of the prisoners stood by expressionless while this carried on. But he knew why no one did anything to stop it. If the other prisoners got involved they'd receive worse themselves. And if he intervened, he knew he might end up never leaving this place himself.

'Come on, let's get out of here,' whispered Frans, pulling Cas along by his arm, but he twisted back to get a look. Frans's grip was firm. All he could think about was the fate of that young man. Would his punishment be to suffer in the rose garden like Theo? He had no time to reflect on this as they arrived at the commandant's office. Briefly, he regretted coming, so shaken up was he by what was happening yards away. He should never have dragged Cas into this. The poor boy was shaking so violently that Frans dropped to his knees and gave him a fierce hug.

'Come in with me, but you won't have to say anything. All right?' He touched his brother's quivering chin. Cas nodded, fighting back tears. Frans took his hand and gave it a squeeze. Ignoring the commotion from beyond the arch, he drew breath and knocked on the door, waiting to be allowed to enter.

The commandant looked up from his desk, his shiny black pen poised over an open ledger. 'Evert. Do come in,' he said with a smile, before realising his mistake. 'Ah, Frans. You know you really do look like your father. Did he ask you to come and see me?'

Frans felt his mouth go dry, suddenly lost for words. He'd met the commandant only once before, the first time he'd come to the camp. On that occasion, his manner had been courteous, almost friendly, because he was on good terms with Pa, Frans had imagined. But now, as Frans stood before the commandant, whose thin lips were curved into a cruel smile, he wondered if he'd been mistaken. What could he have been thinking, coming in here to confront the commandant who ran this terrible place?

'Is there a problem?' asked the commandant irritably, picking up his pen and tapping it on the desk.

Then, by his side, Frans felt Cas give his hand a faint squeeze. He squeezed back, grateful for this tiny gesture that meant he wasn't having to face this situation alone. Closing his eyes briefly, he drew in a breath, remembering how his father had told him that the commandant was a reasonable man once you got to know him.

Despite the deep sense of injustice he felt about Theo, he must try to be friendly but firm, he told himself.

'I've come because a prisoner was sent to the rose garden. I was collecting the potato peelings when it happened and I'm sure he did nothing wrong. He was helping me with the bins as normal and the guard thought he'd hidden something in them. But it wasn't true. I was there the whole time and I would have seen him do it.'

The commandant stood up and paced over to the window, his boots making a metallic click with every step. 'Herr Meiss informed me of the disturbance this morning. The prisoner was showing disrespect to Herr Meiss and has received a fitting punishment.'

'By being made to go and stand in the rose garden all day?' asked Frans.

'The prisoner knew it was against the rules to speak and refused to obey the command to search the bins.'

'But it's not true.' Frans tried again. 'We were there and that's not what happened. Was it, Cas?' Cas had shown his support once and he desperately needed it again. The boy looked terrified but managed a tiny shake of his head. 'He hasn't been in the camp long and maybe didn't know about speaking out,' Frans continued, his heart pounding. He was afraid that he'd gone too far, and he followed the commandant with his eyes as he paced up and down, tapping the pen into the palm of his hand. After a long pause, the commandant swivelled on his heel.

'You must realise that I'm not running a holiday camp. Each and every prisoner is brought here because of their criminal activity. It's our job to punish them. And we find the rose garden an effective way to make them see the error of their ways. It offers' – the commandant paused, as if searching for the right words – 'a period of reflection on their misdeeds. It's an experience that few wish to be subjected to more than once.' He pushed back his sleeve to glance at his expensive watch, and said, 'Nine hours is sufficient this time. I will arrange for the prisoner to be released to his post.'

'Is Theo a criminal?'

Cas shot a sideways look at Frans, who'd been waiting for his brother to ask this question. If truth be told, he'd been wondering about it himself, however much he wanted it not to be so. Theo had been so open and friendly that it was impossible to imagine him capable of carrying out some terrible act. But according to his father, the prisoners were in there for all kinds of reasons, some very minor – because they were the wrong type of people, or simply because they had spoken out against the Nazis. Pa said you could tell what category they fell into from the colour of the badge they were forced to wear on their clothes. There were so many different types that it was hard to remember what each of them meant, but there were two he instantly knew: the big red circle stitched onto the back of a prisoner's shirt denoting they were an escape risk, and the distinctive yellow star singling out anyone who was a Jew. Frans tried and failed to remember what the symbols meant – red, white, brown, black and green – and which colour Theo was forced to display. Whatever crime he'd committed had landed him in deep trouble.

He urged the horse to go faster, till the cart was rattling along at such an alarming rate that it was in danger of toppling into the ditch. On and on they went, bouncing over potholes and in and out of sudden dips in the road. Cas clung on with all his might, until the turning towards the farm finally came into sight. Frans sighed out a long 'whoa' and reined in the horse to a shuddering halt just before the junction. Leaning forward, he patted its rump, which glistened with sweat. Only then did he turn to look at Cas, who was trembling and biting down hard on his lip. He shouldn't have let his emotions run away with him like that, especially with his little brother by his side.

'I'm sorry, I shouldn't have gone so fast,' he said, shoving a hand roughly through his hair, then sighed. 'Theo isn't a criminal any more than any of the prisoners in the camp.'

'But why are they locked up?' ventured Cas in a small voice.

Frans jumped down to attend to the horse, which was still agitated by the whole episode and snorting heavily while jerking its head up and down. He pulled a carrot from his pocket, letting it snuffle gratefully in the palm of his hand.

'That's a question I can't easily answer,' Frans said, choosing his words carefully. He was trying to remember a similar conversation he'd had with his father when the prison had been taken over by the Nazis three years previously. His father had been angry on that occasion, not only because of the incessant searches of the cart, but because of the senselessness of locking up so many people for no good reason. As Frans considered his father's words, he felt he owed it to his brother to be honest with him, just as Pa had been with Frans himself.

'The Nazis aren't like us. Things are black and white to them, right and wrong, with nothing in between. All I know is that many prisoners in there haven't done anything wrong, but they don't fit into Nazi ideals. And many don't deserve to be locked up, because they haven't committed any crime. Have you noticed the ones with a yellow badge in the shape of a star stitched to their shirts?'

'Is it because they've been good?' said Cas, his eyes lighting up.

'I'm afraid not. The Nazis make them wear a yellow star because they are Jewish. It's because they think they are different from the rest of us.'

'And special?'

'In a way,' said Frans, struggling to get across what he wanted to say. 'The Nazis believe that being Jewish is a crime. But Cas, I want you to know something really important.' He walked round to Cas's side and gently raised his chin so he could look him in the eye. 'Jews are good, hard-working people with families and lives.

Remember Ma and Pa's friends, the Bermans, who ran the *apoteke* in town? They were lucky, because they moved away at the start of the war, so the Nazis didn't go after them. But the ones in this camp are the unlucky ones, arrested only because they're Jewish. But they're not criminals. The criminals are the *moffen* who want to punish them.'

Cas ran his tongue over his lip, which had become swollen from all his biting. He sucked and sucked on it and frowned as he listened to Frans's words. 'I don't think Theo is Jewish,' he said in a brave voice. 'Theo has a red triangle on his shirt. What does that mean?'

Ah yes, of course. The red triangle stitched crudely onto Theo's prison-issue shirt, just like all the other prisoners on the kitchen unit who wore the red insignia, symbolising that they were in there for acts of resistance against the Nazis.

'No, Theo isn't Jewish,' Frans answered firmly. 'The coloured badges all mean something different, so Theo… well… he probably got caught doing something he shouldn't have. It could be something as small as being out after curfew.' It sounded pathetic but was the best he could come up with. 'Look, I've probably said too much. You mustn't be too worried about what goes on in there. Now, let's get home and give the cattle their feed. Mama will be wondering where we've got to.'

'All right,' said Cas in a small voice that suggested he was far from convinced. 'Frans?'

'What is it?' Frans felt himself tense up. The conversation wasn't over yet.

'You know that letter you took for Theo. What if the guards found out? Will they lock us up?' Cas's eyes had grown round with fear.

'No. No. Of course not,' said Frans, reluctant to admit that the very same thought had been troubling him too. 'That definitely won't happen.'

Chapter Thirteen

The more time Frans spent at Kamp Amersfoort, the more he needed to speak to his friends. It seemed incredible that so much was going on right under their noses without their knowledge, but he thought that if they all got together they might work out a way to help some of the people who were most at risk. Frans couldn't speak to his father about why he needed to see his friends, nor would Pa understand why Frans had taken such a risk with Theo's letter. It was his mother who managed to convince Evert to let him out of the house, pointing out that Frans was a young man now, that he'd be able to keep himself safe in town.

It was two miles to Saskia's house. Frans sped along on his bike, on the back roads that skirted low-lying fields edged with water-filled ditches, passing through two villages, no more than a scattering of cottages, until the church tower came into view. He slowed down to turn along a rutted track leading to a low farmhouse with a deep roof that touched the tops of the ground-floor windows. He hadn't realised how much he'd missed Saskia since their meeting at her father's shop the previous week, and his heart beat fast as he propped his bike against the gate and waited for Saskia to appear at the back door, keenly anticipating the prospect of being alone with her for a few short minutes before joining Aart.

She came out and gave him a beaming smile along with a little wave. He waved back and watched as she jiggled her bike key into the lock to release it before wheeling the bike towards him.

'You're late,' she said teasingly, pursing her lips. 'I've been waiting for you.' She leaned in for a kiss, her hair brushing his cheek. He breathed in the scent of her soap, relishing the sensation of being close to her. 'I've missed you,' he murmured into her ear and gently traced her face with his hand before kissing her.

The distant church clock struck the hour. 'Come on. We'd better go,' she said, drawing away from him with a sigh. She mounted her bike and pedalled off. Frans hurried to catch her up, but she pulled ahead with an amused shake of her curls.

'I've so much to talk to you about,' she said when she eventually slowed down so they could ride abreast. 'The latest is that my mum thinks I should leave school. Now that my father's out of work, she says I could be more use to her helping with the housework. She takes in sewing and mending and wants me to help with that too.' Saskia pulled a face.

'And that's not what you want?' asked Frans.

'Of course not. I'd much rather get my qualifications. But it's not just that. I couldn't bear to be stuck at home all day listening to Mum getting paranoid about the raids all over town. It's making me jumpy too. We're quite remote out here so we should be fine, but she just hates the idea of me being out of the house and going off to school each day.'

She glanced over at Frans, who nodded, remembering their conversation when she'd expressed her worries about being arrested, and wondered if she'd told her mother.

She screwed her forehead into a frown. 'If I leave school now, I don't think I'll have another chance to complete my education. What do you think I should do, Frans?'

Frans didn't want to upset her by saying the wrong thing, but he didn't see the point of staying on at school whether there was a war on or not. He'd made his decision to leave school to work on the farm, so the question of furthering his education had never arisen. Besides, his father thought getting qualifications was a waste of time, an indulgence, for anyone prepared to do real work. There was no arguing with him. This was how things were done on the farm, so Frans had never given his education much thought. Now he wondered if Saskia would think any less of him if he were to admit any of this, so decided against mentioning it. But hearing her talk like this allowed him to understand how much it meant to her.

They were approaching a bend in the road and he let her ride ahead for a while before catching her up. 'You can always go back to your studies once the war is over,' he said.

'Hmm. I suppose you're right. There are rumours the school will be closing anyway, so I'd have to study at home and I can't see my mum allowing that. But I have been thinking about the shortages. Our neighbour Mevrouw Smit's husband is away fighting and she has four children to feed and clothe. Father has plenty of old remnants of material and needles and thread I could let her have. At least she'd be able to darn and patch up their old clothes. And I can think of quite a few other families who are also in need.'

They arrived at Aart's house, a big place on the outskirts of Amersfoort, set back from the road, part hidden behind thick laurel bushes. His father had stopped pruning them since a Nazi contingent had moved in and taken over the grammar school down the road as their headquarters. Fortunately, they never ventured in their direction, always heading for town where they were more likely to find someone to harass. Their old haunt, the *De Singel Café-bar*, had been taken over by Nazi soldiers as their local drinking den, so meeting at Aart's house was a good alternative. They could share a beer, swap news and enjoy a chat in privacy.

They wheeled their bikes side by side up his driveway. 'I think it's a really good idea helping people,' said Frans. 'The Nazis keep taking from us and we get nothing but misery in return. We've got no idea how much longer all of this is going to go on for, but I'm sure we could make a difference, however small. I've been thinking about how to smuggle more letters into the camp. I think there's a way I can do it safely and without being caught.'

A little way down the road a car approached and slowed down. A soldier in German uniform peered over at them but didn't stop. They watched as he turned into the school grounds.

'I don't think we should hang around outside any longer,' said Saskia nervously.

'You're right,' said Frans, but suddenly felt uncertain about arriving with Saskia as his girlfriend. He hadn't seen Aart since they'd last met at the café in town and hadn't had a chance to speak to him about their new relationship. 'Shall we just not say anything to Aart about us for now?' he asked tentatively.

She nodded, but not before giving him a swift passionate kiss.

Chapter Fourteen

'Come on in. Dad and Mum are out and I've found a bottle of jenever in the cellar,' said Aart, greeting them with a broad smile.

They went through the scullery into the spacious kitchen, where a bottle and three small glasses were lined up on the scrubbed kitchen table. It was just like Aart to polish them up ready for his guests, thought Frans. He'd only been in here once or twice and was slightly daunted by how neat everything was compared to the farmhouse. There were no boots or clogs kicked off by the back door, no clutter of dishes piled high beside the sink, or pot simmering on the stove, and everything seemed to have its place, even down to each chair with its own matching red and white striped cushion. Then he remembered that Aart's parents were busy doctors and had a domestic help to keep the place neat and tidy – so that explained it.

'I nearly forgot. I've brought a little bit of cheese to go with our *borrel*,' said Frans, remembering his manners and pulling a crumpled greaseproof packet from his jacket pocket. 'It's not much, but Ma insisted I bring it to share with you. It may be a bit old as it's been sitting in our cellar since the beginning of the war.'

'Cheese – how wonderful! I can't remember when I last had some,' said Saskia. She carefully unwrapped the paper and stared at the thin triangle, which was crumbly round the edges. She held it to her nose and inhaled deeply. Her eyes sparkled with gratitude and love as she leaned over to give Frans a kiss on the cheek.

'It's nothing,' he said, embarrassed at how grateful she seemed and wishing he'd cut off a large slice for her to take home and share with her parents. Food was becoming so scarce these days that there was barely anything left to buy in the shops or even on the black market. With the closure of his shop, Saskia's father must be finding it even harder to feed his family.

'Come and sit down,' said Aart, pouring out three shots of the jenever.

They chinked glasses and tipped back the fiery liquid, hands in front of their mouths as they tried not to cough. The first one always had that effect, but by the second, they were sipping and savouring the drink with relish. Frans sat back as Aart and Saskia chatted about various friends from school, people he'd long forgotten about. He wasn't really listening, as he glanced at Saskia and thought how lucky he was that this beautiful and vivacious girl actually liked him. For now, he was simply happy to enjoy the company of his friends, but after a while, Saskia noticed his silence.

'Aart, we should talk about something else. I'm sure Frans doesn't want to hear us going on about school,' she said, nibbling on a corner of the precious cheese.

Aart, who had begun to embark on another anecdote about someone Frans only vaguely knew, looked up in surprise. 'You're right. It is boring. I'm sure your life is far more exciting these days, though I can't say I envy you going into that camp. There's been talk about them building a firing range where they'll be executing prisoners. It's making a lot of people on the town side nervous about getting on the wrong side of the *moffen* and ending up inside.'

Frans shifted in his seat. He hadn't talked much about his work in the camp and the cruelty he'd witnessed by the guards towards the prisoners. He hadn't wanted to upset Saskia with the details, but he'd seen a side to her today that showed him how much she cared about the people around her who were suffering, so perhaps it was time to be honest. 'I haven't heard about the firing range, but I have heard that they're expanding the camp to take in more prisoners. I'm afraid things will probably get worse for a while.'

Saskia nodded, widening her dark eyes. 'You must be scared.'

Frans held her gaze for a long moment. 'I'm scared every time I go in there. But the horse and cart are a familiar sight, so they don't hassle us. Unless there's a new guard on duty, then they like nothing better than to throw their weight about and search the cart.' He shook his head. 'Of course they never find anything, though it's really prisoners trying to escape they're after. One or two have tried their luck in the back of delivery vans. But they always get caught. It's horrible when it happens. I've seen the guards make everyone line up in the prison yard and check each one by making them call out their numbers. If anyone gets it wrong, the guards think nothing of beating them with bats.'

'I'm not as brave as you. I don't think I could do it,' said Aart, blowing out his cheeks. He moved his chair back so he could stretch out his long legs.

'I suppose I'm getting used to it,' said Frans, glancing at Saskia, wanting her on his side as he spelled out his idea to them both. She lifted her eyebrows at him to continue. 'I'm not prepared to stand by any more and see them suffer like that,' he said. 'I can't intervene – that would be madness – but I can do something. Recently, a prisoner called Theo passed a note to me for his girlfriend. With Saskia's help, we contacted her and managed to get a letter back to him. I saw how much it meant to him and I want to do the same for others. I've thought of a plan that I think could work, but it will need Theo's cooperation to hand over letters from other prisoners without being seen. No one takes much notice of Cas when he's with me. He's quick and nimble and could easily stuff letters down his socks or in the waistband of his shorts. Then if the guards on the gate tell us to turn out our pockets or do a search of the cart they won't find anything.'

'Sounds too risky to me,' said Aart, with a look of shock. 'If you got caught, they could lock you up.'

But Frans wasn't listening. 'There's so much more I could do. What if we could also get a few food parcels in for the weakest prisoners? They're literally starving. You've no idea how little they get to eat – watery cabbage soup, day after day, and bread hard enough to break your teeth on.'

'Don't you go in there to pick up the potato peelings? Who gets the potatoes?' said Aart.

Frans snorted. 'Not the prisoners, that's for sure. They go into the bellies of those arrogant *rotzakken* who run the place.' He turned to Saskia. 'You think it's a good idea, don't you?'

'I do, Frans. It's a fantastic idea and I know you can make it work,' she said, gazing at him with shining eyes. 'Just imagine how elated prisoners would feel receiving a letter and knowing they haven't been forgotten. It's got to be worth it.'

Curfew was minutes away and it was time for Frans and Saskia to leave. Aart poured one last glass of jenever. 'It sounds like you two have made up your minds. If there's anything I can do to help… you know… you only have to ask.' He spoke half-heartedly, making Frans think he didn't really mean it.

'Me too,' said Saskia enthusiastically. 'I've got my bike. I can help by delivering the prisoners' letters—'

'Saskia, you don't need to do this,' Aart butted in. 'Think about the consequences. They'd be severe if you were caught.' Aart went to lay a hand on hers, but she quickly pulled back.

'I'll decide for myself whether it's too dangerous. Just because other people are too scared to do anything – but I'm not other people. I refuse to stand by and watch those evil men destroy people's lives.'

Frans felt a mixture of pride and fear as she spoke, delighted to have an ally in Saskia, but with a sense of anxiety too that she could be putting herself at risk.

It was starting to get dark and the sky was turning from light to dark blue as they set out for home. Saskia was in a hurry to get back and they pedalled quickly away.

'I'm not sure Aart agrees with us,' she said. 'He doesn't really mean it when he says he'll offer to help. None of it really affects him. He's shielded from it, living in his nice house with two working parents. What does he understand about real hardship?'

'No more or less than we do. But don't be too hard on him,' said Frans, willing to give their friend the benefit of the doubt. After all, he'd known Aart since they were both six, and he was always kind and caring. He'd been a good friend to Frans.

'Hmm,' Saskia exhaled, as if she didn't agree. They carried on in silence till the turning to her house. By the gate, Saskia dismounted and flicked her bike stand down. 'I shouldn't let it get to me, Frans, but things haven't been easy at home with my father here all day and my mother worrying about every small thing.'

Frans leaned his bike against the fence and walked over to her. The evening had turned chilly and he swept her into a comforting hug.

'I know it's hard for you, but remember you've got me now.' He lifted her chin so he could look into her soulful eyes. *My determined, brave Saskia*, he thought.

She gazed back, pressing her lips together tightly. She looked as if she was trying not to cry.

'Saskia, is that you?' came a querulous woman's voice from the house.

Saskia let out a ragged sigh. 'I'd better go,' she said, and kissed him hard on the mouth with a passion Frans hadn't seen in her before. He responded, kissing her urgently, until she broke away.

'Frans, I meant it about helping with the letters.' Her face was still close to his, but it was too dark for him to read her expression. 'We'll do this together.'

Chapter Fifteen

Frans and Cas sat up on the cart, bowling along the avenue towards the camp. While his brother chattered away beside him, Frans remained quiet, ruminating on how he could put his smuggling plan into practice. They'd run through it many times, till he was confident his brother could pull off hiding the letters down his socks without arousing the suspicions of the guards. Their plan was all in the letter Frans now carried in his pocket, waiting for the right moment to hand it over to Theo. He'd written it with Saskia's help, describing how they would build a network of contacts in and around Amersfoort to organise the receipt and delivery of letters through Frans. Inside the camp, Frans would distract the guards while Cas slipped over to the bin store; Cas and Theo would exchange letters for Cas to conceal in his clothing, and the guards would be none the wiser. But would Theo agree to be their go-between inside the camp? Frans knew this part was risky, as he might refuse to cooperate. But without Theo the plan would fail, along with his hopes of finally being able to help the poor souls imprisoned inside. And that was the problem. Frans had no idea of Theo's wheareabouts since he'd been sent to the rose garden. The place was still a mystery to him and he had no idea what kind of punishment took place in there. If Theo had been left to stand for hours under the sweltering sun, that was bad enough, but what if they'd beaten him so badly that he'd been left to die?

The usual guard wasn't on the gate. His replacement asked a perfunctory few questions about the purpose of their visit. Satisfied, he waved them through. At this early hour, there were few people about and Frans was acutely aware of the penetrating gaze of guards high up in the watchtowers. Hoping he was of little interest to them, Frans fixed his attention on steering the cart through the concrete arch and over to the kitchen block. To his relief, there was Theo, who he recognised from his tall angular frame even though he was sitting with his back to him. The clatter of hooves caused Theo to turn his head and he gave Frans a tiny nod, before returning to his potato-peeling.

Frans and Cas began work, removing the empty containers from the cart and dragging them across the yard to the bin store. The kitchen containers were overflowing with peelings and they had difficulty emptying them without spilling the contents everywhere.

'Here, do you need a hand?' Theo appeared beside them. His eyes darted back to the yard, but there were no guards in sight. From where they were standing they were obscured from the nearest watchtower in the far corner of the compound, so relatively safe from prying eyes.

Frans peered closely at Theo, alarmed to see a greenish-blue bruise blooming under his cheekbone. He told Cas to take the bin back to the cart, so the two of them could have a few words in private.

'What happened to you in the rose garden?' said Frans, conscious he was staring at Theo's bruise.

Theo winced, the memory evidently still fresh in his mind. 'There was barbed wire all around me, ready to tear me to bits. I stumbled but I managed to stop myself falling on to it. The guard wasn't too happy so he punched me in the face. Twice.'

Frans gasped in shock. Since he'd last seen him, Theo seemed thinner and his shoulders sagged beneath his oversized prison shirt. 'Are you sure you're all right?' Frans said quietly.

Theo gently touched his own cheek as if to check, and gave Frans a wan smile.

'I went to the commandant to get you freed,' said Frans, desperate to show his concern.

'You did?' Theo lifted his brows and a light seemed to flicker on in his tired eyes. His suffering was almost unbearable to witness. Frans turned away and fumbled in his pocket for the folded sheet of paper he'd been waiting to hand over.

'Another letter from Annelies?' said Theo eagerly.

'No, I'm sorry. Not this time. This one's from me and Saskia.'

Theo tilted his head questioningly, but Frans knew he was running out of time. He'd grown increasingly nervous the longer they'd been out of sight of the guards. 'Read it and give me your reply tomorrow.'

The following morning, there were too many guards roaming around for Frans to engage Theo in conversation. Frustrated, he went about his work while the guards stood over the prisoners, barking out commands to work faster. From the size of the pile of potatoes in the middle of the table Frans guessed there had just been a delivery.

'I need help lifting the bins. This prisoner can help,' said Frans to a guard standing next to Theo.

The guard gave Frans a fierce stare, as if he was about to object, then seemed to change his mind. '*Schnell!*' he yelled at Theo. 'And don't take your time over it.'

Theo scrambled to his feet and hurried to fetch the large kitchen container. Frans stood to one side with his empty bin, not daring to disappear round the bin store after him. Theo came towards him rolling the kitchen bin and together they filled both as the guards watched closely. Then Theo walked round so the bin was between himself and the guards, and quickly touched Frans's hand, transferring to him a scrap of paper he must have been holding. The two men locked eyes for the briefest of moments and Theo gave Frans the faintest of nods. It felt almost like an electric shock.

Frans screwed the paper tight in his fist, not daring to transfer it to his jacket pocket. Without another glance at Theo, he took his bin back to the cart, where Cas was waiting to help him load it. Only when they had cleared the iron gates and were well away from the all-seeing watchtower did he allow himself to read the single sentence scrawled on the torn sheet, which read, 'Yes, I will.'

Chapter Sixteen

A week later, Cas fished the crumpled notes out of one of his long socks and handed them over. Frans looked at the first and searched for a name and address, though it made him uncomfortable reading this man's private note. It was signed 'Lars'. Frans knew he was the prisoner who helped with the bins. His eyes scanned quickly over the words – *My darling girls, I hope it won't be long till I see you both again.* A wife and daughter who must be beside themselves with worry that he'd been locked away, he realised sadly. Suddenly, the note assumed an even greater importance than it had had moments before.

The second note was an untidy scrawl that looked like it had been written in a hurry. He had to read it through for an address, which he eventually found on the reverse.

> *Lieve Toesie, I'm so sorry. The moffen found me hiding in the coal hole and dragged me out – it was such a shock. Someone must have told them, but who? But you mustn't be worried. I'll be home before you know it. Please write soon and tell me you're all right. Liefs Joost.*

Frans shook his head sadly as he folded the note over, trying but failing to imagine himself in Joost's position. He found it hard to believe that innocent men like this had been imprisoned with no prospect of being freed any time soon.

'What are you going to do with them?' asked Cas, who'd been waiting impatiently for Frans to say something.

'They'll need envelopes and then they'll be ready to send off,' Frans said wearily. He went over to his mother's bureau, where she kept her red leather writing folder. He found several small envelopes and a pen in one of the desk drawers and proceeded to copy out the addresses. Slipping each letter inside, he licked the edge of the envelope and pressed it down with the heel of his hand.

'I wonder how many others want to do the same,' he said, more to himself than Cas, who was standing at the window watching his sisters digging up carrots for lunch. 'Off you go and help, Cas.' Frans smiled. 'And thanks for what you did today.' But Cas wasn't listening – he was already halfway out of the door.

Cas had played his part well and Frans was more determined than ever to help as many prisoners as he could stay in contact with their loved ones. Together, Frans and Saskia sounded out acquaintances in town and beyond who were unsympathetic to the Nazis in order to set up a secret network to deliver letters. Once the word spread about what Frans and Cas were up to, he'd been surprised how keen everyone was to help. Before long, what had started out as a small act of defiance against the Nazis became a lifeline for those most in need.

Frans knew he'd have to tell his parents. Mama had turned out to be one of his most enthusiastic supporters, though Pa needed more persuading.

'I can't understand why you're using Cas as a carrier. Your job is to make sure he's safe,' Pa grumbled. He sat across the table opposite Mama, Frans and Cas.

Mama jumped to Frans's defence. 'You've always said no one in there takes any notice of a child picking up food scraps. You should know that after all the years you've been going in and out of that place.'

'Pa, I've thought it through and I'm not going to stop now,' said Frans in a resolute voice. 'Already I can see what a difference it makes. Those people stuck inside never receive news from their loved ones. A single letter… just think of the hope it gives them.'

'And with such a small thing, we can give a little happiness to these poor people deprived of love and kindness,' said Mama, warming to the theme. 'In fact, Nelly and I were talking about it only the other day. She wants to help too and has acquaintances in Limburg she thinks would be willing to deliver letters on our behalf.' Mama's cheeks grew red and a strand of hair came loose and fell over her cheek. 'I agree with Frans. He must carry on. I don't think we have any choice.'

'I still worry that you'll get caught,' said Pa, though the fire had gone out of his words. He looked down at the cigarette he'd been rolling, which lay unlit on the table in front of him, and slotted it between his lips. Frans waited for him to say something else, knowing his rejection simply came from fear for his family. He caught his mother's eye with a smile. At least he had her support.

Cas watched, fascinated by the cigarette that waggled between his father's lips. He reached for the box of matches, struck one and held the flame steady while Pa sucked on the end of the cigarette till the tip glowed red. Pa often let Cas do that when Mama wasn't around to scold him. Today, she said nothing.

'It's actually been bothering me too.' Pa spoke in a gruff voice. 'People know of the harsh conditions inside the camp and send in parcels with food, soap and medicines. But they never reach the prisoners as they're confiscated by the guards to be distributed among the *moffen* to enjoy.' He sucked on his cigarette and let out the smoke in a long sigh. 'You're right, Frans. We have to help them, but it must never be at the expense of your and Cas's safety. Understand?' He turned to Cas. 'You've been brave hiding letters and keeping calm. But remember, this isn't a game. Make sure it's just letters and that nothing changes hands when any of the guards are about,' said Pa, back to his stern self.

Cas bit his lip. 'Yes Papa. I'll be careful, but look how stretchy my socks are. I reckon I can get loads down without anyone noticing.' He demonstrated by shoving his hand down one of his long socks and wiggling his fingers inside it. It made Frans and Mama laugh and even Pa smiled.

'I'm sure you can, but don't get carried away. It's a serious business. And, Frans, I'm relying on you to be extra vigilant.'

'Don't worry, Pa, I'll make sure we keep it top secret,' said Frans, delighted that Pa had finally bought into his idea. He remembered Theo's expression when he'd received that first letter from Annelies, and imagined the relief Lars and Joost would feel, knowing their loved ones were safe. He couldn't wait to do more.

Chapter Seventeen

Before long, the Koopmans house became the nerve centre for all the incoming and outgoing mail. The small sitting room was turned into a busy makeshift post office and the armchairs were pushed against the wall to make way for a trestle table in the middle of the room. In one corner, Pa had strategically placed a large wooden chest on an old Persian rug that concealed a hiding place he'd made beneath the floorboards. It was the place he kept the illegal wireless set that he brought out each evening so the family could huddle round and listen to Radio Oranje, which broadcast from London with news and information to counter German propaganda. The space was easily big enough to hide the letters and parcels, should any German soldiers come snooping.

The twins were marshalled by Frans into ensuring each letter from the camp was ready for delivery by sorting the letters into piles. Cas's job was to take the letters, many just tattered and torn scraps of paper smelling strongly of the disinfectant used in the camp against fleas and lice, and scan each for the recipient's name and address, which he wrote onto a clean envelope. The post was then ready for delivery through their network of trustworthy volunteers, including Saskia, who promised Frans she would be careful and only cover a small area close to home during daylight hours.

Nelly came once a week, travelling by train to Amersfoort from her home town of Limburg, wearing a large leather bag strapped to her body. No one would have guessed it contained illicit letters hidden in the secret pocket underneath. She also carried a wicker basket with some provisions her mother had packed for the Koopmans family, and half a Limburgse *vlaai*, a delicious fruit tart the Koopmans children were always thrilled to receive. If stopped and questioned, she could easily explain they were for her relatives in Amersfoort. And treats were such a rarity these days that the children always awaited Nelly's arrival in a heightened state of excitement as if *Sinterklaas* himself was about to arrive with a bulging sack of gifts.

The smuggling operation was turning out to be a success, but almost too much so. Each week, Nelly came with more letters, but there was a limit to the amount Cas could conceal about his person. It had been so easy when there was just the occasional letter, but once relatives heard there was a way they could get post to their loved ones they began to send parcels too – packages of food and small items of clothing. Frans made it clear they wouldn't accept anything larger than a slim book, until one arrived that was too big and bulky to be concealed in Cas's clothing. Straight away, Frans recognised the name on the package: *Lars Brandwijk, Kamp Amersfoort* – and his resolve broke. Lars, with the wife and daughter, who relied on him to deliver their precious letters – of course he would make sure Lars received it. But he would need to break it down into two smaller parcels if he was to get it past the guards without them knowing. Nothing had been discovered by the camp guards yet, so perhaps he could take the risk of delivering something larger. He untied the string holding the brown paper together and found a woollen vest, a pair of long grey socks, a notebook and pencil. When he came to refold the vest, he found a letter wrapped up inside. Careful not to look too closely, he parcelled up the items so they lay flat, one on top of the other.

Frans waited up on the cart for Mama to finish with Cas, watching as she carefully pushed a letter down each of Cas's socks. It took an age as she smoothed and patted the sharp corners of the envelopes to make them less conspicuous, a task made more difficult as he kept fidgeting to get away from all her fussing. 'Keep still, will you,' she said, with a quick slap to his leg.

'You're scratching me,' whined Cas. He bent down to shift one of the envelopes that was bothering him. Stooping down again, she straightened out the offending sock. Cas squirmed free and ran over to the cart, where Frans was waiting and worrying whether the parcels he'd concealed in a tin box and screwed beneath a wooden slat on the cart would be discovered.

The cart shook as Cas climbed up and sat down next to Frans with a thud. They were ready to go. Frans clicked his tongue and the horse shifted the cart forward.

'Be careful!' called Mama, seeing them off with a wave.

'Of course, Mama. We always are,' said Frans, waving back. 'Cas, go on, wave.'

Cas seemed to emerge as if from a daydream and lifted his hand half-heartedly.

'You're very quiet today.' Frans gave him a sideways glance. 'You're not having second thoughts, are you?'

'What? No, I want to do this,' said Cas in a firm voice, but Frans wondered if he was more fearful than he let on. Everything had gone so smoothly when all Cas had done was exchange a few letters with Theo. At that point, the thrill of deceiving the guards and not getting caught had seemed like a big adventure, but Frans had been pushing Cas to take on more, perhaps too much, without considering how he was feeling.

'Under the tarpaulin there are two packages,' said Frans. 'They're hidden in a tin box under the floorboards. I'll park up by Block IV. We won't be seen there. But if the guard is about, I'll distract him and we won't go ahead.'

Cas's face had turned pale and his hands began to tremble. *This won't do*, thought Frans. 'If it looks as if the guard is at all suspicious then we won't go through with it,' he said. 'I'm not going to force you do to anything you don't want to. We can always try again another day.'

As fate would have it, Frans recognised the guard, a fearsome individual called Meiss, but he was determined not to be intimidated by him. Frans had grown used to the frequent requests to search the cart and hoped that he'd eventually get the message that they were hiding nothing incriminating.

'Open up! Let me see what you're trying to get past me today,' said Meiss with a smirk, and he banged his fist on the side of the cart.

Frans got down and nodded to Cas to do the same. He obliged by letting down the side and hoisting the empty bins out, followed by the tarpaulin. The floor of the cart was completely bare. Meiss stared with a disgusted expression on his face, as if this were a complete waste of his time. He sniffed deeply. 'You won't fool me with your tricks. When you come back, I shall undertake a thorough search. For now, you may enter,' he said in his harsh clipped voice and went over to unbolt the gate.

Frans headed straight to the hospital block, which stood directly behind the bin store. Theo had observed that few guards ever ventured in that direction; they were paranoid about catching an infectious disease off the prisoners, so they kept well away. It gave Frans and Theo the perfect opportunity to exchange a few words and smuggle items. Meanwhile, Theo had got to know and trust the doctor in charge, who was only too willing to help out. His job was to look after the prisoners' health and well-being, but he was delighted to have the chance to help them keep in touch with their families. He stored the packages inside his office, where only he had the key. Together with Theo, he ensured they reached the right recipients without the authorities having any idea it was happening.

Theo was waiting by the bin store for Frans as he parked the cart close to the hospital block. He watched as Frans climbed up and lifted up the tarpaulin to reveal a square black tin box screwed in between the floorboards. The lid squeaked as he slid it back, removing the two small packages wrapped in brown paper. He handed them over to Theo, who put them inside his shirt for safe keeping. His jacket hung loosely over the top, hiding the incriminating evidence.

'Those are for Lars. Some warm clothing,' whispered Frans. 'I had to open the parcel and make two smaller ones so they fitted in.'

'Thank goodness,' said Theo. 'His bed's next to mine and he often talks to me about his wife and baby daughter. He misses them so much, he'll be so pleased.'

Frans motioned to Cas to hand over the letters concealed in his socks. Glancing at one of the envelopes, he saw it was addressed to Theo. 'One from Annelies. Saskia went to see her.'

'The second this month. I was worried she'd given up on me. She's so good to me.' Theo kissed the envelope and stuffed it along with the others into the waistband of his trousers. He disappeared through the door of the hospital block while Frans replaced the tarpaulin. When Theo returned, the three of them worked speedily to load up the cart with the potato peelings before any guards became suspicious.

They were on their way to the exit when Frans spotted the commandant deep in conversation with the entrance guard by the gates. His heart sank at the sight of the two men. *Had Meiss called the commandant over to conduct a search of the cart together? What did they hope to find?* he wondered, reining the horse to a halt. He told himself to remain calm. He no longer had any parcels on the cart and Theo hadn't given any letters to Cas that day.

'Ah, good morning, Frans,' said the commandant, his stern face breaking into an insincere smile.

Frans wondered if Berg had forgotten to salute. 'Good afternoon, Herr Commandant,' he said.

'You've met Herr Meiss, I believe?'

Frans glanced over to the guard, whose face was twisted into an unpleasant smile.

'He searched the cart on the way in.' Frans forced a pleasant smile back at him.

'Ah. Searches will now be a formality, you understand. Herr Meiss has joined us from Dachau where every vehicle is checked on entry and exit. I have decided we should do the same here.'

'Indeed. People who think they can get away with smuggling in stuff won't get past me,' Herr Meiss said and rapped his swagger stick against the palm of his hand.

'Thank you, Herr Meiss,' said the commandant, a note of irritation in his voice. 'I'll take over from here. It won't be necessary to do the exit search on this occasion.'

Frans waited while the guard clicked his heels, saluted and marched back to his post. *Good riddance*, he thought with a shudder. But the commandant wasn't finished.

'May I have a word in private? It won't take a moment,' he said. 'Your brother can wait here.'

Frans hesitated, unwilling to leave Cas by himself, but didn't think he could refuse. 'I won't be long, Cas, I promise,' he said, handing him the horse's reins. Cas sat up straight, his lips white with fear. Frans had no choice but to follow the commandant to his office. It was one of the low brick buildings that overlooked the yard. Frans imagined him standing at the window, his eyes like searchlights sweeping the yard, not missing a thing. He wondered if that was what this was all about – he'd been found out and was about to face the consequences. Looking quickly towards the concrete arch, he was relieved to see it was just out of his sight line. The commandant would have to stand outside his office to be able to see through to the kitchen unit, but knowing this wasn't enough to stem Frans's growing apprehension.

'Please sit.' The commandant closed the door with a click. His office was sparsely furnished, just a large, empty, polished desk in the middle of the room with two chairs on either side. Frans sat down and looked up at a large poster, impossible to miss, of the *Führer* staring out at crowds of people, all gazing up adoringly, arms held high in a stiff salute. He quickly averted his gaze, disturbed by the image and what it represented. It wasn't that he didn't know about these rallies attracting thousands of people who swore allegiance to the *Führer*, but seeing it so starkly portrayed made him realise just how far the dictator's influence had spread.

The commandant walked round the back of the desk and unlocked a drawer. 'As you know, it's become necessary to check anyone coming into the camp, which is why I've put my most senior guard in charge. We have tradespeople who come to the camp and he spends a good deal of his time conducting searches of their vehicles. I'm pleased to say he has stopped goods from being smuggled in on behalf of the prisoners and has thwarted several who were attempting to escape.'

Frans felt himself grow cold and kept very still.

'Now, I've known your father a long time. He's been coming into the camp since long before I was here and I've never had a problem with him. I trust him. As he's your father, I trust you too.'

Instead of relaxing at the commandant's reassuring words, Frans found himself tensing up. Was he trying to trick him into an admission? But the commandant wasn't looking for Frans to say anything. He kept on talking.

'I have something I think will make your life easier. You won't have to come through the front entrance and be searched.' He placed a small metal box onto the desk and extracted a rusty key from it. 'This will open the gate to the back of the camp. Only two exist and I have the other one. Make sure you don't lose it.'

Frans stared at the key, which lay cold in the palm of his hand. The only words he could find to say were, 'Thank you.' He hardly dared believe he was being granted entry whenever he pleased.

'You must not abuse this privilege,' said the commandant, his voice menacing. 'If you are ever seen trying to enter the camp other than to pick up food waste, there will be serious consequences.'

Frans's heart was light as he walked away from the commandant's office with the key in his trouser pocket and his mind brimming with possibilities. The key represented something much more than a means to open the gate – it would give him the freedom to concentrate on his smuggling operation and make a real difference to prisoners' lives.

Chapter Eighteen

Saskia

Hoevelaken was a little out of the way for Saskia, but after Annelies introduced her to a few local families increasingly anxious for news from relatives in Kamp Amersfoort, she was soon making visits every week. Dropping in on Annelies became a highlight, when Saskia could let her guard down after the strain of knocking on doors while watching out for German soldiers, and she was able to relax in her new-found friend's company. The girls found they had much in common, despite the four years that separated them, and could easily while away an hour of two chatting in each other's company. After years of German occupation, it was a relief to be able to share the thoughts and concerns they carried with them every day.

Annelies was waiting for her and opened the door before she had a chance to knock. 'I saw you coming,' she said. 'Come on in. I've put the kettle on. My neighbour has made some biscuits.'

'Biscuits? How on earth did she manage that?' said Saskia, wrinkling her nose at the idea. The grocers were out of all the ingredients everyone took for granted before the war and people had to make do with whatever they could lay their hands on. Baking without flour, fat or sugar tended to be a hit-and-miss affair.

'She didn't say, but she told me she was pleased to find some spice left over from Christmas. Don't say I didn't warn you,' Annelies said with a knowing smile.

Annelies poured two cups of ersatz coffee and placed them on the table along with a plate of the biscuits. Saskia took one and gingerly bit into it. It was rock hard and when she eventually managed to bite off a corner it flew out of her hand and bounced across the table. Annelies could do no better and they both collapsed into fits of laughter.

'Guess what?' Annelies said, her eyes bright. 'I've got a job giving lessons to the neighbour's two children. She was beside herself when their school was shut by the Germans and didn't know how she would cope with them at home, as she works all hours as a seamstress. I never imagined I'd find work here.'

'That's wonderful news. And you're doing something you love,' said Saskia. Although she seemed brighter with every letter she received from Theo, Saskia sensed that Annelies was still not herself. Not only must Annelies be consumed with worry for Theo, but she was dealing with the loss of her teaching job in Utrecht and the move to this quiet town where she had no friends.

Annelies nodded. 'The children were a bit unsettled at first, but the routine is doing them good. Me too, as it helps keep my mind off Theo. And my mother's stopped nagging me to find something useful to do with my time.'

'I'm not sure my mother would approve if she knew what I get up to,' said Saskia, as she reflected on how anxious her mother was since her father had been forced to close the shop. 'She frets every time I go out of the house, so I don't tell her the whole truth. She knows I'm helping Frans deliver a few letters in the village, not that I'm going much further afield. If she knew, she'd only try and stop me. Am I wrong not to tell her?'

'Not as long as you're careful and don't take unnecessary risks,' said Annelies carefully.

'I don't think I do. At least, not compared to Frans. Sometimes, I can't bear the thought of him going into the camp with letters hidden on his cart and being stopped and searched. I'm scared of turning up at the farm and his mother telling me they've locked him up in there.'

'You mustn't think like that,' murmured Annelies.

'I'm sorry to go on about it,' said Saskia, realising that her concerns must be making Annelies feel even worse about her own situation. Then she remembered she had a letter, a folded piece of paper, from Theo and dug it out from the bottom of her bag where she had hidden it between the leaves of a notebook. 'For you,' she said, handing it over.

'Oh,' said Annelies, suddenly serious. 'I do hope he's all right.' She frowned as she read the letter. Folding it back over, she shook her head and sighed. 'He talks about how he's been able to get letters to the prisoners with Frans's help. He wants to do more. Sounds familiar, doesn't it? But he's in such a precarious position, it could get him in even worse trouble. I hoped by now he would have learned his lesson.'

Saskia listened as Annelies spoke of her fears, which had started long before Theo had been arrested. When he'd first mentioned the Resistance meetings Piet had been attending, Theo had said they didn't interest him, but Annelies had suspected otherwise. She had tried to warn him of the dangers of getting involved, but he had brushed away her concerns, even promising her that he would never go along. 'I see now he didn't want to worry me, but Piet was so persuasive, he got sucked in. And now Theo's paying the price,' Annelies said sadly. She began fingering the piece of paper again. 'I don't know what I'd do without these letters.' When she looked at Saskia, there were tears in her eyes. 'Your visits mean so much to me. And it's not just the letters. You're the only person I know who understands what I'm going through. Will you promise to come, even if there's no news?'

'I wouldn't miss coming for anything,' said Saskia, and really meant it. 'I promise.'

Chapter Nineteen

Frans

Whatever lay ahead, Frans always enjoyed the ride to the camp, the soothing clip-clop of hooves striking the path, the splinters of sunlight piercing the tops of the tall beech trees bristling with chirping birds, and Cas riding alongside him. And today he could enjoy it more, knowing that he had the commandant's key. Finally he had the chance to do even more than he had before.

He had to remind himself that the main purpose of his trip was to collect the potato peelings, without which they would struggle to keep the cattle fed, but his main concern was ensuring that the precious cargo hidden in the cart would arrive safely. What if one of Berg's more nasty guards was waiting for them at the back gate ready to undertake a search? He knew he would never get away with it. It was easy to fool them when he'd concealed just two small packages in the tin box. But half a dozen bulky packages under a pile of blankets and covered by a tarpaulin? There was no way he could stop now given the volume of letters and parcels they were handling. Nor did he want to. The prisoners had come to rely on his efforts to bring words of comfort and small packages from their loved ones – every single one of those prisoners was deserving, even if he couldn't help them all. It was up to Theo to single out those most in need, such as Karel, the 55-year-old man whose 'crime' had been to trade in black market medicines. The medicines were to treat his wife's cancer, but she had sadly died not long after he'd been detained at Kamp Amersfoort. After months of incarceration and weakened from malnutrition, only his sister-in-law's kindness helped him survive. Frans made sure that her parcels of bread, tins of meat and cheese always reached him.

Up ahead, the watchtower loomed into view, large and forbidding inside the barbed-wire fence. There was one at each corner, providing a view down into the prison yard and also onto the path outside the fence. The shadowy form of an armed guard inside these wooden structures was the only suggestion that they were manned day and night.

Frans stared straight ahead. The horse slowed, awaiting instructions to turn right along the perimeter fence topped with razor wire. They arrived at the back gate. Frans hopped down, patted the horse and pulled the key from his pocket. The tall gate was in shadow and at first, Frans didn't notice the shiny padlock. It was attached to a heavy metal chain wound several times around the bars of the gate, securing it to the wire mesh fence. He stared uselessly at his key, knowing full well it wouldn't fit. Were they deliberately trying to keep him out? He felt a wave of panic, knowing that Theo would be waiting over by Block IV and wondering where he'd got to. He had no choice but to turn round and go to the front entrance, where that terrifying brute Meiss was sure to be waiting.

'Change of plan – looks like we'll be going in through the front today,' he told Cas in as cheerful a voice as he could muster, though he worried about being intercepted and found to be carrying an illicit cargo.

They were turning onto the avenue when a raucous bellowing erupted from inside the fence, followed by a high-pitched scream. Frans tensed up, expecting to hear gunshots from the watchtower, but there were none. Cas was chatting to the horse and seemed oblivious to the ruckus, but Frans suspected some awful maltreatment was taking place just out of sight over the wire fence. There'd be no avoiding it today.

Cas deftly brought the horse to a halt by the gates as Meiss came striding towards them, spine upright and hand held high in a salute. Frans thought it best to salute back. Now was not the time to show any signs of defiance.

'The key I was given by the commandant doesn't fit the lock on the back gate. Can you tell me why?'

'It's out of bounds. A security risk we can't afford,' said Meiss, an unpleasant smile curling his lip.

'But the commandant only just told me—' Frans began. Before he could continue, the scuffle of feet and shouting of voices caused the horse to whinny and stamp its feet. Frans leapt from the cart to quieten it. A group of men approached, dragging three men in handcuffs through the dust. All of them were in camp uniform. Behind them marched two SS officers, yelling and lashing out with their swagger sticks. Two massive black dogs prowled alongside, straining at their leashes and growling menacingly with bared teeth.

Instinctively, Frans grabbed hold of the reins. He no longer cared that he had a job to do – all he wanted was to get away. But Meiss had other ideas. 'Tie up the horse and come with me,' he snarled at Frans with a sly smile.

'We'll come back later,' said Frans, his foot already on the wooden step up to the cart.

'No, I want you to see this. And bring the boy.' Meiss grasped Frans tightly by the arm and wouldn't let go till he'd fastened the reins to a nearby fence post. Cas crawled down from his seat and cowered next to Frans, and together they watched the three handcuffed prisoners making painfully slow progress towards the entrance gates. Each had a yellow star displayed prominently on their chest. Frans grasped Cas close against him, pressing his head into his side so he wouldn't have to watch. At last the group passed through the gate, followed by their minders. Meiss locked the door of his sentry box and propelled Frans and Cas towards the spectacle that was unfolding.

Hundreds of prisoners were filing into the yard, hurriedly lining up in rows. The three handcuffed prisoners were kneeling on the ground at the front, their heads bowed down on their chests.

'Those three dirty Jews tried to escape but we found them,' hissed Meiss, with undisguised delight. 'Watch and take note. Just remember, you Dutch will receive the same treatment if you ever try to disobey an order from the German authorities.'

Frans flinched at the words, a harsh reminder of how little it would take for a man like Meiss to turn against him. He reached down and clasped Cas's hand tightly. Meiss grabbed hold of his other arm as if he didn't trust him not to run away.

'Look now,' he growled.

Frans couldn't bring himself to stare at the poor kneeling wretches, so scanned the rows instead for any sign of Theo. His eyes darted from one man to the next, but they all looked so similar with their shaven heads, deadpan expressions and loose-fitting prison clothes. Their faces were inscrutable, but Frans noted how many had their eyes fixed on anything but the three men kneeling before them. From where he and Cas were forced to stand, he could see the victims shaking with fear as they awaited their fate. Then, out of the corner of his eye, he saw the Nazi officers arriving with their dogs. When they spied the three prisoners, the hounds set up a frenzied barking.

Surely they wouldn't? Would they?

No sooner had the thought formed in his mind than the dogs were released with a terrifying roar, their fangs glinting. They leapt onto the men, ripping at their clothes. Meiss appeared mesmerised by the spectacle and loosened his grip on Frans long enough for him to cover Cas's eyes. The attack seemed to go on and on, but was probably over in less than a minute. Their work done, the dogs were brought back under control – as far as that was possible – and were led away, slavering and growling.

For a long moment, nothing seemed to happen. The rows upon rows of prisoners stood as still as statues. Frans plucked up courage to open his eyes. Cas trembled against his body, but he was unable to comfort him. Frans dared not look too closely at the three inert shapes, though he could see their clothing was now stained red. With a gasp, he fixed his gaze on the long concrete building at the far end of the compound, and became transfixed by a scraping, scuffing noise. Half a dozen prisoners appeared, dragging a large lumpy straw mattress along the ground as if they were pulling a reluctant person with them. With difficulty, they hauled it across to where the three men lay. The two SS officers came marching over, this time without the dogs, and barked out the command to remove the 'vermin'. Several minutes passed as the prisoners tugged and pushed the motionless shapes onto the ancient mattress, now spilling its grubby contents onto the ground. Frans choked back his tears.

'Come. One more thing you should see,' said Meiss, his face so close Frans could smell his rancid breath. He took hold of Frans's arm again and marched him back through the arch, Cas clinging on in his haste to keep up.

At the entrance gates, a lorry was idling, acrid black smoke filling the air, with its back down. A guard stood by smoking a cigarette, which he quickly stubbed out when he saw them approach. Meiss ordered Frans to wait. A minute passed, then two, before the ghastly procession came into view, slowly making its way towards them. It was the same group of prisoners, now heaving the mattress along with its gruesome cargo. They looked exhausted, but the SS officers in charge kept beating them on the back of the legs each time one of the bodies threatened to roll off onto the ground. With an unpleasant smile, Meiss stood by and watched, slapping his swagger stick in his palm. Finally, they reached the lorry and the unfortunate men were ordered to heave the bodies into the back.

Frans didn't wait. Grabbing Cas's hand, he ran across the road, quickly untied the horse and scrambled on to the cart. His only thought was to get away from Meiss as fast as he could before he could taunt them further. Meiss had wanted to show him that the Nazis would stop at nothing in their desire to crush the human spirit, that they were always watching…

Chapter Twenty

Ever since that terrible day at the camp Frans had been scared to return, but now his desire to help became too strong to ignore. It took him days to figure out his plan, but he knew what he needed to do. The back entrance was no longer an option – it was clear to him that Meiss would not allow it to be used – so he knew he had to find a way to enter through the front. Until he could do that safely, he would come alone.

The previous night, Cas had woken with a start, screaming and shouting, until Frans went to lie beside him and hold him till he quietened down. It was enough to wake the girls on the other side of the wall and their whimpering cries brought Mama from her bed, too. After everyone had settled down, Frans lay awake, listening to his brother's breathing and occasional sobs, and knew he couldn't put him through this any more. His thoughts were confirmed by Mama the next morning.

'I suspect that it's all getting too much for Cas. It's best he doesn't go on the cart with you for now. But Frans, is it safe for you?' She gazed fearfully at him.

Frans didn't want to worry her more than was necessary and was reluctant to say anything about the horrors Cas and he had witnessed. 'I'll be fine. The horse and cart are such a familiar sight around the camp and the guards don't take much notice of me. I have to carry on, for Pa's sake and for the prisoners. They all rely on me now.' But even as he said the words, he felt apprehensive that things weren't going to be quite that simple any more.

Frans had been going into the camp long enough to know how the shift system worked. Meiss always knocked off at six o'clock on the dot, handing over to Roel, a local Dutchman Frans knew, who worked the night shift through till six in the morning. Roel had been a casual labourer working at all the farms in the neighbourhood, including the Koopmans' at harvest time. He was a hard worker and Frans got on well with him, but he had left when he received his call-up demand. He'd said he intended to work for the Germans at a munitions factory over the border, but was persuaded to come and work as a guard at the camp. It wasn't uncommon for local men to join the SS, who ran recruitment drives promising a regular wage and good career prospects, whatever they might be in a place like Kamp Amersfoort. But Frans wondered if Roel had been aware what horrors went on behind the gates before he'd taken the job.

Frans waited a little way down the road between two large beech trees. He could hear Meiss exchange some words with Roel, before lighting up a cigarette, turning up the collar of his coat and walking away in the direction of town. He waited a few more minutes, till Meiss was out of sight, before giving the horse the signal to move off.

Roel had his back turned as Frans drew up alongside and announced himself.

'Frans! I haven't seen you in a while. Are you still doing the potato run?' he said.

Frans nodded. 'I had a key to the back gate. That is until they changed the padlock. I have no idea why, as the commandant had agreed to give me access. Do you know anything about it?'

Roel shook his head. 'I don't get told much. Probably because I'm on nights. But it's good to see a familiar face. As you can imagine, there aren't too many round here. I miss working on the farms with all the lads. I don't suppose there are many left now.' He looked wistful as he walked over to the gate and rested his hand, as if he wanted to keep talking.

'We were down to three men last harvest. The ones left aren't old enough to be called up. I'm also safe for now,' Frans said with a dry laugh.

Roel came a few steps closer so he could speak more quietly. 'None of us are safe. I'm only doing this job because it pays regularly and I can help my family, but those Nazis can turn on anyone if they feel like it. You should be careful when you go in there. You might be too young to work for the Germans, but they'll find any excuse to lock people up. I've seen lads in there not much more than sixteen. It's not right.'

Frans knew there was truth in Roel's words, but he had a job to do. 'Do you work shifts every night?'

'Except Sundays. My day off. If I'm here you won't get any trouble from me. Not like Meiss—' He stopped himself from saying anything further.

'I know. He's from Dachau. I've heard they do even worse things than here. You must be careful, Roel.'

Roel nodded in agreement and patted him on the shoulder. 'Thank you, Frans. And you too.' The gate made a loud screech as he pushed it open, and he waved him through.

Frans had a dozen more questions burning in his mind. But first, he needed to find Theo.

He took his time crossing the yard, warily avoiding the penetrating gaze of the guards high up in the towers. He didn't want to attract their attention by his presence, so fixed his attention on steering through the concrete arch. A handful of dejected-looking men were at work peeling potatoes, but there was no sign of Theo as he set about removing the empty containers from the cart and dragging them over to the bin store. He was wondering what could have happened to him when he heard a door opening and Theo came out of the hospital block. His face brightening, he gestured to Frans to follow him round the back of the building that faced the perimeter fence, beyond which a line of trees was visible, the tops of their branches swaying gently in the breeze. Here they were both hidden from the view from the nearest tower in the far corner.

'I'm sorry they made you watch,' Theo said, staring outwards at the wire fence. 'And Cas too. They shouldn't have done that.'

'So you were there? Everyone looks the same when they're lined up and I couldn't make you out.'

'Yes, I was there. Along with the whole prison camp. But why were you?' asked Theo.

Frans leaned in to whisper. 'If they hadn't changed the padlock on the gate, we wouldn't have been. I'm sure it was Meiss's idea – he seemed to be waiting for us when we came round the front. I haven't been back since. Especially after seeing those three men murdered… I still can't get it out of my head. But Saskia and Nelly keep bringing in post and I can't just leave it piling up. Promise me you'll keep helping, will you?'

Theo looked worried, but nodded his assent. 'We can store the post in a locked cupboard in the doctor's office till it's safe to hand out. Do you have anything with you today?'

'No, I was too scared to bring anything. But I've spoken to Roel on the front gate and he'll let me in without searching the cart.'

'Does he know what you're doing?'

Frans shook his head vigorously. 'No, there's no need. The less anyone knows about it the better.'

They both jumped at the sound of a door slamming, followed by the clack of footsteps running off, before dying away.

'You'd better go. We can't be seen here,' Theo said urgently. 'Go back to the bins and I'll wait a few more minutes till the coast is clear.' He laid a hand on Frans's arm and held his gaze. 'I'm sure we'll make it work.'

Chapter Twenty-One

Theo

Theo was exhausted, but sleep refused to come. He tossed from side to side, unable to find a comfortable position on the lumpy mattress that conspired to keep him awake. He crooked his arm to support his head and stared down the long line of bunk beds stretching the entire length of the hut. Every single one was occupied. The moans and shouts that erupted from them throughout the night were another reason he was unable to sleep, coupled with the harsh light emanating from lightbulbs hanging down from the ceiling that seemed to burn through his closed eyelids.

He had no way of knowing exactly how long he'd been locked away in this camp, but guessed from the darkening mornings that it must have been at least six weeks, possibly longer. Panic flooded his chest. Six weeks during which he'd never been told the reasons for his arrest or how long they intended to keep him here. The fact that none of the other prisoners knew anything about their own fate and seemed no longer to care only made things worse.

When he'd first arrived, he'd been in denial. He told whoever was prepared to listen to him that the authorities would realise their mistake and release him very soon. His enthusiasm was met with sad looks and silence from the sorrowful-looking men who sat with shoulders drooped over their work, peeling potatoes hour after hour, day after day. Slowly, it dawned on him that nothing was going to change. Hunger, exhaustion, threat of punishments and dread at what could be in store for him began to take its toll.

His thoughts turned to Annelies and how he hadn't been entirely honest with her when he'd scribbled that note saying he'd only be away for a few days. But he'd only been trying to protect her from the truth. And maybe he'd even believed it himself at first. Before he'd arrived here he'd never even heard of Kamp Amersfoort, let alone the ill-treatment of innocent people held prisoner behind its wire fences, so why would she have any idea of how bad things were? He'd spared her the details. And in her letters to him, Annelies never blamed him for what he'd done, just promised to do all she could to get him out of his prison; but they both knew his prospects for release were low. Theo clung to the memory of his dear sweet Annelies. She didn't deserve to be put through this.

And now there was the increasing guilt he felt because he had it so much better than all those prisoners who didn't have someone looking out for them. He was one of the lucky ones who had a connection with life outside the camp, all thanks to Frans and Saskia, who were prepared to risk so much for so many. Theo realised his options for escape were limited, and it was all he could do to muster the energy to keep going, but keep going he must.

At one point, he'd considered approaching the guards, but had quickly realised this was a bad idea. Their job was to keep order, prevent anyone from accosting them and dole out punishments whenever they felt like it. So soon after inciting their wrath and ending up in the rose garden, he knew it would take little for him to be branded a troublemaker. He suspected they'd find any excuse to punish him again. In his current state, he wasn't sure he could endure another gruelling spell standing stock-still for hours on end, a punishment designed to break the toughest of men.

These dark thoughts continued to rob him of his sleep, until out of the blue an idea came to him. It might backfire terribly, but if he could prove he had committed no crime, it might offer him the means to escape.

*

It was just after midday and the yard had emptied out. The guards had disappeared off to enjoy the kind of cooked lunch Theo could only dream of and the prisoners were lining up at the canteen to receive their miserable portion of watery soup. Theo, at the back of the queue, slipped away unnoticed. He kept close to the perimeter buildings, making sure he was out of sight of the watchtower, though he suspected that the guard up high was more interested in his cheese sandwich than anything Theo was up to. His mouth watered and his empty stomach clenched uncomfortably at the memory of sinking his teeth into fresh bread and the taste of creamy cheese. He hurried on, eager to get his assignation over and done with.

The commandant was examining a map of the camp pinned to the wall.

Standing in the doorway, Theo cleared his throat to speak, and the commandant swung round to face him. A fleeting look of annoyance passed across his face as if he'd been expecting someone else, but he quickly composed his severe features, which were accentuated by immaculately cut dark hair slicked into place above a pair of thick black brows.

Theo drew in a sharp breath, almost losing his nerve. He had to remind himself that Frans had stood up for him on this very spot and persuaded the commandant to release him from the rose garden.

'Herr Commandant. There's something I wish to ask you,' he began nervously. 'There was no one else I could think to ask.'

'Don't just stand there. Close the door if you're going to come in,' said the commandant in an irritated voice. 'Your number?'

Theo had been about to introduce himself, forgetting that prisoners were only ever addressed by their numbers. He pushed the door shut behind him. '25764,' he said, reciting the number stitched to his uniform.

'What is it you wish to ask me?' The commandant stared at him and knitted his brows together. It was obvious he was annoyed he'd been interrupted at work. Theo dropped his gaze, before remembering why he was there.

'I want to know why I was sent here. It's been six weeks and I've been told nothing. There must have been a mistake as I've done nothing wrong. I was hoping you would be able to look into the matter…' His voice trailed off as he realised how ridiculous his rambling words must sound. Why would the commandant take the slightest interest in Theo, a nameless prisoner among hundreds, possibly thousands, under his command? Theo waited for the commandant to bawl him out and call one of the guards to haul him away, but was surprised to see him nod as he stood listening. He turned to pick up a fountain pen from his desk and began twirling it between his finger and thumb, as if contemplating Theo's words.

'Repeat your number again,' he said as he began leafing through the black ledger that lay open on the desk. Once he'd located the entry, he fell silent. A deep frown line appeared between his brows.

'It's written there, isn't it? The reason I'm here,' Theo blurted out, his nerves replacing his earlier boldness.

'Correct,' said the commandant and looked down, as if to check. 'Utrecht, 8 September 1944. Participation in an illegal gathering of individuals intent on undermining Nazi activities.' He paused as if expecting Theo to say something, but Theo kept his face very still, sensing, dreading there was more. The commandant stared at him a moment longer, before continuing. 'Utrecht, 9 September 1944. Involvement in mass attack on municipal Nazi-occupied buildings, including the hurling of missiles and chanting of anti-Nazi abuse.' He looked up again, a callous smile curling around his lips. He shut the book with a decisiveness that suggested the matter was closed.

'It's not true,' cried Theo, though he realised he'd been cornered. It was inconceivable that his attendance at that Resistance meeting would be enough grounds for deportation to this camp; the accusation of the attack had blatantly been made up to strengthen the case for his arrest. 'I wasn't involved. I had nothing to do with it,' he pleaded, desperate for the commandant to believe him.

'I suggest you save your words, young man,' growled the commandant nastily. 'Your insolence since you arrived here has already been brought to my attention. First you addressed a guard without being spoken to and again when you were in the rose garden.'

'All I said was I hadn't done anything wrong,' pleaded Theo, remembering how he'd shouted out in pain at the guard who had hit him in the face, only to be struck again.

'Quiet! I firmly advise that you stop answering back and that you avoid denying the truth about your actions. If I hear you continue to show such lack of respect to my men, the consequences will be severe.' The commandant walked over to the door and waited for Theo to leave.

Fortunately, Theo could find no words to convey the burning injustice he felt at that moment, but had the sense not to answer back. His resolve crushed, he walked despondently away from the commandant's office and back to a life of misery without end. He knew he'd made a terrible mistake.

Chapter Twenty-Two

Frans

Saskia's occasional visits to the farm became a welcome distraction and Frans always listened out with keen anticipation for the squeak of her bike when she rode into the farmyard. Before even speaking, they would always hug each other close, as relief washed over them that they were safe in each other's arms.

Over cups of tea in the kitchen, Saskia told him about the families of prisoners who were so grateful for any news and who tried to press small gifts of food on her, which she always refused. Everyone had to go short these days and she couldn't bear to take from those who were suffering more than most. She listened as Frans confided his worries about the constant arrivals of prisoners, the harsh work regime they were subjected to and how little they were given to eat. He told her that Roel, the sympathetic guard, had been a good ally, keeping him informed of when Meiss was off duty so he could move freely in and out of the camp without being searched. As a result, the whole process tended to go a lot more smoothly. Even the guards on duty were less strict with the prisoners knowing that their superior wasn't about to criticise and cajole them. Once Frans realised they hated Meiss as much as the prisoners did, he became a little less fearful himself.

But it took a little longer before Cas was ready to resume trips to the camp. Neither Frans nor his mother wanted to force Cas into doing anything he wasn't ready for, but watching his older brother go off on the horse and cart with the letters made him change his mind. He was much quieter these days, no longer so cheerful and chatty, so Frans came up with 'beat the horse', a game that they would play after leaving the camp, and a reward of sorts for accompanying him into that wretched place. Running through the trees and undergrowth was the distraction Cas needed, helping him let off steam and regain his infectious enthusiasm for life. And when Cas was happy, so was Frans. He needed his help inside the camp if the smuggling operation was to be a success.

'Are you ready?' said Frans, as they approached the tree that was the starting point for Cas to jump down, race down a parallel path and emerge through the trees before Frans arrived with the horse and cart.

Cas bobbed his head with excitement and jiggled up and down in his seat. At Frans's word, he leapt down and shot off into the trees.

Frans knew exactly how long it took for Cas to reappear, so kept the horse going at a steady trot – until a loud thump from the back of the cart grabbed his attention. Frans had to yank hard on the reins to stop the horse from bolting.

'Whoa boy! Gently now, it's all right,' he called out as calmly as he could.

Whatever had caused the noise continued to agitate the horse, so Frans was forced to halt the cart and go to try to steady it, but it just pawed at the ground and neighed frantically, setting up a commotion that echoed through the trees. Frans held on tightly to the reins and tried to calm the horse with soothing words, as well as offering the carrot he carried for emergencies.

'What's going on?' cried Cas, running towards them in a panic.

'It's all right, nothing to be worried about,' said Frans. 'A dog or something disturbed him, but he's fine now.'

The horse munched the carrot contentedly by his side. But not for long, as a rustling from the undergrowth caught their attention. It didn't sound like the scuffles of an animal through dead leaves. The horse whipped its head round and Frans tugged on the reins to stop it from rearing up. Then from the corner of his eye he saw a man emerge from the bushes. His eyes were wide with fear and he held a finger to his lips. Frans jumped back in shock, causing the horse to snort and toss its mane. He stared at the sunken-eyed man, a forlorn figure in tattered jacket and trousers that hung off his skeletal frame. Just visible on one lapel was the faint outline of a star, where a badge had once been stitched.

'Have you come from camp? On my cart?' he gasped, shocked at how terrible the man looked.

The man held a hand up apologetically and glanced anxiously behind him. 'Please, I can explain everything,' he said in an accent Frans didn't recognise.

Frans was growing more apprehensive. They were no more than half a mile from the camp and anyone might come across them, especially anyone on the hunt for an escaped prisoner. But he didn't have time to ponder this thought, as the horse began playing up again. He knew if he let go of the reins, it'd bolt down the avenue and most likely overturn the cart.

'Can I help? I know a bit about horses,' said the man in a tentative voice.

Frans nodded. He held the reins while the man pressed his face against the horse's mane, whispering to it in a low voice. It gave a couple of quick snorts before dropping its head.

Frans watched in astonishment. 'Where did you learn to do that?'

'Back home in Poland. My father used to train horses. He taught me tricks when I was a child. I love horses, but it's a long time since I've had one,' he said with sad eyes. 'This one, he's a beauty.' He looked at Frans quickly. 'I'm sorry to put you to all this trouble. When I jumped off, I was going to run off, but I came back when I saw you were struggling.' He lifted his palms in a gesture of helplessness.

'No, it's fine. But I can't believe you made it out on my cart. How did you?'

The man gave an embarrassed smile. 'I've been watching you come and go these last few days. You're from the farm down the road, aren't you? The orderly told me when he came to take my temperature and found me staring out the window. Block IV. I was there recovering from a bout of pneumonia. He came yesterday and told me they were sending me back to the building commando today. We have to shift concrete blocks all day without a break. But I have no strength. Of course, they know that. They're always looking for an excuse to shoot prisoners.' He glanced apologetically at Cas, but he was listening transfixed to the man's story and the earlier look of panic had left his face.

The man continued. 'I watched you come with your cart and worked out how I could slip on board and hide under the tarpaulin. When I saw you filling up the bins this morning, I knew it was now or never. When your back was turned, I crept on board and managed to squeeze into a corner without you spotting me. My plan was to jump off the cart once we were well away from the camp and disappear. I don't suppose you could give me a ride to somewhere a bit safer?'

Frans stared at the man, realising he'd underestimated him. The man must have been terrified for his life, but had the guts to overcome adversity and stand up to his tormentors. Frans was impressed, but his admiration was short-lived – he now realised the magnitude of the problem facing him. The thought of turning up at home with an escaped prisoner in the back of the cart sent a fresh wave of panic through him. He had no idea what to do, but they needed to move quickly.

'I'm so sorry…' he blurted out. 'But we'll get caught.' Without warning, tears filled his eyes and he tried furiously to blink them away.

The man peered at him with a concerned frown. 'Of course. I didn't mean to cause you any trouble. I'll leave you now and you can forget any of this happened. Thank you for helping me get out.' He gave a small bow and patted the horse one last time on the muzzle before turning away.

'Wait,' said Frans, suddenly filled with remorse. 'I didn't mean… what if I…' He grappled for the right words. How could he abandon this man after all he'd been through? But he couldn't say no, he simply had to help him. 'I can't take you into town – it's too dangerous, for both of us – but I could get you closer to Hoevelaken, which will be safer. Do you think you can make your own way if I drop you off?'

The man looked relieved and came back over so he could pump Frans's hand. 'Thank you, thank you. You've done so much for me. When this is over, I'll come and thank you properly.'

Frans gripped the man's thin bony hand and wished he could do more for him. At least he would be taking him to safety.

'Let's go,' he said, after the man had clambered aboard and crawled under the heavy tarpaulin.

'Thank you,' came his muffled voice from behind. Frans raised his eyebrows and exchanged a brief smile with Cas. The horse broke into a fast trot and, once they'd put a good distance between themselves and the camp, Frans let out a long breath. When they reached the outskirts of Hoevelaken, Frans searched for somewhere inconspicuous to drop his unexpected passenger.

'Will you be all right here?' he called back, halting the cart next to a ragged clump of trees at the edge of a field. He vaguely knew the family who lived in the smallholding just visible at the far end. He really didn't want to put them at risk, but knew he couldn't take the man any further. Steadying his nerves with another deep breath, he pointed across the field and said, 'Head over there. They'll be able to help you.'

The man began thanking him again, but Frans made a dismissive gesture with his hand, anxious that he should get away as quickly as possible. With Cas at his side, he watched the man hesitate at the field's edge before stumbling over the ruts to the line of trees before disappearing from view. He didn't look back.

'Will he be all right?' said Cas in a wavering voice.

'I hope so.' Frans kept staring at the empty field until he could be sure the man wasn't coming back.

Unwilling to delay a moment longer, he set off for home before anyone could notice the horse and cart rattling along the bumpy road.

Chapter Twenty-Three

The incident had shaken Frans up. These days, before leaving the camp, he checked under the tarpaulin for stowaways. All it would take was for Meiss to turn up on the gate and search the cart, and it would all be over. He hid his concern from Cas, saying that it was extremely rare that prisoners tried to escape. Even so, they agreed they should stop playing 'beat the horse'. Instead, they sat rigidly side by side as they rode along the long avenue, alert for anything out of the ordinary. For the first few days, Frans nervously stopped to check his cargo in a clearing a little way from the camp. He couldn't be too sure.

Frans's thoughts often returned to the prisoner he'd helped escape. No news must mean he'd got away, so Frans could only hope he'd had a sympathetic reception from the Bos family. It was a criminal offence to hide anyone from the Germans and many were so fearful of reprisals that they had no misgivings about turning away someone showing up on their doorstep looking for shelter. Taking in Jews was exceptionally risky. And Frans thought the star left in outline on his dusty shirt might once have been yellow. If the man had been turned away, his chances of staying safe were slim. Frans shuddered to think of him wandering around the countryside lost and hungry before being discovered and hauled back to Kamp Amersfoort to be executed in full view of all the prisoners. And it would all have been Frans's fault…

He decided to mention the matter to Theo the next time he handed over the post. The guards were always hanging around, but turned a blind eye to Cas as he nipped back and forth between the bins and the cart. He liked to play his part in this secret operation and had mastered the art of concealing letters and small items down his long socks and the waistband of his shorts, hastily swapping them for any outgoing post with Theo by the bins. When there were bigger items, Theo gave Frans a signal to drive the cart behind the bin store on the pretext that the bins were too full that day to drag them into the yard. It was a delicate manoeuvre involving the three of them keeping watch as they exchanged gestures and winks so that no one could guess what they were up to. They relied on the stupidity of the guards not to notice their method of communication, while the kitchen unit were so immersed in the monotony of peeling potatoes that they failed to notice what was happening under their noses. Cas was good at keeping watch, allowing Frans and Theo to disappear out of sight.

When Frans asked Theo if he'd heard about the prisoner's efforts to escape, he was surprised to learn he knew all about it.

'Jozef used to watch from up there.' Theo pointed to a small window set high up in the wall of the hospital block. 'He'd been planning his escape for some time and noting the time you come each day. He watched us talking below his window, imagining we were planning *my* escape.' Theo scoffed, as if such an idea were ludicrous. 'I told him I couldn't help him, but I never imagined he'd do something like this after what happened to those three Jewish prisoners. We're all getting so scared now, so ill and hungry… I don't know how long we can all survive.'

Frans remembered he had a letter from Annelies, given to him by Saskia that morning. He knew it was the only thing that could cheer Theo up. Theo gave a wan smile as he took it and hid it down his trousers. Frans stared at him and took in the purple shadows beneath his eyes, his thin angular face and his shoulders slumped beneath his baggy prison-issue shirt, and wished there was something more he could do to help him. But what? He was already putting himself and his family at risk by smuggling in post, but it was obvious that Annelies's letters and the occasional parcel were simply not enough to sustain him. For the first time, Frans was really worried for his friend.

Theo seemed to misinterpret his concern and kept talking about Jozef. 'It was a risk he had to take. He knew he hadn't much chance of survival once he'd been released from the hospital. This place makes men do desperate things, that's if it doesn't break them first. And if I'm truthful, there was another reason. I saw helping Jozef as an experiment. If he could get out, then maybe I could too.' He held Frans's gaze expectantly.

'No, it wouldn't work,' said Frans backing away. 'Smuggling letters is one thing, but if you think I can get you out… I just know it'll end up badly for both of us.'

'Shh, keep your voice down.' Theo darted a look in the direction of the yard, but the guards were otherwise occupied. Cas was taking his time securing the containers to the cart and cast a fleeting smile in their direction. All clear for now. Still, nothing could be taken for granted in this place.

'You're right of course.' Theo sighed. 'I'm sorry – you're already doing so much for us.'

'It's not like that, Theo. I would do more, honestly.' But Frans felt powerless to do anything.

'Sometimes I can't believe how I ended up here.' Theo spoke so quietly that Frans had to strain to hear.

'You've never told me. What did happen?' Frans had thought he knew Theo so well as he'd been with him most days and was acutely aware of how desperate he was to get back across the wire fence to the girl he loved. But truthfully, he knew very little about him.

'My boss asked me along to a meeting,' Theo replied. 'I didn't want to go, but when we got there, it was crammed full of people who'd come to hear a speech by someone who heads up a Resistance group in Utrecht. He got up on the rostrum and urged us all to stand up and fight the Nazis. It was electrifying. It opened my eyes to what's happening to our country. I had no idea about all the things the

Nazis were doing – it's hard to believe everything the speaker said. Then the meeting was cut short when a load of Nazi thugs stormed the building. I was one of the unlucky ones who got arrested. It all happened so fast and days later I found myself in here. That's when I realised that everything I'd heard that night was true.' Theo spoke quickly and kept glancing over anxiously to see where Cas had got to.

'Stop. I can hear voices,' hissed Frans urgently and laid a hand on Theo's arm. 'You'd better not be seen with me. Go.'

Theo managed to slip through the door of Block IV just as Meiss came marching over, fury etched on his face. Frans pretended to brush some dirt off his hands and looked up with a smile that belied the thumping in his chest. 'I'm just finishing off here,' he said in a level voice.

'Where is the other one?' growled Meiss, then went to prowl over by the bins and thwack his swagger stick against them. The metallic clang reverberated throughout the small space.

'We were putting the bins back. Then he went off,' said Frans as firmly as he dared.

Meiss frowned so deeply his brow almost covered his tiny eyes. 'Where did he go?' he snarled, so close that spit landed on Frans's cheek.

Frans blinked hard. 'He didn't say. He just went, maybe off to do another task. Now, if you excuse me, I have to go.'

Meiss grunted as he stepped aside, but was clearly put out and continued to bang on the side of the bins as if expecting his quarry to be hiding inside.

Frans hurried over to Cas, who was waiting by the cart, looking anxious.

'Why didn't you give me the sign?' he hissed as the horse began moving off.

'I tried to, but he just turned up,' said Cas. 'He was in a hurry and walked straight over to where you were. Like he knew you were there. Sorry.'

Frans shook his head. 'It's not your fault.' But it bothered him that Meiss might know about their secret activities. Already on edge, he started violently at the sound of a klaxon blaring out across the compound announcing roll call.

'We'd better go,' said Frans, urging the horse towards the exit. Meiss was in a temper and no doubt brewing up for another confrontation with Theo. They left, with Frans feeling torn between leaving Theo to face Meiss's wrath and his desire to protect Cas from another gruesome spectacle.

Chapter Twenty-Four

Theo

The astringent smell of disinfectant made Theo catch his breath. The corridor stretched out in front of him, with grey featureless doors on either side. Quietly, he crept along the scoured tiles until he reached Herr Doktor's office. The door was ajar. He peered through the crack, but there was no sign of the doctor, who was probably seeing to patients on the main ward. Entering, he checked to see that he was alone and walked over to the window, where he could hear Frans's voice and the clipped tones of the guard. It was a strain to make out the words, but he desisted from opening the window for fear of drawing attention to himself. More pressingly, he needed to find a place to hide in case the guard decided to come searching for Theo himself.

In one corner of the office was a small storeroom. It was officially used for medical supplies, but was also the place where the doctor hid the parcels before they were distributed to the prisoners. Theo was familiar with the room, having come in here to help Herr Doktor sort the parcels onto the shelves. He knew it would be locked, but he also knew where the doctor hid the key. Locating it in its usual place, tucked away in a packet of cigarettes in the bottom drawer of the desk, he kissed it, and set about unlocking the door.

From inside he could make out that the voices had ceased, but from the sound of it, that idiot guard was making a fool of himself by beating his stick against the bins. Theo made himself small by crouching behind a stack of cardboard boxes. Only then did he stop to think what he'd got himself into. All he'd done by coming in here was to buy himself extra time. His only hope was that Meiss would be too scared of catching something contagious if he came looking for him inside Block IV. But he must remain vigilant, for even if the doctor were to discover him hiding in his office and take pity on him, he would still have to go back and explain himself.

The decision was taken from him when the raucous alarm of the klaxon rang out, the summons to roll call that he simply could not afford to miss. His absence would be noted and he'd be in even greater trouble. Reluctantly he left his hiding place and made it out of the office. He was going back down the corridor to the front door when a voice rang out, commanding him to stop. Theo froze, his hand on the door handle, and turned to see the figure of Herr Doktor, white coat open and flapping, as he hurried towards him.

'Have you come to see me? I'm sorry I wasn't there,' he said, then, staring at Theo's stricken face, said, 'Is everything all right?'

'Not exactly, but I can't say anything more right now. I need to get over to roll call.'

'Of course. But come back soon. I've been too busy on the wards to sort through things.'

Theo nodded. He knew he was referring to the packages.

'I'm worried there are perishables in some of them,' the doctor continued.

'I'll come as soon as it's safe to do so. Must go,' Theo said with an apologetic smile.

He was out of the door before the doctor could say anything more, grateful that this slight delay would mean that Meiss had gone off to attend to the masses filing into the main compound. It was a laborious task fitting in all the prisoners from the entire camp, the only time that the women and children were allowed contact with the men, however fleeting. The rest of the time the two halves of the camp were segregated by the high wire fence.

Theo caught up with a few stragglers and managed to slip in at the end of a row near the back. No one dared utter a word as a deathly hush descended on the yard. It was the usual rigmarole of humiliation that could last for hours. Up to half a dozen guards prowled up and down, staring down the rows, ready to pounce on anyone they took exception to. Anyone with any sense ignored them and kept their gaze rooted firmly in front of them. But no matter how many times he stood there, Theo was always terrified he'd be picked on next.

Row by row, each prisoner was commanded to call out their number. If anyone stumbled over the words, the guards made the whole row repeat theirs, sometimes starting all over again with those standing at the front. Then, at random, they'd pick on someone, forcing them to come forward and jump up and down in time to the guards' chants until they were too exhausted to carry on. Several whacks to the back with a swagger stick were the final punishment before they were allowed back into line.

Theo let his mind wander to the conversation he'd had only minutes before with Frans. If there was some way that Frans could get him out of here, perhaps with Roel's help… His mind jolted back to the present when he heard the prisoner next to him recite the last digit of his number.

'*Nächste!*' roared Meiss, fixing Theo with a malevolent glare.

His number should have slipped off his tongue – he'd repeated it often enough – but he faltered on the fifth digit.

'…*zwei fünf sieben sechs v-vier…*'

A look of pure delight mixed with malice crossed Meiss's face as he marched towards Theo and hoisted him out of his row by the arm. His vice-like grip was so painful that Theo squirmed to wriggle loose, but Meiss only clenched tighter. Wincing, Theo bit down hard on his lip and allowed himself be propelled to the front, where he was made to face the sea of impassive faces before him. A sudden fear of impending death shot through him as he waited for the blows to start raining down. But nothing happened, until a roar erupted that seemed to split the air in two.

'*Zum Rosengarten. Sofort!*' Meiss screamed, his voice hoarse with excitement.

Theo glanced quickly at all those pairs of eyes watching him and detected a shiver that seemed to ripple along the rows.

Two granite-faced guards stepped forward and escorted him to the place every prisoner in Kamp Amersfoort regarded with dread.

Chapter Twenty-Five

Frans

Frans brought the horse and cart to a halt at the front gate and braced himself for a disagreeable confrontation with Meiss. There'd be no avoiding him this morning as it was his day for the morning shift. Frans hoped he would have forgotten about the day before and be more lenient about searching the cart. But to his immense relief, it was Roel who emerged from the sentry box.

'Haven't you heard?' said Roel, his eyes red-rimmed and small from lack of sleep. 'Two prisoners escaped late last night and the place is in chaos. Meiss made me stay on the gate as he's heading up the search. They've been out all night scouring the woods. You surely heard the gunshots?'

Frans was shocked. 'No, I didn't, but the farm's quite a way from the woods. Cas, did you hear anything?'

Cas sucked on his bottom lip as he thought about it. 'The search-lights woke me up with their blinking. They seemed closer than normal. I saw them sweep over our field. But I didn't see anyone.'

Frans was surprised he'd slept through without noticing, but maybe he was getting used to the nightly light show. The security breaches at the camp were happening more frequently, but it was still rare for a prisoner to escape. Usually, they were caught before realising that climbing the perimeter fence could only end in disaster.

'I've been told not to let anyone in to the camp today.' Roel spoke quickly, his eyes darting nervously about him. 'I've already turned away two vans delivering food for the officers this morning.'

'Look, I have a job to do and if I'm not allowed in, the cattle won't get their feed.' Frans spoke more confidently than he felt. He'd rather turn round and go home, but his father relied on him to collect the peelings. And Cas had half a dozen letters hidden in his socks, including another from Annelies. He had to stand his ground.

Roel glanced at his watch and gave an uneasy nod. 'All right. I don't think Meiss will be back for a while. But hurry. If he discovers I let you in I'll be in for it.'

Frans felt sorry for the young man, not much older than himself, who'd landed a job where he was under constant surveillance from his overbearing superior. He watched as Roel went to open the tall iron gate, which made a loud whine not unlike an animal in pain. It made Frans wince, but fortunately there were no guards about to hear the metallic screech. Frans wasn't sure what to expect inside, but it wasn't the chaos Roel had described. The yard was almost deserted, apart from a couple of men peeling potatoes in their usual position at the kitchen unit.

There was no sign of Theo. Frans hoped he'd escaped harassment the day before and was over at Block IV fetching letters from Lars and Karel for him to send to their families.

As he looked around, he noticed that a couple of grim-faced guards were pacing the yard, hands tightly gripping their rifles. Together with Cas, he attended to the bins, aware they were being watched. 'Take this over to the cart,' he told Cas, wheeling one of the tall metal bins towards him. He walked over to the two prisoners at work. 'Can you help me with this one?' he addressed one of them, then in a softer voice asked what was going on.

'Two prisoners escaped this morning on their way to the forest commando.' The young-looking prisoner looked frightened and spoke so quietly Frans could barely hear him. 'The guards were furious and took it out on the rest of us. We're the only ones left.'

'What's happened to the others?' asked Frans, forgetting to speak quietly. His heart beat fast at the thought that Theo was somehow involved.

Neither man replied, but, with fear in his eyes, one jerked his head in the direction of the front entrance. Frans opened his mouth to ask if they'd been taken out of the camp, just as one of the guards came up behind them and poked the prisoner who'd been speaking with the end of his rifle.

'What are you talking about?' he growled.

Frans gave a start. He didn't recognise the guard and wondered if he'd been drafted in specially following the escape. His colleague sauntered over and, before he knew it, had Frans and the two men surrounded. Frans cast an anxious glance at Cas, who'd had the sense to climb back onto the cart.

'I'm here to pick up the waste,' said Frans, as firmly as he dared. 'I come every day. It's been agreed with the commandant.'

Both guards towered over him, smirking unpleasantly. Frans flinched at the sound of a rifle click. But they weren't interested in him. The rifle was pointing at the prisoner who'd been whispering to him. He'd gone extremely pale and dropped his hands by his sides as if accepting whatever was about to come to him.

'You will tell me what you were discussing,' said the guard, pointing the rifle.

When the prisoner didn't answer, Frans spoke up. 'I was only asking him where everybody was. There are normally seven or eight men working here,' he said with a boldness he didn't feel. He kept his gaze directly on the guard.

'Who works here is none of your business and I suggest you leave now.'

'But I have to finish the job. My cattle need their feed. The commandant knows that,' said Frans, panicking.

'We give the orders here.' Both guards took a step towards Frans, who retreated to the cart and slammed the back shut in a hurry.

He realised there was no point arguing – if they turned on him there was nothing he could do to stop them keeping him there. He glanced back at the two prisoners, who'd slunk back to their seats to resume their work. No doubt they'd be punished as soon as the horse and cart were out of sight.

But it wasn't over yet. Roel must have seen them approach and had opened the gate to allow them through, but now he seemed to be distracted by something just outside on the road. As Frans drove through and turned onto the avenue, he almost ran into a large group of dishevelled-looking men, women and children, new arrivals to the camp. The horse whinnied in fright and reared up, almost upending the cart. Frans and Cas leapt off, Frans holding onto the halter, Cas, face pressed into its mane, attempting to calm it with soothing words. And then Frans caught sight of Theo just visible through the barbed-wire fence. He was standing ramrod straight and staring right at him. Theo was back in the rose garden, and this time Frans knew there was nothing he could do to help.

Chapter Twenty-Six

Theo

When they finally released Theo, he was close to collapse from exhaustion, hunger and thirst. Hour after hour he counted the chimes of the clock tower in his head, eventually losing all sense of for how long he'd been made to stand upright with no respite. How he yearned just to squat on his haunches to relieve the pain in his legs, or briefly lie on the hard ground and snatch a few moments of sleep. But that would defeat the object of the punishment, designed to browbeat prisoners until they lost their balance from exhaustion so they became entangled in the wire spikes with horrible, even fatal, consequences.

Twice, the darkening night sky lightened with the dawn and when the sun came up it beat down on him as he stood upright on his concrete patch surrounded by sharp wire spikes. From time to time, prisoners were brought in to stand alongside him, only to be released a few hours later. Theo tried to work out why his punishment was so much longer, but his mind kept drifting. All he could think was that Meiss must have something to do with it.

Theo was jolted from his stupor when the metal gate creaked open and two guards entered. They had come to release him. One on each side, they dragged him out of his wire cage into the yard. His legs didn't seem to work as he stumbled between them. They passed several prisoners, who either kept their heads down or shot him a sad look. They all knew it could so easily be them.

Theo was marched to the detention block and was locked in an airless, dim cell furnished with only a dirty mattress, a blanket and a tin bucket. From the rank smell emanating from the bucket, he guessed it couldn't have been emptied since the last occupant. But he was so relieved to be out of the sun and able to lie down, he no longer cared. He lowered himself painfully onto the dirty mattress, too exhausted to care about the stains. From the direction of the corridor came the muffled sounds of scuffles, footsteps, raised voices and cries, followed by the occasional thud of a door swinging shut and the grate of a key in the lock. Outside the tiny barred window halfway up the wall he could hear that evening roll call had started. He was grateful he no longer had to suffer that humiliation.

His mind drifted till he was on the edge of consciousness, but he wasn't quite able to let go. The shouts of the guards as they barked out their unending commands were like some form of new torture. *Eins, zwei, drei… Halt! Nochmals!* Over and over again.

But after enduring his latest punishment in the rose garden, he was no longer frightened. Exhaustion and thirst from being forced to stand for hours in the blazing sun, followed by a sharp drop in temperature at night, had left him stripped of all emotion. At least he could rest. He shivered and pulled the scratchy blanket round his shoulders, trying to force his mind back to happier times before he knew that such a terrible place existed. He closed his eyes and thought of the walks he and Annelies took on Sunday afternoons to the nearby park, sitting on their bench beside the duck pond. If he thought hard enough he could remember the softness of her hair that flowed down to her waist and the scent of her skin when he leaned in to kiss her. Had he told her he loved her? He couldn't even remember. Reaching down, he touched the letter Frans had given him before he'd been banished to the rose garden. It had lain pressed against his skin all this time, but he needed to regain his strength before he could bring himself to read it.

A fresh wave of despair gripped him as his thoughts moved to Frans and his selfless efforts to bring post in and out of the camp at personal risk to himself and his little brother. Theo had leapt at the chance to help and make a difference to the wretched lives of his fellow prisoners. It was the perfect scheme, fooling the camp administrators and guards and providing a lifeline for them. And the younger farmer's boy's bravery astonished him – the way Cas never gave anything away and brazenly concealed letters down his socks and parcels on the cart without the guards ever suspecting a thing. They were incredible, reflected Theo, as he remembered everything they had already done for him.

He twisted his aching body into a less awkward position. As he lay in the darkening gloom, he resolved that if he ever got out alive, he must find a way to thank them.

Some time later, a raging thirst woke him from a fretful sleep. For a short blissful moment, Theo forgot where he was, but the sound of footsteps approaching his cell abruptly brought him back to the present. He scrambled to his feet, trying pointlessly to make himself invisible against the cold damp wall of his cell. Was this it? Had they come to kill him?

The door swung open and he just had time to catch sight of the green triangle stitched onto the jacket of the guard, who, with a grunt, pushed a tin cup of water and lump of bread along the floor before slamming the door shut. Theo fell on the cup and sucked greedily, heedless of the taste of mildew – or something else he dared not think about. He could easily have drained the lot, which wasn't much, but he left an inch in the bottom, in case this was the last he'd get for some time. He did the same with the bread, so stale he could barely bite down on it until he dipped a corner into his precious supply of water to soften it. It was hardly a meal, but was the first sustenance he'd had for two whole days.

It was morning. That much he could guess from the trickle of light seeping in between the bars of the window. Before long, it would be roll call. But before that, the low rumble of wheels and clip-clop of hooves announced Frans's arrival to collect the bins. In two steps, Theo was at the window, and pulled himself up by the bars so he could see out. He did a quick scan of the yard before calling out as loud as he dared. But his voice came out as a hoarse whisper and it was obvious that Frans couldn't hear him above the clatter of hooves and rattle of the cart as he headed towards the kitchen block.

The muscles in Theo's arms trembled and he slid back down onto the cold concrete floor. Despair enveloped him. His hopes dashed, he gave up hope of ever reaching Frans again.

Chapter Twenty-Seven

As the days passed, Theo pondered on what lay ahead. After two gruelling sessions in the rose garden, he knew that it was unlikely he'd escape severe punishment a third time. Both times he'd been lucky and singled out for relatively minor misdemeanours, but if the guards were to discover what really went on behind the kitchen block, it would be the firing squad for him. He shuddered, but clung on to the belief that what he was doing for others was the right thing to do. His act of defiance had also brought him closer to Annelies, but he couldn't bear to think that his lifeline to her had been cut.

Lying back on his mattress, he was determined to conserve what little strength he had, but it was so hard. All he received in the way of food was leftovers after the other prisoners had received their own meagre bowl of lukewarm filth, but he had to force it down if he was to be in any fit state to survive. And he needed to build his muscles to get stronger if he was to endure whatever gruelling regime the guards had in store for him. At first, all he managed before his arms quivered and shook were five tentative press-ups. He nearly gave up but, instead of focusing on the futility of it all, he kept Frans, Cas and Annelies in his mind's eye as he pushed on. Little by little, he increased the number until he was able to do fifteen without stopping. After five days he switched to the bars of the window, which he used to hoist himself up. Soon, he was able to do half a dozen pull-ups with ease. Only slightly out of breath and feeling pleased with himself, he had just rolled onto the mattress to rest when a thought slowly took root in his mind.

With trembling fingers, he searched under the mattress for the blue envelope and stared at the writing as he plucked up courage to open it. The writing was smudged and faded after being pressed against his damp skin all the time he'd stood in the rose garden. He slid it open with his finger, making a ragged tear. Inside was a single sheet of paper written on both sides. He quickly turned it over and, seeing 'Annelies', written in her familiar hand, caught his breath.

Lieve Theo

How are you coping, my love? I still can't believe you're still locked up for something so minor and pray they're not treating you too badly. But I'm so worried you're not getting enough to eat, so I'm saving my coupons to send you a parcel of food. There are shortages all over now, but I'm putting a little aside for you when I can. Last week, I went to buy some potatoes and found the greengrocer was closed. A neighbour told me he's been forced to hand over all his produce to the Germans. I now have to cross town to queue up at the only greengrocer that's still in business.

Oh Theo! Every time I write I worry my letter won't reach you, so I pray this one will. I want you to know I think of you night and day and the time we'll be together again. If this one reaches you, please try and get a message to me through Saskia. She comes like clockwork even when there's no letter in case I have one for you. She says it's worth her while as she has a few 'customers' in the area. We've become such friends. I've come to depend on her for news as she also brings her copy of Het Parool. *It doesn't make for easy reading but at least I'm able to follow any news about the camp.*

Theo my love, please stay strong. I miss you so much.

Your one and only Annelies xxx

Tears streamed down Theo's face as he gently placed the letter back in the envelope. He folded it until it was small enough to hide in his trouser pocket, a reminder that Annelies still cared for him.

The following day, not long after a tin cup of lukewarm coffee and lump of stale bread had been shoved through the door of his cell, Theo heard the scrape of a key in the lock. He froze when he saw the guard filling the doorway with his bulk, then caught sight of another equally hefty man standing behind him. Both wore the green triangle on their jackets, signifying a history of criminal violence and singling them out as prisoners that people should fear within the camp. Everyone knew that they were given special privileges in exchange for doing the guards' dirty work, including the most vicious of assignments. Theo was nearly as scared of these prisoners as he was of the SS guards. No prisoner ever dared cross someone bearing a green triangle.

'You're to come with us. Get out, now,' growled the first in a thick Russian accent. Both men stepped inside the cell, one on either side of Theo, almost lifting him off the ground.

'Where are you taking me?' gasped Theo, almost paralysed with fear.

'Shut up,' the two men snarled in unison.

They marched him along a dark corridor of locked cells and out into the bright sunlight, which caused him to stumble. He took great gulps of the crisp fresh air and looked up at the clear blue sky. It was a beautiful morning.

There wasn't time to mull over where he was being taken as he was dragged across the empty compound. At least it wasn't roll call, he thought, blinking in relief. Perhaps he was being given another chance.

They arrived at the commandant's office and the two bullies deposited him inside the door before retreating.

Berg was at his desk, writing in a ledger with his black fountain pen. If he was surprised at the noise made by Theo being dumped on the floor of his office, he didn't show it. He slowly screwed the cap onto the pen, thanked the guards and dismissed them.

Theo squirmed inwardly as he remembered the previous occasion he'd gone to confront the commandant in his office, and wished he hadn't been so impulsive. All he'd achieved was to draw attention to himself as a troublemaker.

'I think you know why you're here.' Berg rose from his chair and began pacing up and down. 'Twice you've been sent to the rose garden. Not many prisoners are awarded that privilege.' He smirked. 'I've been updating my records and have come across only one other prisoner in the past six months who has visited the rose garden. He's no longer with us, but I think you know of him.' Berg gave the prisoner's number and Theo clenched his fists in recognition. He knew the man's name to be Ezra; he was one of the three Jewish prisoners who'd been beaten to death. But Berg appeared lost in thought as he circled the room, stopping every so often to make a point.

'He made a run for it and was punished accordingly. He was foolish and arrogant.' Berg swung round to look Theo in the eye. Theo managed not to blink. 'No, I don't believe you are that foolish and arrogant. I think you're more sensible than that. A little high-spirited at times, mm?' He paused, waiting for a reply.

Theo gave the faintest of nods. He had a feeling this was about to take an unpleasant turn. The commandant moved a step forward, thought better of it and went over to the window, where he stared out over the yard.

'You know, you remind me a lot of myself when I was a young man. I could also be headstrong and often got into trouble. Joining the *Hitler Jugend* made me the man I am now, though I was resistant at first. I quickly learned from my mistakes and saw that a rigorous regime made me resilient under pressure. And it was all down to physical hard work. I'm willing to give you a chance to prove yourself. And maybe become a useful asset to the camp.' The commandant tilted his head and gave Theo a sly smile. Theo felt a chill spread through him. He didn't like what he was hearing. At first he'd thought he was in for another punishment, but now he wondered if the commandant was planning something even worse.

'I'm proud of what we've achieved here at Kamp Amersfoort, and so is the German high command,' continued Berg, walking over to Theo so he could stare him in the eye. 'Plans are under way to expand the site and make the camp the largest this side of the border. It'll be magnificent. But we need plenty of capable young men – young men like you. So, I want you to start work tomorrow with the forest commando who are clearing woodland for the purpose. You will return to your barracks and will have no further contact with any of the prisoners on your former work unit. Do you understand?'

Theo had no choice but to give his assent.

What would happen to the letters and parcels piling up inside Herr Doktor's office? He knew he'd let Frans down. And how would he let Annelies know he was still alive?

Defeated and deflated, and as if from far away, he heard the door open and the commandant give the guards the order to take him away.

Chapter Twenty-Eight

Frans

Frans blamed himself for Theo's banishment to the rose garden. He'd been too careless in assuming that it was safe to talk, losing track of time as he'd listened to Theo's distressing account of how he came to be arrested. Frans had expected Meiss to be off duty, but that should not have been an excuse. Meiss was a sly, nasty piece of work, capable of springing surprises with devastating consequences.

Catching sight of Theo in the rose garden had been a huge shock. Prisoners sent there often didn't survive and when Theo hadn't turned up for work for several days, Frans became increasingly worried.

The atmosphere inside the camp was now so much more tense. There'd been no opportunity to ask any of the prisoners about Theo as there were guards circling close by, who constantly queried what Frans and Cas were doing and kept a close watch on their movements between the bin store and the cart.

Saskia was the only one Frans could talk to who understood what he was going through. As often as he could, he went to meet Saskia at her father's empty shop, where they could talk in private and spend precious moments together. They sat cross-legged on the bare floorboards, mulling over ideas on how Frans could find out anything about Theo's whereabouts, but they struggled to come up with a solution. They resigned themselves to having to wait.

*

One morning Frans was wheeling his bin across the yard when the doctor came hurrying towards the hospital block with an armful of folders. Frans recognised him from Theo's description of a small man in a white coat with a bald head and thick-rimmed glasses. As he was passing, one of the folders slipped loose and landed at Frans's feet.

'I am sorry,' he said.

At the same time as Frans stooped down to retrieve the folder so did the doctor, almost dropping the others.

The guards were watching but seemed uninterested.

Frans handed him the folder and saw his chance. 'Have you seen Theo lately? He's always here to pick up the post, but I haven't seen him for days,' he said urgently.

The doctor looked startled. He pushed his glasses up his nose so he could take a good look at Frans. 'You must be the Koopmans boy,' he said softly. 'It's a plucky thing bringing in parcels under the guards' noses. The prisoners are very grateful for what you do.' He gave an approving smile.

Frans responded with a nod, struck by the sudden realisation that everything was all about to fall apart. 'Well, I've had to stop bringing in parcels as Theo's no longer here. They sent him to the rose garden, but that was days ago.'

The doctor drew in a long breath and frowned. 'I haven't seen him either – it's a shame – but that's not uncommon. They move prisoners around all the time. I'm usually the last to know.'

Frans felt a wave of disappointment as the doctor returned to his pile of documents, which he managed to shuffle into some kind of order. Then he peered at Frans again. 'Please don't stop bringing the post. The prisoners rely on it and it gives them such comfort. I have a stack of letters waiting to go out. Would you mind waiting while I go and fetch them?'

Frans glanced nervously at the guards, who were berating several prisoners at the table for not working fast enough. The heap of potatoes in the centre was as large as ever. Cas was over by the cart and some other guards were in one corner of the compound talking among themselves.

'All right. I can take a few this time, but I need to be careful.'

'Splendid,' said the doctor, nodding his head as if pleased to have solved the problem.

But the problem was far from solved. Frans was reluctant to restart the smuggling operation without the help of Theo to take parcels off his hands. The doctor asked if Frans could deliver the parcels himself to the door of Block IV, but he refused, saying he couldn't take the risk. The scheme only worked when he had an intermediary prepared to share the risk. Briefly, he considered roping in another prisoner, but who could he trust? Besides, there was no opportunity as there were always guards close by, watching and waiting, always suspicious. With a heavy heart, he realised he would have to stop.

Unexpectedly, the decision was taken out of his hands when Nelly came to the Koopmans' home with the week's parcels. Frans was in the post room, as the family called it, surveying the parcels piled up in the middle of the table. He was wondering how on earth he was going to get them delivered when Nelly's voice rang out from the kitchen.

'*Goedemorgen*, Mevrouw Koopmans.'

'Nelly! It's good to see you. What have you got for us today?' his mother replied.

Frans shifted some parcels to make space for the inevitable stack Nelly brought with her each week. He took no notice of the murmur of their voices coming from the kitchen until it stopped, when he went over to investigate. Nelly had placed her basket on the table and was lifting an enormous tart onto the large blue-patterned plate his mother always provided. Knife in hand, his mother portioned it into eight pieces. He noticed that the basket, normally filled with parcels, was empty.

'Frans, I've brought an apple *vlaai* today. It's your favourite, isn't it?' Nelly's words came out in a rush and her cheeks seemed pinker than usual. She caught him looking at her basket and cleared her throat. 'Let me explain.' She pulled out a kitchen chair and lowered herself down heavily. 'I'm afraid I won't be coming any more after today,' she began, her voice cracking. She looked anxiously at his mother, who lifted her eyebrows a fraction. Frans guessed they'd been discussing her announcement moments earlier.

'It's my father.' Nelly's voice was thin, as she tried to hold back her tears. 'He's had a bad stroke and is paralysed down one side of his body. It's too much for my mother to look after him by herself and I simply can't be away from him. I'm so sorry.'

'Nelly, you've nothing to apologise for. It's not your fault,' said Frans's mother, taking her hand and stroking it.

'But I've let you all down, the people in the network and all those poor people in the camp waiting on news from their loved ones. What will you do?' Nelly pressed a handkerchief into her eyes.

Frans exchanged a quick glance with his mother. They'd already discussed the difficulties of the smuggling operation and agreed to tell Nelly that things must change. She gave him an encouraging nod.

'Nelly, perhaps it's not such a bad thing,' he said quietly. 'I can't carry on smuggling bulky items on the cart any more. We've never been caught, but I can't take any chances, as there are many more guards trained now to search vehicles going in and out of the camp. So far we've been lucky and had a prisoner who helped us inside and made it all happen, but he disappeared a few days ago. He's left me with no one to do the job.'

Nelly finished drying her eyes and forced a rueful smile. 'I suppose it was too good to be true. Word's been spreading about the work we do in getting much-needed essentials to the prisoners and more people have been dropping off parcels with me. I'm sorry I didn't realise the pressure you were under. I hope the prisoner is okay…'

'Delivering parcels has always been more risky,' said Frans. 'The only way to get them in safely is to hide them on the cart. Letters aren't so much of a problem as they're less easy to detect, and Cas has perfected the art of carrying several at a time stuffed down his long socks. It's letters that the prisoners need most and give them the most comfort. I've seen first-hand the pleasure they bring. It's vital we keep delivering letters.'

Nelly looked at him miserably. 'I can see that, but I can't do it any more, so all those prisoners will miss out.'

'Listen, there is something you can do,' said Frans, leaning forward, motivated by the idea forming in his mind. 'You can give me the names and addresses of all the people you know who correspond with someone in the camp. I'll make sure that their letters get through, even if I have to deliver them myself. But you must tell them it can only be letters from now on. No more parcels.'

Chapter Twenty-Nine

With the wind on his back, Frans rushed along the back roads towards Saskia's house. His bike rattled over the bumps in the road, reminding him that he needed to patch up his dilapidated tyres. They were so tattered that they were close to failing, but the bicycle shops were now all shut so he couldn't replace them. When the time came, he would decide whether to cut up pieces of old rubber to make makeshift tyres, or do without and ride on the hard wooden rims. Neither much appealed to him.

His mind turned to Theo again. Frans knew Theo had been punished because he'd been in the wrong place at the wrong time – his story about how he ended up at Kamp Amersfoort went round and round in Frans's head. With the things he and Saskia had learned, he could imagine the two of them attending Resistance meetings themselves, they were so desperate to do something to help. Theo's fate could so easily have been theirs.

If Theo had survived what was happening to him now, what state would he be in? Frans tried to put his feelings of fear aside as he pictured what Theo must be going through. As he approached Saskia's turning, he thought of how he would feel, separated from her by an impenetrable wire fence. It was unimaginable.

Frans scuffed his feet along the ground to slow down, aware he also needed to fix his brakes. He jumped off and wheeled his bike up to the gate, thinking his tyres definitely wouldn't last five minutes if he tried to ride over those ruts.

Saskia was crouching beside her bike, with an oily rag in one hand.

'*Hoi!* What's the problem?' called Frans, leaning his bike against the fence.

'The chain was loose, but I fixed it,' she said, straightening up and looking pleased with herself. She wiped a hand across her brow, leaving a dirty smear.

'Come here,' said Frans, smiling. He took out his handkerchief and tried to rub it off. 'Sorry, I've only made it worse.' He pulled her into his arms and breathed in the familiar soapy scent of her neck as she relaxed against him. He was reluctant to let go as the unwelcome image of a wire fence separating them came to him again.

'Hey, is everything all right?' Saskia said, laughing, wriggling round so she could look at him. Frans laughed too, embarrassed to share his foolish thoughts. 'Of course. Just happy to see you.' He kissed her warm soft lips and let his worries subside.

'Are your parents in?' he murmured.

'Aren't they always?' Saskia sighed. 'My father rarely goes out these days since he's shut up shop. He just sits in his chair reading bits out of *Het Parool* to my mother. He's scared to leave the house now…' She looked sadly into the distance. 'It gets him really het up every time there's something about the *moffen* arresting innocent people. Luckily, he has Mum, and I just try to keep out of their way.' She gave a shudder and went on, 'I don't want to go back in. We'll only have to sit around making polite conversation. It's so nice this afternoon, why don't we go for a bike ride instead now I've fixed my chain?'

'Sounds a much better idea. But first, I've got something I need to talk to you about.'

'What is it?' she said, with a flicker of anxiety.

'I can't say out here,' he said, even though they were well away from any prying eyes.

Saskia suggested they went into the back garden where they couldn't be heard and they walked over to an old wooden bench below the branches of a gnarled apple tree.

Frans kept his voice low as he confided his worries about Theo's whereabouts, Nelly's decision to stop coming and his concerns about whether he could keep the smuggling operation going by himself.

'Then you must let me do more to help,' Saskia said, before he had a chance to ask her the same thing. 'I have a lot of contacts locally and can be very discreet. Annelies will vouch for it,' she went on, then noticed the look of concern on Frans's face. 'What's the matter?'

Frans reached into his pocket and pulled out the creased letter he'd been carrying all this time. 'This is the last letter you gave me for Theo. I thought I'd be able to get it to him, but it seems hopeless now. Will you tell Annelies?'

Saskia pursed her lips. 'Of course, but I don't want to worry her too much. I tried to offer her some words of comfort when Theo disappeared, but I could tell she wasn't reassured. Leave it with me. I'll do what I can to keep her spirits up.'

Frans gazed at her keen face, her beautiful dark eyes. Every moment with her was so precious and the last thing he wanted was for her to take on more than she should. But she was a strong-minded young woman and he knew he could rely on her. So he went back to his plan. Saskia would take over from Nelly, but only accept letters, not parcels.

'Leave it with me. I know I can handle it,' she said. 'In fact, I desperately want to get out of the house and do something constructive. School's a waste of time now the best teachers have gone and a lot of the time they just send us home. So, this is *my* plan. I know Amersfoort and its surroundings like the back of my hand. I can make house visits to collect post without the *moffen* suspecting.' She tilted her head in anticipation of his reply.

Frans hesitated. He was relieved he no longer had to shoulder all this on his own, but her plan made him uneasy. Would she be taking on too much? And how could she be so sure her movements wouldn't be detected?

'You must promise not to do anything that puts you in danger,' he said solemnly. 'And if you have any suspicions about anyone you meet, you must tell me.'

'As long as you promise to tell me everything that's going on in the camp. You've been keeping things to yourself for far too long,' she said, with gentle reproach.

'All right. I promise.' He leaned in for a lingering kiss, then hugged her to him, keeping his eyes tightly shut.

Chapter Thirty

Saskia

Saskia yawned and looked up at the clock in the corner of the room as it struck ten. She closed the book she'd been reading. That was when she heard the crunch of footsteps in the lane and the squeak of the gate swinging open. She froze. Her mother looked up anxiously from her darning and her father came out of his study and peered over his glasses at them.

'We have absolutely nothing to worry about,' he said calmly and walked over to the bureau where the Dekker family kept their identity cards. Saskia knew he was trying to reassure them, but guessed he was as terrified as she and her mother.

They all flinched at the thump of something heavy and metallic pounding against the door accompanied by harsh German voices demanding they open up.

'Wait here while I deal with them,' whispered her father, as the thumping and shouting continued. Saskia was afraid for him and leapt from her chair, determined to face whatever was about to confront them together. Her father tried to gesture her away, but she stood her ground as, seconds later, three German soldiers came bursting through the door.

'Paul Dekker,' snarled the one who seemed to be in charge and took a pace towards her father. It was not a question.

Her father held out his card, ready to prove his identity, but they ignored it.

'We have orders for you to come with us.'

'What orders? He's done nothing wrong,' cried Saskia, unable to contain her anger.

'Except being Jewish,' spat the soldier, grabbing hold of her father's sleeve. The other two moved inside, their bulk filling the small hallway.

'Stop. There's been a mistake. My father… none of us are Jewish. We have the papers to prove it. Father, show him.' She grabbed his card from him and thrust it at the soldier, before racing into the sitting room where her mother was standing, her hand to her mouth. From the hallway, she could hear the demands of the soldier and her father's pleading voice. Saskia's head was in turmoil. Everything her father had feared was coming true, and the thought came to her that whoever had accused him of being Jewish and driven him to shut up his shop must be behind this.

'Wait in here,' she whispered, as she seized their identity cards from her mother. Through the door, she saw her father being held by two of the soldiers with his hands behind his back, while the third kept on with his questions.

'Leave him,' said Saskia, erupting with rage, as she pushed between them. 'Have you even looked at his card?'

The German looked unsure of himself and glanced down at the card he was holding. There it was, everything as it should be, the photograph taken with his left ear showing, the thumbprint that they could easily check from a database in the Hague. And there was no large black J stamp. Saskia shoved her own and her mother's card at him so he could see that they were no different.

After he'd shut and bolted the door behind the departing Germans, her father came up to her and squeezed her tight. 'Thank you for what you did,' he whispered.

'Are you all right, Papa?' she said, twisting round to look up at him.

'I am now,' he said, pursing his lips. 'I've been expecting this to happen for some time, but no one's safe any more. We have to be constantly on our guard.'

Saskia nodded her agreement, but her anger took longer to subside. Having personally witnessed her father's intimidation at the hands of German bullies, she threw herself into her illicit activities with renewed energy. Too many people were being wrongfully arrested and deported to the camps for crimes they did not commit or simply for being who they were. Their families were made to suffer too, left behind in anguish without knowing the true nature of why their loved ones had been taken from them and left to cling to a sliver of hope that they would emerge alive.

From then on, Saskia knew she needed to actively seek out families with relatives locked up in Kamp Amersfoort and was determined to provide some solace through the letters and parcels she hid in her bag, which had been adapted for the purpose by an acquaintance of her father who worked in the leather trade. He had crafted a spacious secret storage compartment at the base, accessed by means of a concealed zip. She resolved to take control of the smuggling operation with an urgency she hadn't previously known.

Chapter Thirty-One

Frans

'Evert, Frans, come quickly!'

Frans's mother's skirt billowed in the strong breeze as she stood at the edge of the field where Frans and his father were turning over the soil in preparation for planting.

'What's happened? Is it one of the children?' cried his father. They both threw down their spades and ran to her. There were no shouts or screams, usually the sign that something was amiss. Frans remembered how only last week, Elsje had been playing in the hayloft with Cas, lost her footing and come tumbling down the ladder onto the barn floor. Her screams had been so piercing they could be heard all the way down the field where he'd been working with his father. Frans had raced over and found Cas comforting his loudly sobbing sister, who had seemed no worse for wear. When Pa had turned up, out of breath and angry, he'd told the children off for being so foolish and forbidden them from using the barn as a playground.

'There's a German on a motorbike coming along the drive,' Frans's mother cried out, wringing her hands in agitation. 'What have we done wrong?'

'Shh!' commanded his father, as the motorbike skidded to a spluttering halt in the yard.

The uniformed German heaved the bike onto its stand and removed his cap and black leather gloves. He raised his hand in a stiff salute and barked out, '*Heil* Hitler!'

Frans shrank back when he saw who it was. What on earth was the commandant doing coming all this way to see them? Instantly, he thought he'd been found out. His mind raced feverishly back to recent visits to the camp and his disappearance into the hospital block to exchange letters with the doctor. He'd been so careful... surely he hadn't been spotted?

Frans's father touched the brim of his cap in greeting. '*Goedemorgen*, Herr Berg. This is my wife, Janke, and my son Frans. He takes the horse and cart into the camp.'

Berg turned his head to stare at Frans, his eyes flickering in recognition. 'I remember,' he said. 'Potato peelings you collect, isn't it?'

'Yes sir, that's correct.' Frans nodded. He thought it best to avoid supplying any more information in case the commandant took exception to the arrangement.

Berg bowed his head. 'I'm here to discuss a business matter,' he said importantly.

There was a pause as Frans's father considered his words. 'Why don't we go inside and discuss this over a cup of coffee?' he said finally. 'Frans will join us. The farm is his business too.'

Frans's father put an arm round Frans and led the way along a dark corridor filled with piles of muddy clogs. Berg cast his eye around the property while keeping a smile pinned to his face.

'You keep a nice home,' Berg told Frans's mother when she placed a cup of coffee in front of him. 'How many children do you have?'

'Five, sir.'

'Do they all work on the farm?'

'Oh no, sir. The girls are all under five and mainly get under my feet. Cas is a help, he's ten, and goes with Frans to pick up the cattle feed.' Her cheeks flushed pink, as if she regretted saying so much.

Frans looked down at his hands, embarrassed for her, wishing Berg would cut out the small talk and get to the point of his visit. He was still only mildly reassured that Berg hadn't come to question him.

'If you will excuse me, I must get on with my work,' said Frans's mother after leaving a polite gap in the conversation. It was obvious she was finding it awkward.

'Of course. Thank you for the coffee,' said Berg, glancing at his untouched cup.

With a slight nod, she left the room and Frans's father took a seat opposite him. Berg placed his hands on the table, one on top of the other. He began to explain that he was in charge of ensuring that the prisoners were all given jobs, both inside and outside the camp, and proudly described the deal he had struck with a firm that made signalling devices in Hilversum, which had set up a workshop inside the camp where radio cabinets were assembled by prison workers. But Berg's efforts to introduce more initiatives like this were being hampered, he explained, by the arrival of many more prisoners into the camp.

As Frans listened, he surmised there must be hundreds, possibly thousands pouring into the camp. He wondered how they'd all fit in. The prison blocks were full to bursting and the new barracks under construction were some way off being ready. He tried to imagine all those prisoners crammed into the low huts, forced to lie on hard wooden bunks without mattresses. Distracted by his thoughts, he almost missed the commandant's request.

'I am of course aware that the situation here in Holland means that many businesses are short of manpower. So, I was thinking that you might be able to do me a favour,' he said to Frans's father with a small cough. 'I've drawn up a list of local businesses. I can provide them with workers. Here, tell me what you think.' He dug a small black notebook from the top pocket of his uniform jacket, which was covered in various insignia and badges. He opened it at the list of contacts and slid it across the table.

'Most of these names are familiar to me,' said Frans's father, after scanning the list. 'Suppliers and businesses I've had dealings with.' He eyed Berg warily. 'What is it you want from me?'

'That you put in a word for me. I think they would be more amenable to the idea if it came from you,' said Berg, remembering to smile.

Frans's father sat back and folded his arms. 'And if they think I'm working for you?' He sniffed loudly. 'How do you think that would go down?'

Berg frowned. 'I appreciate that things aren't easy, but we'd all be doing our bit for the community. And,' he coughed again, 'I can make it worth your while.' He drummed his fingers on the table as he waited for a reply.

His face impassive, Frans's father stared at the commandant. 'I don't want payment. A lot of us are struggling. All our young men have left for Germany, either because they had no choice or because they believed that working over the border was a good idea. Without workers, our local businesses are barely surviving.' He let out a sigh of resignation. 'But they might consider an offer of help. I will visit a few locals and tell them the camp is offering to let prisoners come and work for them. They can make up their own minds and approach you if they want to go ahead – but I don't want anyone knowing you've been speaking to me directly.'

Frans watched the commandant's demeanour and was gratified to see he looked uncomfortable. He was proud of the way his father was calmly handling the situation, but knew it must be an effort to keep his temper in check and hoped he wouldn't let it get the better of him. Of course, no one wanted free labour – nobody wanted the prisoners at the camp at all – but the commandant didn't understand that. The idea that they would be uncomfortable about these poor men and women working for free was foreign to him.

'Of course, I will be discreet. And there will be no question of a bribe.' Berg emphasised the word as if he found it distasteful. 'As I say, I need to find employment for a lot of prisoners. I'm thinking you might use a few prisoners on your farm. And I will make sure you are compensated for your cooperation, so you won't need to worry about any cost to yourself. What do you think?'

Frans couldn't believe what they were being offered. These men weren't Berg's property to send wherever he wanted.

But looking at his father's face, he knew what he was thinking. It was months since the last reliable farmhand had left for Germany, and they hadn't had any requests from casual labourers looking for work.

And perhaps it would mean the men would be free of that barbaric place, even if for just a few hours a day. They could give them rest, food, letters, parcels… This could be the answer to the problems Frans had been facing trying to smuggle correspondence safely in and out of the camp.

'It's a good offer, my friend. A dozen men. Will you accept?' Berg said impatiently.

Frans waited for his father to answer and recognised the look on his face that suggested he was hatching some plan.

'A dozen,' he said at last. 'That would be a good start. The ditches need digging out and the potatoes need harvesting. But I won't accept payment. These men will be treated fairly and kindly like all workers I employ. I insist on paying the men myself. A guilder a day. And from now on, I will keep everything we produce.'

A silence fell between them. Frans wondered if his father had gone too far. If he refused to hand over his valuable produce, would Berg punish him? But Berg merely nodded and waved his hand, as if he were pleased to have solved his problem. Evert's suggestion seemed to be of no consequence to him. His mind had moved on. 'I will arrange for the men to be brought from the camp every morning. They will be accompanied by guards who will stay to supervise their work.' His chair scraped noisily over the tiled floor as he stood up to go. 'I'm sure the arrangement will be of benefit to us both.'

They shook on the deal, and as an afterthought, Berg offered his hand to Frans.

Chapter Thirty-Two

In the days that followed, Frans prepared for the prisoners' arrival with a mixture of fear and excitement. A small part of him hoped he might see Theo. He'd had mixed feelings as he'd stood with his father watching the motorbike roar away down the track in a cloud of dust that day. He was sure Berg had left convinced he had achieved what he'd come for, but Frans couldn't but help reflect on the state of the prisoners. His father hadn't been into the camp in some time, and he felt he needed to remind him.

'I'm not sure this is such a good idea,' he said to his father. 'From what I've seen most prisoners aren't in any fit state to be working out in the fields all day. Some are so weak from malnourishment they can hardly stand.'

Evert slowly shook his head. 'I know. It's terrible it's come to this, but as long as the *moffen* are in charge, it's the best we can hope for. Those poor prisoners may not be able to work as well as the men we're used to having around the farm, but I'd rather try to improve a few lives than worry about productivity at the moment. Don't you agree?'

Grateful to be asked his opinion on such an important matter, Frans gave his approval. He began to think of what they could do to alleviate the men's suffering when they were on their land. At least they could make sure they were well fed and had breakfast when they arrived and a proper cooked lunch. Mama would be quick to help out.

But Frans's concerns were proved right when the workers arrived. None were in any fit state to be undertaking manual labour, especially when driven at the pace the accompanying guards expected.

They didn't just look on, they drove the prisoners hard in a way that Frans and his father would never have done. And there were no tasks on the farm that weren't physically exhausting.

Frans's mother did her best by doling out large plates of porridge to the men when they arrived, but they never managed more than a few spoonfuls before the guards were cajoling them to get to work.

'It's not working,' she said tearfully on the third morning when Evert and Frans walked through the door to grab some breakfast themselves. 'No sooner have I given the men their breakfast than the guards come in. It's like they derive some sadistic pleasure from stopping them from eating.' She pointed at the abandoned plates with spoons half-submerged in thick porridge. 'I feel terrible. What am I to do?'

'I'll deal with them. I'll make sure it doesn't happen again,' said Pa, with an air of resignation. 'Come on Frans. It's important they know who's in charge round here.'

Frans sighed wearily. He'd also seen how vicious these guards could be and dreaded a confrontation – what if they ended up in trouble themselves? But he knew better than to argue with his father.

They put their clogs back on and plodded down to the corner of the field, where several scrawny men were clearing out the ditches. Four guards surrounded them, menacing-looking individuals, barking out orders to work harder and faster. They stood by, beating time by slapping their thighs with leather straps, which they flicked over the back of any prisoner deemed to be slacking.

'That's not how things are done round here,' shouted Evert.

The four guards hadn't seen him approach and turned to face him in surprise.

'This is my farm and I do not allow my workers to be pushed around,' he went on. 'Now, please step aside and I will issue the instructions.'

The cluster of men stopped to watch the scene unfold, their bony shoulders slumped with weariness. This didn't escape the notice of one of the guards, who brought his strap down hard on the back of the head of one man, causing him to yelp in pain.

Frans's father refused to be intimidated by this show of bravado. He stepped forward and folded his arms. 'If you continue to beat my workers I will have no choice but to ask you to leave.'

'You will, will you?' said one of the guards, a smirk curling at his lip. 'Well, Mr Koopmans. If you want us to stay and get the work done, you'd better accept this is the way we do things.'

Terrified, Frans stood by, convinced that standing up to the steely-eyed, square-jawed guard would turn out badly for his small thickset father. If it were to come to a fight, he wasn't sure his father would win; but he hoped he could win the argument. The two men sized each other up, both as formidable as the other in different ways.

'May I remind you that this is my property and I have invited you here,' said Evert, without shouting. 'And I am paying the men their wages,' he went on, his voice resonating with authority.

The guard darted a look to his colleague and spoke to him in rapid German, while Evert looked on patiently.

'Understood,' said the guard finally, though his disgruntled expression suggested he wasn't happy about it.

'Get back to work!' barked the guard, turning to the prisoners, who resumed hefting large clumps of sodden vegetation onto the side of the ditches in which they stood, their feet submerged in freezing water.

Frans hated what he was seeing and made his way back to the house while his father kept watch over the men to ensure they weren't being maltreated. He could hear the shouts of the guards, goading them to go faster, but they no longer appeared to be lashing out. As he kicked off his clogs by the back door, he realised his father hadn't said anything about giving the men enough time to finish their breakfast. Probably best left for now, he thought with a sigh. There were bound to be more confrontations with this lot.

*

He didn't need to wait for long. Later that morning he was attending to a cow and her newborn calf when he heard a commotion from outside the barn. The noise of thudding boots approaching the yard alarmed the cow, who scrabbled to her feet, almost trampling her calf. Frans pulled it out of harm's way and stuck his head out of the door to see what was going on. The men, many in a distressed state, were being chased into the yard by the yelling guards. *What now*, sighed Frans to himself as he stepped out to block their path. The men lined up, a ragged, exhausted-looking lot, some barely capable of standing. Frans could hardly watch as they staggered in their ill-fitting clogs. But he would have to deal with the situation himself; his father had left him in charge while he went to discuss Berg's proposal with several acquaintances in town.

'Is this absolutely necessary?' said Frans, his heart pounding, as he stood before the guard from their earlier confrontation.

'Absolutely,' the guard said. 'The men have a ten-minute lunch break, so we can't have any dawdling.'

'All this noise is frightening the animals,' Frans said. As if on cue, the mother cow began to bellow and kick against the barn door. The calf tried to stagger to its feet.

Frans held the barn door to behind him, determined to have his say. 'These men shouldn't have to run to earn their lunch. In future, they will walk here. And they will have fifteen minutes for lunch from the moment they sit down.' He wasn't sure where the courage came from to say these words, but he was quickly brought back down to earth.

'Is that what your papa told you to say?' said the guard and spat on the ground.

His heart still beating fast, Frans stood firm. 'No, it's what I say. I'm in charge here,' he said in an unwavering voice.

The guard threw him a sceptical look and herded the men into the kitchen. Frans quickly finished off attending to the animals and went in after them.

His mother was placing steaming plates of food in front of the men, who were squeezed in around the table. Each worker received a decent-sized portion of meat and potatoes with plenty of gravy. Frans resolved to stay until they'd eaten every last morsel. The guards stood by watching. The tension in the room was palpable. Frans pulled up a chair so he could sit between two young men, barely out of their teens, and asked them where they were from. Out of the corner of his eye he saw one of the guards step forward to object, but Frans refused to engage with him.

'We're brothers, from Hilversum,' said the one to his left with a glance at his brother, who was more intent on shovelling down his food than speaking.

'How are you finding working on a farm?' asked Frans quietly.

'Hard work, but it's a relief to get out of that place,' said the first, lowering his voice. 'And thank you for the meal. It's life-saving—'

'That's enough.' A guard appeared at Frans's shoulder. 'The prisoners don't have all day to sit around chatting.'

Frans looked up into the guard's cold pale eyes and thought better of answering back. These Kamp Amersfoort guards might only be here because it had been arranged between the commandant and his father, but that didn't stop them from throwing their weight about. 'Of course,' he said, biting back what he really wanted to say. Instead he made sure the men finished their meal before heading off for their afternoon shift looking considerably happier than when they'd first arrived.

Chapter Thirty-Three

Weeks passed and the uncomfortable arrangement between the Koopmans and the camp guards continued, with frequent tussles to determine who was in charge. And Theo never arrived. Saskia tried to reassure Frans, but the truth was that having the guards close by put him on edge and he found himself worrying more about her and her activities, despite what she said. First there was the raid when she'd managed to prevent her father being arrested and now she was talking about someone with connections to the camp who was helping with the smuggling of letters. She refused to be drawn on who it was, merely saying he was reliable and trustworthy. Frans had too much on his mind with the farm to question her further, but the constant feeling of unease refused to go away.

Each morning, Frans and his father took it in turns to accompany the men into the fields, staying a while to keep an eye on proceedings. Their presence was enough to keep the guards from their usual bully-boy behaviour, though Frans was bothered by what might be going on whenever their backs were turned.

One morning, an idea came to him after he had arrived back in the yard and unloaded the bins. Unhitching the horse from the cart, he led it slowly down to the edge of the field, all the while speaking in a soothing low voice. As he approached the men, whose job that day was to clear stones from an area of the field, one looked up and waved as the horse plodded past and another called out a cheerful greeting. This was enough to set the guards off bellowing, causing the horse to pull up short with a toss of its mane and a stamping of hooves.

'He'll behave himself if you don't shout,' said Frans, struggling to hold tight on the reins. He wondered if his ruse had been such a good idea. He pulled a carrot from his pocket and stroked the horse's muzzle and ears till it calmed down. With concerned backward glances, the men returned to work and Frans continued to walk the horse slowly around the field until he was confident the guards wouldn't yell out. After that first unfortunate incident, Frans was pleased to see that carrying out this routine at the start of the day was sufficient to settle the atmosphere between himself, the guards and, more importantly, the men they were tasked to watch over.

Before long, they started to see the fruits of the men's labour. After long neglect, the field left fallow was tinged green as the new crop took hold. Encouraged, Evert negotiated with Berg to take on more workers. Soon the fields were filled with as many workers as he'd had before the war.

But there was one thing that was greatly concerning and there was no obvious way to address it. A number of the workers were Jewish, singled out by the yellow star sewn on their jackets. They were segregated from the others and had their own guard standing by ready to come down hard if they weren't keeping up.

One morning, Frans was in an adjacent field supervising the planting of seed potatoes when he heard raucous shouting from the guard in charge of the Jews.

'Up, down, up down, up down. Faster. Faster, you worthless layabouts,' he screamed.

Frans thrust his spade into the soil and went over to investigate. All five of the men were prostrate on the ground, clearly exhausted from their punishment. He hurried over and tried to help one of them to his feet. 'I don't think I can keep this up,' whispered the man, his face grey with fatigue.

'What do you think you're doing?' Frans's father came running across the field, shouting at the guard, who was slapping his thigh repeatedly with his leather strap.

'I know when someone is deliberately slacking and none of these men were putting their backs into it,' said the guard, with a curl of his lip.

'You won't get any more out of them by making them do these ridiculous drills. Frans, take this man back to the house.'

Frans linked his arm through the man's and, with his gaze on the ground, passed the guard, whose face had turned a nasty puce colour.

'I won't allow it,' hissed the guard. 'These men are under my command. Now get back to work. All of you!'

'The man is not fit to work. I'm taking him off duty whether you like it or not,' Frans heard his father say.

Frans and the man kept on walking. 'I'm sorry,' he whispered to the prisoner at his side. He cast a glance back at his father standing resolute against the guards, however much they tried to hinder his efforts to run the farm on his own humane terms. It made Frans proud of his family and the risks they had all been prepared to take and wondered what more they could do to alleviate the misery of the prisoners working on their land.

The prisoner began leaning heavily against Frans as they approached the farmhouse.

'What's your name?' Frans asked, once he'd sat him down in the safety of the kitchen.

'Jakub,' he said, struggling to hold back tears.

Frans went to the tap to run him a glass of water and waited while he drank it down in small sips. Peering at him with concern, he wondered if Jakub was suffering from more than exhaustion. His skin was so pale, so translucent, and his lustreless eyes seemed to recede into their sockets. He gave the impression of a man close to giving up. Firm action was needed. 'I'm going to take you to the cowshed where you can help clean out the stalls,' said Frans, but Jakub scrambled to his feet, protesting that he had to get back to work. 'If I don't, I'll get thrown into the rose garden and they'll leave me there to die. My brother…' He broke down in sobs.

'Sit down for a moment.' Frans felt himself grow cold at the mention of the rose garden. It had been several weeks since he'd last seen Theo and the longer he had no news, the more he resigned himself to thinking the worst. Now hearing Jakub mention this terrible place, his anxieties resurfaced. Surely if something really terrible had happened to Theo, Roel would have told him? He briefly closed his eyes, wishing there was a way to find out.

Jakub had collected himself, though his eyes were brimming with tears. Frans let him compose himself till he was ready to speak, but as the man's story unfolded, he found himself shaking his head in disbelief. Of course he'd heard stories of persecution – Jews seized from their own homes before disappearing with no warning – but this was the first time he'd heard it from someone caught up in the horror of it all themselves.

'I've lived in Groningen all my life,' began Jakub. Frans knew just how far away Groningen was from Amersfoort and thought how terrible it must have been for him to leave his whole family behind. 'When the Germans moved in, we lost our freedom. We couldn't walk down the street without them constantly demanding to see our papers. When the order came for Jews to identify ourselves, we knew it was too dangerous for us to stay. I always hoped we'd remain together as a family, but my father said it would be safer for my brother and me to go into hiding. He stayed behind with my mother, thinking they'd be safe as he worked at the university as a professor. I worry every day about what happened to them after we left; I just hope they managed to stay out of trouble.' Jakub paused, his breath catching in a sob. Frans waited patiently for him to continue.

'Ben and I boarded the train to Zwolle with false papers. It stopped suddenly in the middle of nowhere and was stormed by a whole load of Nazis. They didn't even look at our papers but forced us to get out. They were prodding us in the back with their rifles. They marched us across fields to a lane where a truck was waiting with its engine running. I don't know how we all fitted on. There must have been at least fifty crammed in the back. We couldn't see a thing, but the sobs and cries told me there were women and very young children in there too. Ben was so angry and kept shouting and banging on the sides. I tried to calm him down but he wouldn't shut up. At the camp, the guards flung open the doors and immediately set on him with bats. Everyone was screaming, me the loudest, but they kept on. Ben, being Ben, refused to give up without a struggle, though I knew the wound on the side of his head must have been hurting. Then in all the commotion, I lost him. It was only later I heard he'd been sent into the rose garden, then to work at the worst of all the commandos, the one where they dig trenches for the bodies of prisoners that have been shot. That's the last I heard—' Jakub stopped abruptly, pain etched into his face.

'I'm so sorry. You mustn't give up hope,' said Frans, though he knew his words sounded hollow.

Jakub shrugged and forced a smile. 'It's better I don't know, but thank you for listening. I feel better now I've talked to you, but I must go back to work.' He stood up and briefly held the edge of the table to steady himself.

Frans moved forward and put an arm around the bony shoulders of this young man, probably not much older than himself, who life had dealt such a terrible blow. Was it enough that men like Jakub who worked on their land received hot meals and were treated with kindness by Frans and his family? Frans could see they had a better deal than most, but could he do more? If there was only a way he could arrange for them to meet loved ones here and in private, it would surely give them a brief respite... Gradually an idea began to seed itself in Frans's mind.

Chapter Thirty-Four

Theo

Dusk was falling when the forest commando finally downed tools and returned to the camp. It had come not a moment too soon for Theo, no longer able to feel his red-raw hands. Thrusting them deep into his pockets in a desperate search for some warmth, he trudged along despondently.

The day had started bitterly cold and stayed that way, making it difficult for the men to keep up with the arduous job of felling trees and sawing them into manageable-sized logs. Their standard issue second-hand uniforms and the wooden clogs into which their bare feet were jammed offered little protection against the harsh wind that blew in from the east. How could the guards comprehend their suffering, wrapped up as they were in thick greatcoats, woollen gloves and knee-high leather boots? Towering over the prisoners, they bawled at them to keep on swinging their axes to split the wood into logs before bawling at them again to load the logs onto carts ready to be dragged back to the camp. Everyone knew the logs would disappear into the SS quarters to stoke the stoves that kept them warm. The men were lucky to have a few leftover sticks of kindling to take the chill out of the air in their own barracks.

It was little consolation to Theo that he wasn't assigned to cart duty today; he'd be asked soon enough.

When the light had almost drained from the sky, they were finally allowed to down tools and return to camp. Theo couldn't say he looked forward to it, but it was the only time each day that he allowed his thoughts to drift to Annelies and imagine it wouldn't be long till he saw her again.

Their march took them past the other forest commando, the one no one had much to do with, the ones working on a project kept top secret. He glanced over, suspecting something sinister was unfolding at this secluded spot, where, several weeks ago, a large contingent of Jews could be seen putting their shoulders into moving large quantities of earth. Each day when Theo's own commando returned to base, he noticed the trench had grown deeper and longer. At first, he'd shuddered at the thought of some kind of large-scale burial ground, but as the weeks went by, it became obvious that something bigger was unfolding. The trench became a long straight avenue, carved deep into the earth and bounded by high-sided banks. Grass was already growing patchily on the sides. Soon there would be nothing to suggest the back-breaking labour that had formed them.

Drawing level with the avenue, Theo slowed his step and peered towards the men who were still shovelling earth. He knew they wouldn't be allowed to stop toiling until long after dark.

'What do you think they're doing?' he whispered to the prisoner next to him.

'Haven't you heard? They're digging a new firing range.'

'What for?' Theo said, though it was a pointless question. Of course he knew.

The prisoner let out an anguished sigh, causing the nearest guard to whack him on the back. Weakened through lack of food and from hours of hard labour, the man crumpled onto the ground where he stayed, whimpering.

Theo dropped to his knees to help.

'Leave him alone and move on!' bellowed the guard, but Theo wasn't prepared to leave the man, who was clearly in pain. It had been his fault for speaking to him. He leaned in closer, but the man didn't respond. Suddenly a sharp pain in Theo's shoulders made him gasp out. He twisted round to see the guard looming over him, ready to strike again.

'Did you not hear me? Leave him!'

A second guard came towards them from the back of the group and, together, the two guards rolled the prisoner into the ditch, where he lay without moving.

'No!' shouted Theo and rushed to help his fellow prisoner, but he wasn't quick enough. Another blow to his back sent him flying on top of the inert body in the ditch.

'I'll get help,' he whispered fiercely into the man's ear, but he got no reply. Theo suspected it was already too late.

'You'll do no such thing. Now get back in line,' growled the first guard. He reached down and yanked Theo up by the lapels. As he stumbled to gain his footing, Theo caught sight of the guard's coal-black eyes. He blinked hard, ice-cold fear flooding his body. The two guards were bigger and stronger than he was and it would take very little for him to end up dead in the ditch. All the fight knocked out of him, he resumed his place in the line of men who snaked towards the main gates and back inside the camp.

One morning before dawn, he was shaken awake by the deafening crack of guns being fired, so loud it seemed to be happening right outside his barracks. Everyone scrambled from their bunks, alarmed at what the firing could mean.

'Oh, God, it's started.'

'What's going on?'

'Have they come to shoot us?'

'Are we being freed?'

Shouting over one another, the men all scrambled for the door. Theo got there first and peered out into the pre-dawn mist that hung over the yard.

'Shush! Stop making such a racket. Do you want them to come for us?' he hissed. He strained to hear any more sounds of gunshots, but it was deathly still. Willem, a friend of sorts as they both worked for the forest commando, came and stood next to him.

'Maybe it's a practice session, you know before they do it for real,' said Willem, drawing on the cigarette he'd lit. *If only*, thought Theo, as he made a scoffing noise.

Dozens of men crowded round, anxious to get a glimpse beyond the door of their hut. 'There's nothing happening. Let's get some sleep,' said Theo, though he knew that was unlikely.

As he settled back on his unforgiving mattress, he regretted he hadn't tried to escape on Frans's cart when there had still been an outside chance he might succeed. This latest turn of events made him deeply uneasy. And at morning roll call, his worst suspicions were confirmed.

There was nothing to suggest that anything out of the ordinary was about to happen as they traipsed out into the bleak yard and huddled against the penetrating cold. The yard was so packed with new arrivals that Theo had to jostle for his place, while trying to avoid catching the eye of any of the numerous guards. Several had brought snarling dogs, always a sure sign something unpleasant was about to unfold. Those in the front row began to shout their numbers in German. The procedure moved along faster than normal as there were so many to get through. Theo, halfway back, kept rehearsing his number to himself, even though he'd recited it correctly hundreds of times. He knew only too well that all it needed was a stumble over his words to be singled out. To his left stood a young man, differentiated by the yellow star stitched crudely to his threadbare jacket. When his turn came and his voice wavered, Theo glanced anxiously at him.

'*Sieben, sechs, vier…*' The man paused as he grappled with the German words.

Theo tilted his head slightly so he could see his number, and spoke the remaining digits to him in as low a voice as he dared.

'*Zwei…*' faltered the man.

'*Halt! Kommen Sie nach vorne!*' shrieked a nearby guard. When the man didn't move, he came over and yanked him out of the row by his collar, marching him to the front next to several others who'd had the misfortune to snag the guards' attention. Theo's turn came and he recited his number faultlessly, though he was certain the pounding in his ears could be heard reverberating across the yard.

'*Nächste!*' roared the guard in charge. Theo was able to disappear into the sea of prisoners.

When roll call was over, at least twenty men, all Jews, were paraded out in front. Their shocked, terrified expressions suggested they had guessed the fate that lay in store. Then, from all sides they were surrounded by a clutch of fearsome-looking guards and their terrible dogs. Amid threats and blows to their bodies, they were herded out of the compound, until the echo of boots and clogs died away.

When Theo lined up with the other members of his commando in readiness for work, the sound of rapid gunfire crackled across the clear blue sky. They all looked up. No one spoke. They didn't need to. Clasping his trembling hands together, Theo bowed his head in a silent prayer for the Jewish man he'd been unable to help and whose tiny error had cost him his life.

That day, the forest commando was led in the opposite direction to the firing range to work on clearing a new area of woodland. Theo was thankful to have something else to focus his attention on and set about felling a sturdy pine tree and sawing it into a pile of logs. When the order came for the men to down tools, he could barely move. He'd thrown himself into his work and paid for it with an aching back and painful blisters to his hands. But it only went some way to stop him from dwelling on the implications of what had unfolded earlier that day.

Chapter Thirty-Five

Saskia

She wore her mother's cast-off long blue coat, which was a little on the large side but with the belt tied tight did a decent job at keeping the wind out. The navy beret was less effective, but she liked it and it helped hide her mass of dark curls. They'd agreed to meet outside the bakery and she arrived just as the station clock pealed out the half-hour. Anxious not to be spotted hanging around, she decided to give it two minutes before heading back home. Then she saw him, a rangy figure in a tan overcoat and matching brimmed hat pulled low over his eyes. He weaved through the crowd towards her. Drawing level, he touched the rim of his hat and murmured, '*Goedenmiddag*'. She waited until he crossed the main road before setting off after him.

The house was like any other on the residential Bankastraat, with a small neat front garden edged with low shrubs and a path that skirted the side of the house. Watching from across the road, she saw him disappear round the back. There was nobody about, but she looked around her all the same before walking up to the front door. First reaching into her bag for the rectangular tin, she rapped on the door three times. It was flung open by a small beaming woman of about fifty wearing a striped apron round her waist.

'My dear, how lovely to see you! How is your mother keeping?' the woman asked.

'She's very well, thank you. I've brought some *koekjes* she made,' Saskia replied and handed over the tin with a smile.

They spoke loudly enough that if anyone had wanted to listen they would have assumed it was a normal social visit. Pleasantries over, she stepped into the hallway, shutting the door behind her with a click. The man she'd followed was visible through the door to the living room. He'd taken off his hat and was smoothing his hair in a mirror above the fireplace.

'Herr Stengel,' she said. 'How are you?'

'I'm very well, Saskia. And you?' he said, catching her eye in the mirror. He turned to face her. 'I'm sorry I'm late. I came as soon as I could but was held up by urgent business at the office.' He spoke with a thick German accent but his command of Dutch was good.

'It's no problem, Herr Stengel,' said Saskia, stepping inside the room. 'Have you many letters for me today?' She looked round as the woman came bustling in, carrying a tray with two cups of tea, which she placed on a small table between two armchairs.

'Mevrouw Jansen, you shouldn't have,' Herr Stengel said, with a smile.

'Ach, Heinz, you know how I like to look after you,' she said, handing him a cup with a girlish laugh.

'Thank you.' He accepted it with a little bow. 'But you already do so much for us. Your generosity in allowing us to meet safely and behind closed doors knows no bounds. Those entrusting us with their messages for their loved ones are enormously grateful for the service we provide and it simply wouldn't be possible without you.'

Saskia pretended to rummage for something in her handbag. Coming to Mevrouw Jansen's house and meeting Herr Stengel still made her tense, though she'd been coming for several weeks. Not for the first time, she had to remind herself that what she was doing was a good and kind thing. Delivering letters took on a whole new meaning when she heard Mevrouw Jansen speak of the joy mothers felt when they received a note from their sons, even if it was sometimes no more than a couple of lines scribbled on some torn scrap of paper. It gave them such hope knowing their sons were still alive.

Today, Saskia wished Herr Stengel would hurry up with his speech so she could get away, and stop off and see Frans on her way home. She hated it when Frans was on edge, which he was so often these days, worrying that something must have happened to her if she wasn't exactly on time. Theo's disappearance had been the catalyst for his anxiety and he was prone to thinking the worst. It wouldn't do to reveal her own fears that Herr Stengel might not be everything he claimed to be. If she was to continue with her work, she had to reassure Frans that Herr Stengel was on their side and also wanted to alleviate the plight of the prisoners at Kamp Amersfoort.

She'd been doing her rounds for several weeks when Herr Stengel was introduced to her by Mevrouw Jansen, whose son, Bernd, had spent three months as a prisoner inside the camp. Bernd suffered from eczema that worsened from the stress of being locked up, so he had gone to the hospital for help. There he found the doctor in conversation with an SS officer who turned out to be Herr Stengel. He discovered that the two Germans had been friends before the war and both had been forced to join the Nazis against their will. They were also united in their desire to help the prisoners in whatever small way they could. After Bernd's release, Herr Stengel wrote to him asking if there was anyone he could trust to help distribute prisoner letters within the local area. Naturally, Bernd thought of his own mother, a pillar of the community, who constantly looked out for the needy and saved her own dwindling rations to make wholesome soups so that neighbours would not go hungry.

'So you see, not all SSers are bad,' Saskia had said, when she explained Herr Stengel's role to Frans. Herr Stengel worked at the administration offices in town and regularly visited the camp, ostensibly on business. Because of his uniform, he was never stopped by the guards when entering or leaving the camp, often carrying illicit letters and parcels in his battered leather briefcase with its false bottom. Mevrouw Jansen vouched for him and persuaded Saskia that Stengel's extensive knowledge of happenings both inside and outside the camp would help them reach more people. Saskia was reassured by Stengel's calm and friendly manner, but she remained wary of him. She never told him anything that was more than absolutely necessary to do her job.

'It's my pleasure to help,' Mevrouw Jansen said to Stengel. 'I only wish more people would do the same. People round here turn their backs on the things that go on. Or think it's their duty to report anything they find suspicious to the authorities.' Her expression hardened. 'Why, I'm sure Herr Telling down the road was behind the arrest of Mevrouw Kuyper's son the other day. The poor boy, he's not a day over sixteen, but they wouldn't believe him, even though his ID card's genuine.' She pursed her lips and shook her head.

Saskia cast Stengel a furtive glance. Such talk made her uncomfortable and made her think of Frans, also sixteen years old. She knew she must not endanger him in any way and vowed never to mention him to Stengel.

Stengel merely nodded and drained his cup, handing it back with the reassurance that he would let her know immediately if there was any suggestion of goings-on around here.

At last, Mevrouw Jansen left the room and they were left to deal with the letters Stengel had brought with him. He pulled out a document case from his shabby leather bag and extracted several items that were interleaved between official-looking papers. There were folded sheets of lined paper ripped from exercise books and a few were in envelopes supplied by Herr Doktor.

'Most are for houses in the centre, but there are one or two for the villages. Will you be all right delivering those?'

'Yes, of course. I'll deliver them on my way home,' said Saskia. She appreciated his concern, but wondered if he didn't quite trust her to do the job. Twice, she'd caught sight of him walking a little way behind her when she was out delivering letters. When she'd confronted him, he'd said it must have been a coincidence as he was in the area on business. What business he never told her, but he often said he was concerned for her safety, so she was inclined to believe he had her best interests at heart.

'Have you any for me?' said Stengel, tilting his head.

'I'm sorry, I nearly forgot,' said Saskia, her cheeks flaring hot. She lifted her handbag onto her lap and turned it on its side. She unzipped the base and reached into the secret pocket to draw out a handful of letters, one of them for Karel, a prisoner Frans had grown concerned about. She knew the letter wasn't much, but it would go a little way to alleviating his suffering, so soon after he'd lost his wife to cancer. 'Just these today. Everyone's getting anxious for any news from the camp. You will make sure the prisoners get them, won't you?'

'Don't you worry. They'll be safe with me,' said Stengel, taking them and tucking them into his document case before fastening it shut. 'And I'll see you at the station next week at the same time?'

'Yes, I'll see you then. Goodbye, Herr Stengel.'

After exchanging a few words with Mevrouw Jansen and retrieving her biscuit tin for next time, she left swiftly, half running to the end of the road, where she was swallowed up by the crowd.

Chapter Thirty-Six

Theo

Theo tried to keep his nerves under control, but his whole body flinched whenever the crack and volley of gunfire started up again. It could last anything from a few seconds to several minutes, but there was never a pattern to the shootings, which could start up at any time of the day or night. None of the prisoners dared discuss what was going on, which only made things worse. Everyone knew they could so easily be next. Then sometimes, Theo would catch another man's eye and the unspoken terror written there would fill him with despair that he would never be free of this place.

One morning, Theo was preparing to leave for another long day putting his back into chopping trees out in the forest when a guard pulled him out of line and told him to go and see the commandant right away. Already on edge as he was, Theo's mind raced back to when Berg had had him transferred. It must have been more than a month ago. Was it because he'd attracted attention to himself by trying to attend to that poor man? Fear pulsed through him as he attempted to steady himself for another confrontation.

Head down, he was halfway across the yard when he looked up. It was Frans. He was gesturing towards a space between two buildings away from prying eyes. Casting about to make sure it was safe, Theo followed him in. It was so narrow that they were pushed up against each other, almost touching. He stiffened, embarrassed at his appearance, his filthy feet rammed into ill-fitting clogs and the smell coming off him. How could he even begin to tell Frans how bad things were?

'I've been so worried about you. Are you all right?' whispered Frans, scrutinising his face.

Theo tried to shrug it off. 'I'm working chopping trees in the forest, but it looks as if that's about to change as the commandant's asked to see me.' He paused. 'I'm so sorry. I let you down.'

Frans looked so sad as he spoke. 'I should never have got you involved. You only got into trouble because of me.'

Theo shook his head vigorously. 'I've been marked out as a troublemaker from the start and they would have come after me whatever I did.' He looked anxiously towards Berg's office. 'I have to go before someone sees me.'

'Wait, I have some good news. Saskia has been visiting Annelies and helping her keep positive. She'll be so pleased to hear I ran into you.'

Theo's dull eyes briefly lit up on hearing Annelies's name. 'Do you think she'll wait for me?' He hardly dared believe what Frans had told him, but it was the best news he'd had in months.

'Well, Saskia doesn't tell me everything, but that's the impression I get.' Frans was looking over Theo's shoulder. 'Stay strong. We should go. I'll try to speak to you again soon.' He squeezed Theo's hand before walking away.

Theo waited a few moments before emerging from the opening, only to come face to face with a thickset guard sporting a livid red scar running from the corner of his right eye to his mouth. His insides turned to liquid as he fought to think of a reason why he'd been standing talking to Frans.

'Who was that man? Do you know him?' the guard growled with such force that spittle sprayed onto Theo's face. Theo flinched. There was no point lying. 'I do. He's an acquaintance and we were exchanging greetings.'

'It's forbidden to speak to any visitors to the camp.' The man bared a mouth full of rotten teeth.

Theo looked away. 'He spoke to me, so I answered him. It would be rude not to.' He didn't like the way the conversation was heading. To his relief, Berg appeared at the door of his office.

'Igor,' called the commandant. 'You can leave him with me.'

'I think you should know he's causing trouble. I caught him talking,' said the guard, narrowing his puffy eyes into slits.

'Thank you. That will be all, Igor,' Berg said brusquely, gesturing to Theo to follow him into his office.

'I wasn't doing anything wrong,' protested Theo, though he knew that being caught speaking to Frans was hardly likely to endear him to the commandant.

'Igor's only doing his job. Now forget about it. I have an important matter to discuss.' The commandant gave him a condescending smile and closed the door behind them. Theo removed his cap and twisted it between his hands as he stood before the commandant.

'I've been keeping a close eye on your progress out in the forest,' began Berg.

Theo's heart began to pound.

'You've been working hard, which is what I like to hear.' He paused. 'But I hear you disobeyed orders to leave a fellow prisoner and were reprimanded for it. You must realise these things do not escape my attention.'

Theo wanted to explain his version of events, but realised it wouldn't serve him well at all. And he had no desire to goad the commandant, who appeared to be waiting and watching for his reaction. Resigned, Theo gave a small nod.

'However,' the commandant continued, moving to his desk so he could pick up his pen and twirl it between his fingers, 'I'm prepared to overlook your latest transgression in the light of developments in the camp.'

Theo was shocked. He remained very still, as if not drawing attention to himself would somehow help his case, but the commandant's mind had moved on as he recounted how prisoner numbers had multiplied since he had transferred from Westerbork, the transition camp for Jews close to the German border.

'More prisoners need more supervision. SS guards from Germany are not the answer as they're hard to come by since the expansion of the camps in newly annexed territories. I have been looking closer to home within the local community and have found that young men are eager to take up roles within our administration. The uniform is attractive, their quarters comfortable and career prospects are good. But unfortunately, I'm unable to find enough recruits as so many have moved away to work for us in German factories.' A look of irritation briefly crossed the commandant's face. 'My solution is to fill jobs from within.'

Theo held his breath as it dawned on him what the commandant had in mind for him. Everyone knew that the SS camp was populated with fervent young Dutch men brainwashed into enforcing Nazi racial doctrine, directed primarily at the Jewish population, in exchange for a secure job close to home. Impressionable young men the Nazis hoped to groom for more senior positions in the party. Was the commandant suggesting that he, Theo, switch over to the other side?

'Naturally, we won't be able to spare you for the rigorous training we provide in order to become a fully fledged guard. You will work at the SS camp, where you will take your meals at the staff canteen. We will also need to change your uniform,' Berg said, looking Theo up and down with an expression of thinly veiled disgust. 'The administrative staff will see to that. You will report to the SS administration building right away.'

He went to his desk and picked up a sheet of paper, which he handed over. Theo stared at it, not knowing what to say. Of course he couldn't become a guard... an SS officer... a Nazi. But what choice did he have when he was already in so much danger? If he questioned the commandant, or even dared refuse, what would happen to him, he thought with mounting dread.

'Mind you perform your job well. Any reports of misbehaviour and I will have you transferred to the shooting range commando. Now, I have other business I must attend to,' Berg said, moving swiftly to the door, where he stood waiting for Theo to leave.

Theo swallowed and mumbled, 'Thank you, Herr Commandant,' though he wasn't sure what for. All he knew was that the document he held was the only thing that might save his life.

Chapter Thirty-Seven

Frans

The gate squeaked, announcing Saskia's arrival, and the cow he was milking gave a loud moo. Frans almost knocked over the pail as he stood up in his haste to meet her. The last few days had been so tense as he waited for her to arrive with news of what was happening in town and whether rumours of hundreds of German soldiers massing in the centre were true. And every day Saskia didn't appear, he fretted that something must have happened to her.

'Saskia, you're here!' he said, relief washing over him as they fell into each other's arms.

'I came as quickly as I could,' she said, catching her breath. 'Oh Frans, I can't tell you how good it is to see you.'

They kissed and for a brief moment forgot all the worries of their time apart. But when she pulled back to look at him, Frans realised there was something troubling her.

'Is everything all right? Is it about Stengel?'

Saskia shook her curls. 'No. But something happened in town today… can we go inside?'

Frans took her into the house, through the kitchen, where Saskia greeted his mother, who was busy preparing the evening meal, and into the room where the post was sorted.

'What's going on?' he said, shutting the door behind them.

Saskia reached into her coat pocket and pulled out a crumpled sheet of yellow paper. Straightening it out, Frans read the word *Bevel* written across the top in thick black lettering. Puzzled, he looked up at her for an explanation.

'I came straight from town. It's true, the *moffen* are everywhere. I had no idea why till I saw this notice lying on the ground next to my bike. Then I saw there were notices all over the place, pasted on trees, lamp posts, shop windows. Frans, you have to read it.'

Frans flattened out the sheet of paper and began reading, his face growing pale as he mouthed the words. It was a decree from the German high command, ordering all men aged between sixteen and forty to register immediately for *arbeidsinzet*, in other words, enforced labour, in Germany. It contained the stark message that only those with a valid reason, such as working for the military or engaging in civilian duties, were excused and must carry their exemption card with them at all times. Anyone attempting to go into hiding or put up resistance would be shot.

'The *moffen* were hanging around looking for men to arrest. And you'll be arrested too if you keep going into that place,' she said anxiously, after he'd been reading for several minutes.

Frans jabbed the notice with his finger. 'Look what it says here. If I can prove my job is essential, I'll be exempt. I run the farm with Pa, so they can't refuse me.'

Saskia sighed in exasperation. 'Even if you manage to persuade them to exempt you, you'd be crazy to go into the camp. You're sixteen,' she exclaimed. 'They're bound to find a reason to keep you inside.'

'But you don't understand. The letters… we finally have a system that's working and if I stop, we'll be letting people like Lars and Karel down.' His eyes darted anxiously to the stack of letters on the table. 'And listen,' he said, hearing his voice getting increasingly desperate. 'I saw Theo in the camp today, the first time in weeks. He's so worn down, so terribly thin, that I barely recognised him. When I told him you'd been writing to Annelies, you should have seen his face light up. I believe that knowing she still cares for him is the one thing that will help him through this. I have to do this.'

Saskia gave him a sad smile. 'Please Frans, you have to think of your own safety now. If it's about getting letters to Theo, Herr Stengel is the answer. None of the guards take any notice of him when he goes in and out of the camp. He's just another SS officer in uniform going about his business.'

'Are you crazy? Every time you go and meet that man, I'm out of my mind with worry. It doesn't matter how many times you tell me you trust him, I can't forget he's a *mof*. Do you honestly trust that man after this?' Frans prodded the notice that lay on the table between them.

Saskia stiffened. 'I'm always careful when I'm around him and never take anything for granted. You've nothing to fear. I can look after myself. But Frans, this isn't about me. You can't be seen in that place. Don't think you're immune just because you have a job to do.' Saskia's eyes took on such an intensity that Frans had to look away.

'It's not just about the letters,' he said. 'All I know is that I have to help Theo get out of there before it's too late. He was on his way to see the commandant. That can only mean more punishments, even harder labour. Saskia, I wish you could have seen him. You'd understand that I can't just leave him in that state.'

'I'm afraid Saskia's right,' said Evert from the doorway. He looked tired and the dust in his hair made it appear greyer than usual. 'You and Cas mustn't be seen taking the horse and cart near the camp, but you'll get an exemption to work on the farm. Berg owes me a favour – they've taken all our best workers. He should be able to arrange for your papers.'

'Pa—' Frans began, about to remonstrate, but his father held up a hand to stop him.

'No, Frans. Arguing isn't going to change anything.' He rubbed a hand up over his face and hair, then left.

Saskia rose to her feet. 'I must go. I need to warn Aart. He's also in danger and I know he's adamant he won't work for the *moffen*. I don't like the idea, but his only option is to go into hiding.'

Frans listened in shock as the reality of the situation hit him. An exemption to work wouldn't help at all – it would simply be too risky for him to leave the farm. He regretted that there was nothing he could do for Aart, but the thought that Saskia was prepared to put herself in even more danger was much worse.

'What do you intend to do about it?' he said, tensing.

'I don't know. But the least I can do is warn him.'

He stood up and took her hands. 'Promise you'll be careful?'

'Please don't worry about me,' she said, but her eyes told a different story.

Frans pulled her into a close embrace, while trying to ignore the pounding of his heart.

Chapter Thirty-Eight

Theo

With a heavy heart, Theo approached the two rows of barbed-wire fencing that separated the prisoners from the Kamp SS compound, conscious he was betraying the prisoners he'd left behind. But he'd had no choice in the matter and it could so easily have gone the other way, with him being selected to face the firing squad on the whim of some heartless guard. A small part of him was grateful that Berg had offered him a chance of survival, but he knew this would be the last chance he'd get.

He looked back at the yard he'd left, but there was no one to witness his departure. He hung his head and thought of the prisoners, of Lars, Joost, Karel and countless others, who had grown to rely on Theo's efforts to bring them news from outside. Out of shame, he hadn't dared tell anyone that he was being offered a marginally better chance of survival.

Take one step at a time, he murmured to himself, his breath catching in his throat.

He walked up to the uniformed man on the gate, who looked up suspiciously as Theo handed him his letter. He scrutinised it with a frown before pointing to where Theo should go. Theo walked through to the other side, acutely aware of the guard's eyes on his back.

The SS compound didn't look so different from his own – several low buildings he guessed were for the administration, some storage buildings, another that looked like the mess and kitchens, and the sleeping quarters. Theo glanced up, as he often did, to check who was manning the watchtower, only to realise there wasn't one. After living for months beneath the invisible stare of guards positioned high up every few yards along the perimeter of the camp, it felt disconcerting. It was then he realised that the reason he'd been allowed to cross the divide must be because Berg trusted him. But the thought did nothing to reassure him – as he stood there, he was aware that he was anything but safe.

'Hey, what are you doing?'

Theo was wrenched from his thoughts by a uniformed officer striding towards him, a hand on his revolver belt. It was just the two of them in the vast empty yard, an SSer in uniform and Theo in his badly fitting prison clothes. Theo glanced nervously back towards the guard on the gate, but he'd disappeared from sight.

'I've been sent to work here. By the commandant,' said Theo shakily, holding up the letter.

The uniformed man gave a snort. 'Show me,' he said and snatched the letter. He scanned it, then peered at Theo for a moment. 'So, you're a new recruit? We've had a few recently, mainly black triangles, working over at the cell block. Is that why you've been sent over here?' He looked Theo up and down. 'You look in better shape than most of that useless lot.' He jerked his head disdainfully in the direction of the prisoner compound.

Theo was reluctant to tell this SSer the details of his meeting with the commandant. But the truth was that he wasn't sure exactly why he'd been singled out to work here.

'Do you know which unit you'll be assigned to?' The SSer sounded impatient.

Theo shook his head, wishing he'd asked Berg before so readily accepting his fate. Prisoners never talked about what might happen in the SS compound, which was considered to be as grim as their side of the camp. And what was the point, when their only thought was getting through each day and staying alive?

'Huh. You'll find out soon enough. Come on, I'll show you where to report for duty. I'm Peter,' he announced. 'And you?'

'Theo.' It felt strange saying his name after months of being addressed by a number. Saying it made him feel more normal, less at a disadvantage, but certainly not an equal.

'How long have you been in the camp?' said Peter with a scrutinising look. Theo had to think. So many days and weeks, all merging into one. He was unable to answer. 'I hear the execution squad is up and running now. Did you hear the shots?' the man went on.

Theo balked at the excitement in the SSer's voice and his breath quickened. 'How could I not? I've seen men digging a deep trench out in the forest. It's obvious they've been preparing for their own deaths.'

Peter fell silent, making Theo wonder if he'd said the wrong thing. After all, this man was one of them, however friendly he seemed.

They arrived at the administration building. 'They'll kit you out in there. No doubt I'll be seeing you around.' Peter performed the Nazi salute and walked away.

Still clutching the letter, Theo opened the door and was met by a wall of warm air the likes of which he hadn't experienced since he'd left home.

'Shut the door, will you – you'll let the heat out,' said a woman in an irritable voice as she looked up from behind the reception desk. Next to her was a large black stove radiating an intense heat.

Theo quickly pulled the door to and took in the scene in front of him. There were several doors leading off the reception area and uniformed women were hurrying in and out, some carrying piles of papers, others calling out instructions to one another.

'Are you going to stand there all day?' asked the receptionist. She had rosy cheeks that reminded him of Annelies – Theo felt a stab of pain shoot through his chest.

'I have a letter from the commandant that I'm to register here,' he stuttered.

'Let me see,' said the receptionist. She barely skimmed the letter before slapping it on the counter. She went to a cupboard behind her and pulled out several items of clothing and a pair of boots. 'These should be your size. Go down the corridor to the far end, you'll see a room on your right where you can get yourself changed. When you're ready, Frau Koch will take you through procedures.'

Unsure of his place among all this activity, he hurried along to the room indicated and pulled the door shut behind him. It was icy cold, but surprisingly pleasant after the intense heat of the reception area. He sank down onto a wooden case, one of several, and examined the uniform he'd been handed. It had clearly been worn before. The jacket was slightly worn at the cuffs, but had a neat black collar bearing an insignia he didn't recognise. The grey trousers were obviously several sizes too big, but there was a leather belt and also a plain cap without a badge. No shirt and no underwear. Had she forgotten to give him any? He certainly had no intention of going back to ask.

Glancing quickly at the door in case someone came in, he slipped the jacket over his own thin one and did the same with the trousers. The belt made a difference, pulled tight into the last notch. It was a relief to discard his wooden clogs, even though his toes were now squashed uncomfortably right up to the ends of the hard leather boots. He decided against wearing the cap, assuming it would be disrespectful to put it on indoors. Walking up and down in the small room, he noticed the small heel made a clicking sound, but the idea of having to go back down the corridor filled him with terror. What if someone saw him as an imposter? The woman on the reception desk had taken his letter and he had no proof of why he had been sent here.

Gulping in a deep breath, he opened the door and came face to face with a thickset woman holding the commandant's letter in her hand.

'*Heil* Hitler,' she said, saluting. 'I am Frau Koch. You are to come with me.' She stared at him with eyes devoid of all emotion. 'I will show you where to go and Herr Westerveld, our Kamp SS leader, will tell you where you will be working.' She spoke in a deep gruff voice that matched her severe expression, sending a chill through him. Later, Theo was to discover she was *Aufseherin* Koch, formerly a brutal guard at Ravensbrück camp, who had been employed by the commandant to oversee the expanding women's section of Kamp Amersfoort.

At the staff canteen, Frau Koch informed him that breakfast and dinner were at six thirty, morning and evening. 'If you're in camp, you may partake of a meal at midday, but you'll have to do without if you're working on the outside.' She didn't look as if she cared about his welfare and Theo imagined her enjoying a comfortable life with plenty of food and heat inside the administration building. When she had finally finished all the details of his induction, Theo was relieved to see the back of her.

Inside the canteen, around half a dozen officers were eating their midday meal. Theo was half expecting someone to come and challenge him, but no one took any notice of him. He guessed the uniform he was wearing helped him to blend in, but he was unable to shake off the anxiety he'd felt ever since he'd arrived.

He went over to the counter, where an orderly handed him a bowl of thick soup and hunk of fresh bread, the sight of which made him catch his breath. So that's where all the potatoes go, he thought, taking his bowl to the nearest empty table. Head down, he tucked in. The potato and bean soup with chunks of meat tasted good and he ate fast till his belly ached. It was the first proper meal he'd had in months. But every spoonful made him feel desperately guilty for the men and women he'd left behind.

Chapter Thirty-Nine

Paul Westerveld was the Kamp SS leader, his title *Arbeitsführer*, and organised the work commandos. He was known to have escaped deportation to a German munitions factory thanks to his acquaintance Berg, the drinking companion he'd met in the early months of the war. Having until then worked as a bank manager in Amersfoort, Westerveld had persuaded Berg he was hard-working and could be trusted to work for the Germans. Berg rewarded him with a senior post and expected him to keep a strong grip on 'the locals', as Berg liked to call the Dutch youths, whose allegiance to German values was of paramount importance. The arrangement suited Westerveld perfectly, allowing him to turn a blind eye to what was happening around him, rather than face an uncertain future across the border.

Westerveld wasn't entirely without compassion. His job was to appoint guards to different work units, based on which groups of prisoners were physically capable of undertaking heavy labour and who would be better off undertaking lighter tasks around the camp. If it had been up to him, he'd have been more lenient towards the Jewish prisoners. But conveniently, that was the role of the *SS Hauptsturmführer*, who invariably put the most vicious and brutal guards in charge of Jews, assigning them to the toughest and most back-breaking of jobs, regardless of their ability or state of health.

'Theo de Groot… let me see,' said Westerveld, flicking over the pages of his thick black book till he found what he was looking for. 'Ah, here we are.' He made a note in black ink next to Theo's name.

Theo sat before him in his office awaiting his decision. He watched as Westerveld wrote and tried to pick up any clues as to what he could expect. Westerveld had already described the guard jobs he was looking to fill, mostly associated with the building of the new section, which was behind schedule.

'It's not often that the commandant transfers prisoners to work in this section of the camp, but we are suffering a shortage of recruits currently. He tells me that you are eager to show your loyalty to the Fatherland.' Westerveld looked up at Theo and waited.

Theo wasn't expecting this. Was it a test? Could this Dutchman be any less bad than the Germans he'd encountered when he was a prisoner? Something warned him to remain cautious. 'I know what it's like to work as part of a commando, so I'm sure I can get the prisoners to cooperate,' Theo said carefully.

'Good. There are a lot of prisoners working on the commandos and they need close supervision at all times. Your role will be to assist the SSers in charge. You will be part of an important team responsible for a doubling in size of the camp. Just imagine how many more prisoners that means. It'll be a terrific achievement and those involved will be justly rewarded.' With a look of satisfaction, Westerveld sat back in his chair.

Theo contemplated the implication of Westerveld's words. It could mean only one thing – that there could be no prospect of the war ending any time soon. And as for being rewarded, he was sure Westerveld had been thinking only of himself. The thought of all those prisoners already suffering such hardship, and others yet to arrive, unsuspecting of their fate, was almost too much to bear. He knew only too well what it was like to suffer at the hands of the Nazis – now he was expected to behave like one of them. A flash of anger towards Westerveld seared through him. But it was pointless. Speaking out would do him no favours. He had no choice but to comply.

Theo was one of four Kamp SS recruits, three Dutch and the fourth a German officer who'd been transferred to the camp after he'd been injured in gun battle when fighting on the Eastern Front. The Dutch ones seemed so young, no more than sixteen or seventeen, and full of zeal for the Fatherland. Theo was wary of them and their tendency to brag about how they made prisoners work hard in order to win praise from their superiors. It made him uncomfortable, their stories reminding him of what he'd left behind and the torture his camp-mates were all still enduring at the hands of their captors.

When any of them asked how Theo came to be there, he kept quiet about the reasons for his arrest, surmising that they wouldn't take kindly to someone involved in activities that opposed the regime they supported so fervently. But after he had worked alongside them for a while, they began including him in their jokes and banter and stopped asking questions.

Early each morning, they took their band of prisoners out of the camp along the perimeter fence, past the entrance to a nearby farm and onto a rough area covered in dense undergrowth and tree stumps, which needed to be cleared to allow the building work to begin. It was back-breaking labour. Herman, the leader, didn't tolerate any slacking and spent his time yelling insults and threats at the men. Theo, used to such behaviour from his time as a prisoner, did his best to keep the men's spirits up with encouraging words whenever Herman was out of earshot.

One late afternoon, a cold drizzle began to fall and the prisoners were flagging. If he'd had his way, he would have told them all to knock off, get back to camp and warm up, but that was never going to happen as long as Herman and the others in charge were throwing their weight about. All at once, the flicker of something moving caught his attention – a figure was approaching through the mist. A stooped woman with skirts that touched her muddy clogs came into view. She was carrying a bulky bag, which she deposited at Theo's feet. She gave him a quick, fearful look. 'This is for the men. Will you make sure they get it?' The woman spoke anxiously and her creased kindly face reminded him of his own mother. How could he refuse?

'I'm not in charge, but I'll make sure of it.' Theo glanced over at the other guards, who hadn't noticed their exchange. 'And thank you, you're very kind.'

The woman gave him a brief shake of her head. 'It's the very least I can do for those poor men. No one should be made to work like this, and in their state too. Look at them, they're all skin and bone.' She then peered at him suspiciously. 'You're Dutch. Why are you working for them?'

Theo felt himself go cold, but before he could answer, Herman and one of the other guards came striding over. 'What's going on? And what is this?' said Herman, noticing the bag Theo was holding. The woman was already hurrying away back down the track to the farm.

Theo opened the bag and they all peered in. Two loaves of bread and cheese cut into slices were ready to hand out. '*Lekker, heh?*' the Dutch one said with a grin and stuck his hand inside the bag, causing Herman to snort and do the same. Theo was furious; their behaviour reminded him of the times he'd squabbled with other children when the teacher handed out treats. But this wasn't a game, nor were these men children. Theo grabbed the Dutchman's wrist, saying, 'We don't need it. Can't you see it's for the prisoners?' His heart pounding, he realised he may have overstepped the mark, but he refused to stop there. The young man looked shamefaced and listened as Theo told him how hard it was for the prisoners to work when their bellies were permanently empty. 'We'll get so much more out of them if they get proper food and not the dregs that pass for it here.'

'It's against the rules. You know that,' said Herman, who didn't look as confident as when he'd been shouting at the prisoners.

'It's a risk worth taking. They'll work so much harder if we do this for them. Believe me,' said Theo, with a courage he hadn't realised he had. 'Michiel – will you go and tell the other guards and get them to agree?' It was the first time he'd called the boy by his name and his pleading must have touched a nerve. For all their bravado, these young men weren't as hard as they liked to make out. He could tell they were persuaded by his argument, though they would never go as far as agreeing with him.

They all stood by and looked the other way as Theo shared out the food among the grateful prisoners.

The next time the woman appeared she came with a little boy, who was eager to help. They weren't the only ones. Word must have got around that this commando was led by SSers who could be trusted. Most days someone would appear with offerings of dried sausage, apples, bread and cheese. Morale among the prisoners improved as they gained in strength – even the grudging guards could see that. And Theo was gratified he was able to help them in some small way. But he knew it wouldn't last long. The men finished the work faster than anticipated and the wasteland was soon ready for the next stage. Before long, the commando was disbanded and another unit moved in to start with the erection of the new buildings.

Chapter Forty

Saskia

Every week when she rode to Amersfoort, Saskia was careful to hide her bike where it wouldn't be found by any passing Germans, who considered it their right to help themselves to other people's property. She'd been lucky so far, thanks to her secret spot by the church. But today as she approached the centre of town, she noticed many more Germans on the streets and decided she needed to find somewhere more safe.

Saskia stopped beneath the bare branches of a tree and rested her bike against her, blowing onto her numb hands to regain some feeling. It was bitterly cold, even for late March, and she wondered when this long hard winter would ever end. Rubbing her hands together briskly, she put her threadbare gloves back on and wheeled her bike towards the bridge, where she was hoping to find a place to leave it. She craned her neck and had seen a spot she thought might be suitable when a German soldier stepped into her path, lifted his hand and yelled out, '*Halt!*'

Saskia's heart stopped. How could she have been so foolish as not to keep her wits about her? He was blocking her path. She had no choice but to confront the German, though her instincts were telling her to jump on her bike and get away as fast as possible.

'*Papiere!*' the man shouted hoarsely.

Unpleasant memories of the last time she was ordered to show her papers gave her a jolt. Her hands shook as she took her ID card from her bag. The German snatched it and spent some moments looking at the photo, then at Saskia. Grim-faced, he handed it back to her and demanded she open her bag for him to conduct a search.

'I have nothing to hide,' she stuttered in German, petrified he would discover the letters hidden in the secret compartment at the bottom.

'I will decide that,' spat the German. He grabbed the bag from her and emptied its contents onto the ground. There was nothing much there: a shabby purse with a few coins, a small hairbrush and the tin she always had with her when visiting Mevrouw Jansen. He opened the purse and shook the coins into his hand, then pocketed them.

'Please don't take my money. It's all I have. I need it to buy my mother bread,' Saskia cried uselessly, as she tried to grab the purse that had once belonged to her grandmother.

But the German callously tossed it over the bridge. She heard it land with a thud on the frozen surface of the canal. 'And now we will see what you are hiding in the tin,' he said.

'You'll find nothing. Just a few *koekjes* for my aunt.' Trembling, Saskia watched as he picked up it up. There was no point resisting.

He prised off the lid, lifted the tin to his nose and sniffed, before taking one of the biscuits and biting it in half. The expression on his face turned to disgust and he spat the contents of his mouth on the ground, before throwing the tin down. Saskia's mother's biscuits rolled into the gutter as Saskia let out a shuddering gasp.

'Hand over your bike,' the German ordered, kicking the tin aside.

All the time she was suffering this humiliation, Saskia had gripped the handlebars hard. She wasn't going to let go now. Finally rage took over.

'You've taken what little money I have and thrown my possessions on the ground. You will not take my bicycle.' Her eyes flashed with anger and her heart thumped in her chest. The German began to laugh, a humourless nasty laugh. He kept on laughing as he prised the handlebars from her hands.

'It's worth nothing. And the brakes aren't working. Please, don't take it.' She hated herself for pleading like this and wished she had the strength to take him on. But all she could do was watch helplessly as the German mounted her bike and rode away.

'No… no,' she sobbed, tears streaming down her cheeks. She bent to pick up her bag, which lay beside the tin, now crumpled where it had hit the ground. She clasped the bag to her, and closed her eyes. He hadn't found the letters. That was all that mattered.

The church clock rang out the hour and she realised she would be late. Setting off at a run, she reached the station ten minutes later. There was no sign of Stengel and the square was teeming with groups of Germans standing around in groups, watching for any suspicious activity. It was too dangerous to stop and wait, so she kept on walking, desperate to reach Mevrouw Jansen's house and safety.

The Bankastraat was sufficiently far from the town centre for there to be no patrolling Germans. Saskia passed one or two people with empty baskets, who probably ventured out every day in the hope of buying a few provisions. Her chest constricted at the thought of the biscuits she no longer had. She still had the empty tin, though, and took it from her bag as she always did before knocking on Mevrouw Jansen's door.

The door was opened immediately by Mevrouw Jansen herself, who seemed to have forgotten their usual pleasantries as she waved Saskia inside.

'We were so worried something had happened to you. Is everything all right?' she said.

Saskia knew she must look a sight, her tear-stained cheeks and hair in a mess, and Mevrouw Jansen's concern only brought on more tears.

'Come and sit down,' Mevrouw Jansen said gently and led her by the arm into the sitting room. Herr Stengel was pacing anxiously up and down.

'I thought something had happened to you. I'm so glad you made it,' he said, relief visible on his face.

'What's going on out there?' said Saskia, brushing the back of her hand over her wet face.

'They are arresting any man over the age of sixteen who lives in the centre of town.'

'But what's that got to do with us?' she said, her thoughts turning anxiously to Frans's safety rather than her own. Was it just here in Amersfoort they were conducting searches, or all over the locality?

'They're angry that so many have refused to report for duty and don't trust anyone who might be helping men to hide. Saskia, did anyone follow you here?'

Saskia's heart began to pound as she tried to remember, before realising she'd been in such a hurry to arrive she hadn't been as careful as usual to cover her tracks.

The sound of a car stopping outside made the three of them look up in alarm.

'Give me your bag. Quickly,' said Mevrouw Jansen. 'We have to hide the letters.'

Saskia handed it over as a car door slammed.

'Heinz, help me,' said Mevrouw Jansen, stooping beside the fireplace and peeling back the rug. The two of them lifted a floor-board and threw the letters from the base of Saskia's bag into the cavity, before banging the board back down. Moments later, the front door burst open and several armed German soldiers came charging in.

Saskia, Mevrouw Jansen and Herr Stengel stood in shock as the men pulled apart the room in front of their eyes, sweeping china ornaments to the floor with a splintering crash, ripping apart the furnishings and hauling back the rugs. When they had finished downstairs, two of the soldiers ran up to the first floor, while a third stood guard over the three of them. Saskia glanced at Herr Stengel, expecting him to do or say something, but he watched silently – he seemed as shocked as she was. Mevrouw Jansen stood beside her, quietly weeping.

After some minutes of thumping and crashing from above, the men came down empty-handed. This seemed to make them even more enraged.

'Don't think you will get away with this,' snarled one of the soldiers, the one in charge. 'Take them away.'

The pain Saskia felt as her arms were wrenched backwards was sudden and excruciating. As she cried out, she felt a blow to her head, before she blacked out.

Chapter Forty-One

Theo

'Have you ever used a gun?'

Theo followed Peter up the steps to the watchtower Theo had always been so careful to avoid. He shook his head vigorously, making Peter laugh. But Theo was appalled – it was certainly no laughing matter.

'Don't look so worried. I can show you. Once you get the hang of it, you'll be fine,' said Peter.

Theo had no choice in this next job, nor did he dare refuse when Westerveld announced that he would be working as a security guard patrolling in the prison yard. But he had never imagined he'd be expected to pull a gun and fire at his fellow prisoners, knowing only too well that feeling of utter terror at being defenceless when confronted with an armed guard intent on harm.

'We're becoming rather stretched now we're at full capacity,' Westerfeld had announced to Theo, after summoning him to his office to tell him about his next assignment. 'With so many prisoners in camp, I need more guards on the watchtowers and along the perimeter fence. Peter is work supervisor and will be in charge. He can show you the ropes.'

As he stood on the wooden steps, Theo tried to hide his fear from Peter. He was reluctant to say out loud he'd never held a gun, let alone fired one. And he was simply unable to contemplate the idea of ever shooting another person.

Theo's father had been a pastor and had instilled in his son the need for compassion towards all fellow human beings. He never tolerated any form of violence. But it was a hard lesson for young Theo, who regularly got into fights at school, returning with cuts and grazes. Once he came home with a black eye, which he tried unsuccessfully to hide from his father. He knew he was a disappointment to him, but was incapable of staying out of trouble. Everything changed the night of the bombardment when they were forced to flee their burning house in Rotterdam with none of their possessions. His father never recovered from the shock of running barefoot for his life. The heart attack had been so sudden – one minute he was drinking his morning cup of tea and the next he was dead on the floor. Theo and his mother were helped through this difficult time by his father's cousin, but Theo was unable to shake off the belief that he was in some way responsible for his father's death. What would his father have made of his only son now, imprisoned in a concentration camp, forced to carry out orders on behalf of the most evil of men?

Theo stared up at the square wooden structure with windows on all sides, offering a perfect view of the prisoner compound and beyond the high perimeter fence. Fixed to the roof were searchlights, which clicked on after dark and swept the terrain for any unusual movement. This was the most dangerous time for any prisoner to be out. Only the most foolish would attempt to escape.

The guard sitting up high was huge and filled the cramped space. On the ledge in front of him lay a half-eaten sandwich, a packet of cigarettes and a rifle. He grunted a greeting before cramming the sandwich into his mouth. Theo's heart lurched as he recognised the man by his livid red scar. He hoped the recognition wasn't mutual.

'You?' The man pointed a grubby finger at Theo, who froze.

'Do you know him, Igor?' said Peter with a frown.

Igor kept looking at Theo as he chewed, finally speaking after he'd swallowed down a mouthful. 'Prisoner! What are you doing up here?' he growled, reaching for his gun.

Theo almost lost his footing as he took a step backwards.

'Calm down, Igor. It's fine, he's working for us. Now, put down the gun,' said Peter, slowly pushing down his palms in an attempt to defuse the tension.

Igor glanced suspiciously from one to the other before lowering his gun.

'Igor is very conscientious and has prevented many prisoners from escaping,' Peter told Theo, with one eye on the guard. 'Theo will be working the perimeter fence. I want you to be quite clear that he is working for us.'

Igor grunted and went back to his sandwich, casting resentful looks in Theo's direction.

'How do you know him?' asked Peter once they were back on solid ground.

'I don't know him and he doesn't know me,' retorted Theo a little too quickly. 'He must have recognised me from my time as a prisoner.'

'Out of all those hundreds of men? He doesn't seem bright enough.' Peter scoffed and laughed loudly. Theo smiled, but was uneasy. Igor certainly wasn't bright, but his killer instinct was the only qualification needed for this job.

Peter sent Theo back to the administration building to be kitted out in a heavy overcoat and leather gloves. 'You'll need these as you'll be out in all weathers,' said Peter, stretching out his hand to catch a falling snowflake. It was a bitterly cold day but the snow flurries weren't settling. Theo looked up at the iron-grey sky with a strong sense of foreboding.

The following morning, Theo started in his new position. In addition to patrolling the perimeter fence, he was one of several guards required to herd hundreds upon hundreds of prisoners into position for roll call. He'd been given strict instructions to reprimand anyone uttering so much as a word to their neighbour and to yell at the 'slackers' who invariably brought up the rear, but he just couldn't do it. Theo knew that they were so ground down they could barely move. During his time as a prisoner, he'd often tried to cover for those weaker than himself, sometimes propping them up with a hitch to their elbow. Now, it was all he could do not to rush forward and lend them a helping hand, so he hung back, trying to avoid being noticed by the other guards.

One morning, he felt a nudge to his arm and saw it was Lars, his former work colleague from the kitchen unit, who had lost his footing and was in danger of falling to the ground. Theo was shocked to see how frail he looked. He quickly put an arm round the other man's scrawny shoulders and helped him regain his balance.

'Can you manage?' he whispered in Lars's ear.

'I have to,' Lars whispered back in a weak voice.

Theo was reluctant to leave him, so continued to walk two paces behind him, making sure he was hidden from the gaze of the other guards. When they reached his row, Lars caught Theo's gaze and gave him a small smile of gratitude.

Once the yard emptied out and the prisoners had departed for their work units, Theo was left to patrol the compound, keeping an eye out for anyone acting suspiciously. The gun that nestled in the holster at his side filled him with fear and he worried constantly it might somehow discharge itself or, worse, that he'd be required to pull it on a prisoner trying to make a run for it. Peter had given him only the briefest of instructions on loading and using it, saying that it was highly unlikely that Theo would ever need to. First and foremost, it was the job of the guards in the watchtower to shoot.

It was another freezing day as Theo began walking briskly round the yard. Alone with his thoughts, his mind went back to Lars. He wished he'd been able to ask if he'd had any news from home, knowing that was the only thing that kept him going. He could only hope that Frans had found someone else to help him smuggle letters into the camp. The thought briefly reassured him, but what if the smuggling operation had broken down? Now that Theo wore a guard's uniform, was there a way for him to do something about the letters? He was briefly buoyed up with hope, but then he glanced up at the watchtower and his heart sank. Igor was up there, recognisable by his enormous bulk. As Theo came closer, he could sense the brute's eyes boring into him. Theo hurried past, pretending he hadn't seen him, but his heart began to race as he realised how futile it was to even think he could evade Igor's watchful gaze.

Next time he approached the wooden structure, he deliberately avoided looking up. There were few people about as most prisoners were outside the camp, toiling away in their work commandos. The only people in the yard were guards and admin staff going about their business. No one spoke, apart from a curt '*Sieg Heil*', and most wore miserable expressions on their faces. *You don't realise how good you have it*, he wished he had the nerve to say, all too aware of the comforts and privileges they enjoyed compared to those they were tasked to oversee.

He turned right onto the section housing Igor's watchtower, and caught sight of two prisoners approaching.

'*Halt*! *Was machen Sie da?*' Theo spoke in German as he'd been instructed.

At that moment, an object came hurtling down from the watchtower. They all looked up and the man nearest dived down and picked it up. It was half a cheese sandwich and Igor could be heard chortling from up above. One of the men grabbed it and began stuffing as much of it into his mouth as he could. The other tried to grab the remains of the sandwich and the two fell onto the ground in a tustle. They were so obviously starving that it hurt Theo to watch. He wished he had more food to hand to them, but that could never happen as long as Igor was up there. Theo shot an angry glance at Igor, who was watching the scene with a stupid grin on his face. Another object flew through the air and landed at Theo's feet. Theo grabbed it before either prisoner could reach it. It was a crumpled cigarette packet containing two cigarettes, clearly meant for the two men. He quickly scanned the yard, making sure there was no one to see him hand them over. He had to warn the men to scarper before they got into trouble.

'Go!' he hissed urgently.

Up above, he saw Igor lift his gun. Theo shuddered and moved away so he didn't have to speak to him. But the incident shook him up and he did his best to avoid any further contact with the brute. In the days that followed, Igor often threw objects for prisoners to squabble over, a game that seemed to give him perverse pleasure.

One evening, he was about to come off duty and was walking towards the gate leading to the Kamp SS section when a gun firing close by echoed across the yard. He jerked his head up. He was sure it came from the watchtower where he knew Igor sat hunched in the half light. Out of the corner of his eye, Theo noticed a dark shadow flitting by the buildings. The searchlight clicked on, sweeping back and forth before picking out Theo with its bright beam. Hesitantly, he put his hand to his gun, too scared even to draw it. Instead he raised his hand to Igor in acknowledgement, but also as a warning not to fire again. He was terrified. Was the shot meant for him? But the searchlight continued sweeping the yard until it reached its target. Theo caught sight of a prisoner, glued against a wall. He must have known he'd been cornered. Theo held his breath as he waited for another shot, but none came. The searchlight swept away. Glancing up at the watchtower, Theo could just make out the outline of Igor sitting up there. He couldn't be sure he'd seen the fugitive.

Then, without a thought for his own safety Theo shouted to the man: 'You need to run! Now!'

The prisoner wasted no time in running towards the safety of the barracks, disappearing inside just as the searchlight reached him again. Theo turned on his heel and ran as fast as he could to the gate. Fumbling to retrieve his ID from his pocket, he waited several agonising seconds before the guard waved him through. Breathing heavily, he steadied himself against the fence to stop his knees from buckling beneath him.

Chapter Forty-Two

Frans

It was early in the morning when he heard the crunch of footsteps approaching. The men weren't expected for another hour. *Saskia! At last…* His breath caught in his throat as he imagined her rushing towards him, her dark curls tumbling across her face and the sweet smell of her skin as they fell into an embrace. He quickly finished filling the pail with milk, lifted it onto a wooden shelf and patted the cow on its flank before going to meet her.

Instantly, he froze at the sight of a tall fair-haired man gazing around the yard. The smart SS uniform and boots polished to a high shine suggested that he must have come from the camp.

'Can I help you?' Frans said, his mind still reeling from the dashed hope of seeing Saskia. As he wiped his hands on his overalls, he felt uneasy at the way the officer glanced around him. His father had mentioned nothing about anyone coming to visit the farm.

'*Guten Morgen! Ich bin SS-Untersturmführer* Oberle,' said the officer, clicking his heels and raised his arm in a stiff salute. Switching to heavily accented Dutch, he asked to see the owner.

'I'm his son,' said Frans with a steady gaze.

The officer frowned. 'And you work here?'

'More than that, I'm in charge.' Frans folded his arms in an attempt to show his authority.

'Where is your father?'

'Out on errands.' Frans managed to keep his voice level, wishing it wasn't just the two of them in the yard. He was reluctant to offer any further information without knowing the reason for the visit.

The officer clicked his tongue and marched over to the gate, where he took in the view of the top field. Frans knew he wouldn't see his father there. He'd already left with the horse and cart.

'I will need to see your proof of exemption,' ordered the officer curtly as he spun back round to face him.

So he's come to check up on me, Frans realised. Telling the officer to wait, he went inside to fetch his papers, knowing he had no reason to be nervous but feeling so all the same. Berg had sanctioned his exemption days earlier in exchange for almost a quarter of the year's potato harvest. But Frans felt bad his father had been forced into this position and had promised to make it up to him by working even longer hours.

When Frans returned, he found the officer with his head inside the door of the cowshed. He cleared his throat just as the cow nearest the door lifted its head to let out a deep bellow at the intrusion. The officer sprang back with a look of distaste, causing Frans to smile to himself.

'I'm sorry, I should have warned you. She does that to strangers,' he said, trying to compose his expression. 'Here you are.'

The officer's face flushed as he snatched the document and mumbled in German under his breath as he studied it for several moments. '*Alles gut*,' he said and thrust it back at him. 'Now, I have orders from Commandant Berg to take a good look round. There have been reports about inconsistencies in the running of this farm. It may not be secure. I'm sure you don't need reminding that the prisoners who work here are all criminals.'

Frans swallowed nervously. He knew he shouldn't get into an argument about the status of prisoners when his own position was so precarious. Even though he had proof of exemption, Saskia had warned him that he wasn't immune just because he had a job to do. He wished she were beside him for moral support.

'Very well, I can show you round,' he said. 'The cowshed is where we teach the men proper animal husbandry. I find they're quick learners. I don't suppose you'll want another look, so let me show you the outbuildings we use for storage and farm equipment.'

Frans let Oberle poke around inside while he waited by the door. Inspection finished, Oberle announced that a guard should be stationed outside to keep watch in case anyone took it into their heads to hide in there.

Frans gave a non-committal shrug. 'Let me take you into the field,' he said, glancing down at Oberle's boots, which had lost their shine after his tour of the farm buildings. It was obvious he'd never set foot on a farm before and Frans had no intention of putting him at his ease. 'I can provide you with a pair of clogs,' he said. 'We always have plenty spare for visitors.'

'That won't be necessary,' snapped Oberle. 'I will stay here and you can point out any weak points along the boundary.'

From where they stood it was hard to see anything against the sun, which shone right in their eyes, but moving would mean walking across the muddy field. Oberle remained rooted at the edge.

'There's no chance of anyone escaping when the guards are here,' said Frans, trying to be helpful.

Oberle grunted and waved towards a clump of trees just beyond the edge of the field. 'What's that over there? Is it secure?'

'Of course. There's a wire fence to stop any animals from getting in and spoiling the crops. And if you look to the left, where the field borders onto the road, there's a wide ditch filled with water. Anyone trying to jump over that wouldn't get very far.'

Oberle squinted at where Frans pointed, before turning to look at him. 'Any breach in security will be taken extremely seriously. From what I've seen today, it would be prudent to bring in more guards. I will make a recommendation to Herr Commandant and you will be informed of any further action.' He raised his hand and barked out, '*Heil* Hitler!' Snapping his heels together, he marched back to his motorbike, which he'd left by the farmyard gate.

Frans walked back to the kitchen, which was coming to life with the buzz of the family's early-morning routine. One after another, the girls came piling in to take their place at the table next to Cas, who was already halfway through his bowl of porridge. On seeing Frans appear at the door, Lien jumped straight up and ran over so she could circle her little hands around his legs in a hug. Frans gave her a kiss, scooped her up and settled her back down in her place. He went over to his mother, who was stirring the large pot of porridge on the stove.

'I heard you talking. Is everything all right?' she said, sweeping a lock of hair back from her face.

'Hard to say,' said Frans, keeping his voice low. 'One of the SS officers came over for an inspection, but he was too bothered about getting muck on his clothes to do a proper search. He mentioned bringing in more guards, but I suspect it's more of a threat than anything. I doubt they'll be able to spare any with all the extra prisoners arriving in the camp.' He took two bowls of porridge over to the older girls, who were trying to get Lien to repeat the lines of a song. She was more interested in stirring a spoonful of syrup into her porridge.

'Settle down and eat up,' said Frans. He went back to stand beside his mother. 'He asked to see my papers,' he said in an urgent whisper. 'It makes me wonder if the real reason he came round was to find out why I haven't signed up. And I'm not the only one. Aart's had to go into hiding at his uncle's house in Friesland – he's been lucky to get away. The soldiers in town are panicking and pursuing anyone my age as they're so desperate for men to work for them. It's making me scared.'

'Oh Frans,' said his mother, stopping what she was doing. 'You've done nothing wrong. Remember that. Everything's been agreed with the commandant. And as long as you don't leave the farm, you'll have nothing to worry about.'

He knew she was right. If the commandant found out that he wasn't on the farm, he'd be sure to be called up and their agreement would be broken. Or worse… he'd be arrested and sent to the camp for defying German orders.

As frustrated as he felt about his own loss of liberty, he was even more desperate to try to find out if Saskia was safe. She'd told him that even if she did get stopped by the Germans, she was always able to give a valid reason, such as visiting an ailing relative or helping a neighbour. But Frans fretted constantly, knowing the risk she took every time she met Stengel in town – the more it went on, the less Frans trusted the man. Saskia was so sure about Stengel, but what if he had some ulterior motive in getting her to work for him? With a shudder, Frans remembered the smaller women's camp attached to Kamp Amersfoort, but quickly pushed the thought away.

Chapter Forty-Three

Theo

Theo woke with a feeling of dread in the pit of his stomach. Knowing that Igor would be watching him from high up on his platform was disturbing, as he never knew what surprise the brute might spring on him. Since Igor had taken a potshot at him, he was convinced that the man was biding his time and waiting for an opportunity to do so again. His only hope was that Igor wasn't on duty. Wearily, he dressed himself and crossed the compound to the SS camp, where he found Peter waiting for him.

'Igor's been transferred back to Dachau,' Peter said with some satisfaction. 'I think we'd all had enough of his pranks, including the commandant. Shooting at prisoners is one thing, but when he heard Igor was taking potshots at anyone who crossed his line of vision, even the commandant thought he'd overstepped the mark.'

At the news, Theo suppressed a smile of relief. He dared to hope that an opportunity would present itself for him to do more for a group of prisoners he had noticed across the fence at the far corner of the compound. A plan began to form in his mind.

The new guard was up in the watchtower, unaware that Theo had changed his route so it took him along the wire fence that segregated the two sides of the camp, men on his side, women and children on the other. Thin mothers attempting to soothe their crying babies paced up and down, while other women sat on the ground in tattered clothes, barely noticing the small children playing in the dirt. Each time he passed, his eyes met those of a young woman, no more than twenty, with big dark eyes set in an angular face, who gazed warily at him. He found it hard to wrench his eyes away, wishing fervently he could help her. She looked so painfully thin, more so than any of the other women. Perhaps she had been here the longest. As he continued on, he knew he couldn't leave her in that state.

The following day, Theo took an extra portion of bread at breakfast and slipped it into his jacket pocket. Before he went on duty he broke the bread into three pieces, small enough to pass through the wire links. He knew that passing food to her posed a huge risk if he were caught, but he would simply have to find a way.

His nerve almost failed him as he approached the fence and looked towards the women sitting, crouching and standing on the other side, but he couldn't see the woman he had seen before. He kept walking past, twice, three times, until he caught sight of her a little way away, cradling her crying child in her arms. She saw him. He gave her a faint smile and carried on.

With his cap pulled low over his eyes, he kept his gaze glued on the guard as he approached the watchtower. He could just make out the newspaper spread out on the wooden ledge. The guard was bent over it and glanced up every so often to scan the yard, which was filling up with prisoners.

Theo's pulse quickened as he hurried on, knowing that this was his chance. The girl was now just yards away from him. He slowed, letting a group of prisoners pass by, hiding him briefly as he stopped with his back to the fence. From here, he checked to see that the guard was distracted, then took a piece of bread from his pocket and pushed it backwards against the fence. He felt her take it. Twice more he passed bread to her as he kept watching the guard for any movement, but he was still engrossed in his newspaper. Theo turned his head and caught the girl's eye. She stared at him unsmiling, giving him only the faintest of nods as she moved away. It was over in seconds and he was able to breathe again.

The next time he brought bread and a small piece of sausage, but when he came close, a woman he hadn't seen before was by the fence, hooking her fingers through the links. She was small, not much bigger than a teenager, but the lines round her eyes suggested she was much older. 'I saw what you did yesterday. Do you have anything for me?' she whispered hoarsely.

'Where is the girl with the young child?' Theo asked, anxiously scanning the yard behind her, but it was so densely packed with women and children that he was unable to see if she was there.

'They took Lily to the rose garden.'

Theo's heart stopped. 'And her child?'

'Rachel's looking after him.' She tilted her head to a woman rocking back and forth beside two young children who were squabbling over a stick.

'I can't stop any longer. Wait here till I come round again,' he said, shaken. Surely it wasn't his fault she'd been taken to the rose garden? But the next time he drew level with the fence, the woman was no longer there.

Theo slept badly that night. Waking early, he pulled on his clothes and slipped soundlessly outside. Breathing deeply, he looked up to see a blackbird perched high up on the roof, its beak trembling as its sweet song filled the chill morning air. Theo closed his eyes, his tiredness lifting as he pictured himself arm in arm with Annelies, far away from this place. Did she share the same dream, he thought sadly, trying to remember the last time he'd written to tell her how he truly felt.

At that moment, he heard the familiar rattle and clatter of the horse and cart from the prisoner compound. He gasped as he recognised the shape of Frans holding the reins.

Theo hurried past the guard, who was dozing at this post, and slipped through the gate, catching up with the cart as it came to a halt by the kitchen commando.

'Frans…' he began, before realising his mistake. 'Where is he?'

Evert Koopmans looked down at Theo with a quizzical look. 'It's too dangerous for him to come, so I've taken over the collection. I'm his father Evert. You're Theo, aren't you?'

Theo nodded vigorously. 'We did the letters together, until they moved me from the kitchen unit.'

'He's been so worried about you,' said Evert, lifting an eyebrow as his eyes swept over Theo's uniform.

'They forced me to be a guard, and if I refuse, I'll be digging graves by the firing range. I would never survive that,' Theo explained. He was desperate that Evert understood this wasn't his choice.

Evert looked pensive, then said, 'They've been sending me prisoners from the camp to work on the farm. I'm told they'll be sending in more guards to supervise.' Theo guessed what Evert was suggesting, but was doubtful he'd be chosen to leave the camp. There were senior guards who would want those positions away from the terrible conditions here. To be in the fresh air, to see beautiful views and smoke cigarettes out in the fields… he'd overheard some officers talking about it.

'I can't see the commandant ever allowing it,' said Theo despairingly, wanting nothing more than to be free of the camp, even for just a few hours a day.

'Let's see,' said Evert.

Chapter Forty-Four

Frans

The flat fields were shrouded in early morning mist that lingered close to the ground. Maybe today the sun would break through, providing a little warmth after the relentless cold of a long hard winter. People had said there'd never been one like it in living memory and the war had only made things worse. After nearly five years of German occupation, so many were struggling to make ends meet through lack of food and basic commodities, and still there was no end in sight.

But today, Frans felt more optimistic than he had in months. He stamped his feet impatiently and blew into his hands, keeping his eye on the track for the arrival of the men. He'd hardly been able to contain his excitement since his father had announced that Theo would be coming to work on the farm, following Oberle's recommendation for more guards.

Finally, they came into view as his father appeared at his side.

'There he is,' said Pa, a rare smile crinkling the corners of his eyes.

The twenty-strong column of men clomped noisily into the yard, followed by a guard wearing a cap that threw his face into shadow. Several surly guards shouted at the men to stand in line and wait their turn for breakfast.

'You made it,' said Frans, moving towards the guard at the back. Theo removed his cap with a grin. Frans let out a gasp as he stared at the friend he'd last seen weeks before inside the camp. Weeks, when he'd had no idea whether Theo had even survived the rose garden. Frans noted how thin he still looked, but the deep shadows under his eyes had almost gone and he had lost his haunted look.

'I can't tell you how happy I am to see you,' said Frans, swallowing down hard.

'Me too. But I'm not free yet,' said Theo, his brow wrinkling as he looked towards the guards.

'Welcome,' said Evert, coming over to shake Theo by the hand. The other guards were still lining up the men, so it felt safe to take a moment with him. 'We're pleased you've come.'

'Thanks to you. I can't quite believe I'm here. And it's my first time outside that place in months. I mustn't forget why I'm here though,' said Theo, stealing another glance at the guards to make sure they weren't eyeing them suspiciously.

Frans watched Theo as he went to join them and hoped that his presence on the farm would result in a more harmonious atmosphere between guards and farm workers. Maybe together they could reduce the men's punishing workload and make sure they were treated better. And with Theo at his side, he would be able to put into action the plan he'd been mulling over for weeks. He understood only too well how much a reunion, however brief, would mean to the prisoners. If they could look into the eyes of their wives or girlfriends for a few snatched moments, they might find a spark of hope to carry on. But could he manage it without Saskia's support? He still hadn't seen her and despite enquiries by his father to acquaintances who knew her there was still no news. Frans could do nothing more than wait.

Over dinner the night before, Frans had spoken about his plan, wondering about their house and all its nooks and crannies, and whether it was possible to clear a space that the guards wouldn't be able to find. A place where a prisoner could meet his beloved in private, if only for a few precious minutes at a time. And with Theo mingling in their midst, there was a chance that visitors could come to the farm without the guards noticing. But how would they get the prisoners from the field to the house undetected? He was thankful to have an ally in his mother, who was determined to play her part and had come up with a number of practical suggestions.

'Remember, we know the workings of the farm better than the guards, even if they do think they're running things round here,' she had said, outlining how she would call on the prisoners' loved ones to explain by what means they could visit in safety. 'They can't be seen near the farm. They'll need to come along the path that runs through the wood at the back. I'll be there to meet them.'

After dinner, the two of them went to investigate the room tucked under the eaves, accessible through a low door. It had been a playroom when Frans was little, but over the years an accumulation of junk meant that it had lain largely forgotten. Together with his mother, Frans sorted through piles of old clothes and blankets dumped on a divan bed that had once belonged to Mama's parents and was used only on rare occasions. Mama covered the bed with sheets, a woollen blanket and a floral bedspread. An upturned crate worked well as a bedside table and she found a lamp with a cracked shade that worked perfectly well.

When they had finished, Frans walked over to the tiny window overlooking the field where the guards would be striding up and down the following day. 'Ma, I'm not sure this room is safe enough. We must find something to conceal the door.'

'I've been thinking the same thing,' she said. 'The idea of those *moffen* tramping through our house and discovering our secret terrifies me. There must be a piece of furniture we can use. Maybe a chest of drawers? No, too heavy and I don't think it would hide the doorframe,' she went on, musing over the options. 'I know, let's go and fetch the bookcase from the bedroom.'

The bookcase covered the doorframe exactly. Anyone coming up the staircase would see the bookcase on one side and a door leading to the attic on the other. As long as the bookcase was in place, no one would have any idea what lay behind.

The next problem was how to get the men over to the house from the fields without the guards blowing up. Again, it was Mama who came up with the answer.

'There are some old milk churns at the back of the cowshed we can put out in the fields for drinking water. They'll need refilling. You tell the prisoner they need filling from the outside tap. Theo stands by to give permission, while I make sure I've arranged for his sweetheart to be waiting in the house. He slips in to be with her and I keep watch. They'll only have a few minutes together, but it's better than nothing. What do you think?'

Frans allowed a smile to form as his mind raced forward with possibilities. Could their scheme actually work? Of utmost importance would be to keep their operation secret from the guards, while Theo kept an eye on the other prisoners to make sure they didn't give the game away. It was high risk, but as Frans looked at his mother he knew they were doing the right thing.

'Let's start with Joost,' said Frans, remembering the letter the young man had sent to his girlfriend after being found hiding from the Germans in a coal hole. He deserved a little good fortune. 'His fiancée lives this side of Amersfoort. Saskia has been picking up letters from her right from the start—' He fell silent, struck by the thought that if Saskia were here, she would be keen to help out.

'Shall I arrange for Joost's girlfriend to come?' asked his mother, who seemed to sense her son's sorrow.

Frans took in a deep breath. It was now more than a week since he'd heard from Saskia. He nodded, unable to shake off the feeling that something terrible must have happened.

'Hurry, we haven't much time,' urged Frans. 'You're to follow Mevrouw Koopmans indoors. You'll see what she's got in store for you.'

'Is this a trick?' said Joost, a slight young man. He looked sick with worry.

'Go on, it's a surprise,' said Frans. 'A good one,' he added. He hadn't expected this reaction. He had a sinking feeling he might have said the wrong thing.

'What is it?' said Joost, now white-faced.

It dawned on him that Joost believed he was walking into a trap, and he realised the poor man was incapable of spotting kindness after his months of harsh punishment inside the camp.

But there was no time to waste and no time to reassure him that the guards had nothing to do with this. 'I can't say – but hurry.'

His mother appeared in the doorway, shielding her eyes for anything that might upset her scheme. She smiled broadly when she saw the two of them.

'Joost, isn't it? I've arranged for someone special to visit. Come inside.' She took the stricken Joost gently by the arm. He was still wary, but he didn't resist as she shooed him inside the house. To Frans, she said, 'Keep watch. Come and tell me if anything looks suspicious.' She closed the door before he could answer. He was disappointed she hadn't let him in. He'd been so looking forward to seeing the look on Joost's face when he set eyes on his girlfriend. All those weeks not knowing when or if they'd ever see one other again gone in an instant and his life would be worth living again. He fervently hoped that Joost's brief tryst was a success, so he could do the same for others.

He carried the churn over to the outside tap and tipped the tepid water down the drain. The minutes ticked past as he let cool water fill the can in a slow steady stream, glancing every so often towards the door and willing Joost to come back out. Already nervy, when he heard the crunch of footsteps approaching he took fright and rushed to the house to warn his mother. In a flash, Joost was out of the door and at his side, just as Theo came striding into the yard.

'Did someone forget to turn off the tap?' he said, reaching for the churn before it toppled over.

'Thank goodness it's you,' huffed Frans as he stretched past him to turn off the gushing tap.

'Calm down, no one has noticed how long you've been gone. I thought I'd come and check everything's all right. It looks like it's been a success,' Theo said, watching Joost emerge from the house with a big smile on his face. Behind him, Frans's mother quietly closed the door and joined the group.

'Thanks for your part in this, Theo. Don't spoil it all by getting caught out by the enemy,' she said with a frown.

'That's not going to happen. All that lot are concerned about is punishing anyone working out in the fields. They won't notice anything unless it's happening in front of their noses. All the same, we'd better get back.'

Joost turned to Mevrouw Koopmans and held both of her hands. 'You've no idea how happy I am to see Toesie. Did you know we'll be getting married next year?' he said eagerly, his face lighting up with pleasure.

'I'm so very pleased for you,' said Mama with a warm smile. 'Now you'd better get back before they notice you've been gone.'

No more than fifteen minutes had elapsed between leaving the field and returning, but it was enough to arouse the guards' suspicion.

Joost was roughly manhandled back to his unit by two of them, leaving the third to have it out with Theo. It was simply too much for Frans. Fired up with anger, he butted in, claiming he'd knocked the water can over and had asked Joost to help him clean up the yard. Pa, who'd been working in the far field, strode over at the sound of raised voices, saying that cleanliness and safety around the farm were more important than the few extra minutes it would take to fetch some water.

'But you were there. Is that what really happened?' the guard snapped at Theo.

'Of course. Everything is under control and I can vouch for the prisoner, who did nothing to obstruct or delay the task.' Theo didn't raise his voice and the guard eventually calmed down, though he seemed determined to have the last word.

'We can't afford any more unrest among the prisoners. I'm relying on you to keep a watch on proceedings.' He prodded his finger at Theo as he spoke.

'Of course you can rely on me,' said Theo, his face not revealing a thing.

'I haven't time to stand around listening to you chatting. There's work to be done,' said Evert, turning to stomp away across the field.

Frans mulled over the implications of what had just happened as he walked back to the house. Had they taken too much of a risk? In his stand-off with the guards, Theo had averted a potentially difficult situation – would they take it out on him next time? But when Frans had seen the look on Joost's face after being reunited with Toesie, he'd known they were doing the right thing. Happiness was in such short supply inside the camp, he was determined to do all he could do give these men a few minutes' respite from their misery. It definitely was worth it, but they must take nothing for granted.

Chapter Forty-Five

Theo

'Go up to the top. It's on the right. I've moved the bookcase to one side. I'll call you if anything changes. And good luck,' said Mevrouw Koopmans, smiling kindly.

Theo stood at the bottom of the steep wooden staircase and held his breath. When Frans had told him Annelies would be coming, it seemed as if the dark cloud that had been hanging over his head for so many months had finally lifted. He'd longed so much for this moment, it was all he could think of. But now it had finally come, he found himself hesitating. They'd been parted for so long; would Annelies be horrified by the changes in him? Only that morning, he'd peered into his shaving mirror and been dismayed to see how pale he was and how his cheekbones protruded. Even after weeks of better nutrition, his face and body still bore the marks of months of hardship and punishment.

Pulling himself together, he surveyed the stairs that separated them and slowly climbed up. The treads creaked with every step. At the top, he knocked so timidly he thought she couldn't have heard him. But then the door opened a crack and Annelies peered round, lit from behind with a halo around her beautiful blond hair, making her expression impossible to fathom.

'Annelies,' he said, his voice faltering. He stooped to enter the small room. 'Annelies, I can't believe you're here.' He touched her chin so he could look at her properly. 'You're so beautiful,' he breathed, gazing into her eyes, as tears wet her cheeks. She lifted a finger and gently traced the contours of his face. He flinched, assuming she was shocked at what she saw. But the look on her face told him otherwise and she silenced him with a long kiss. Gradually, he felt the tension in his body subside. It was like coming home.

The room was tiny, with barely enough space for the neatly made bed covered in a rose-patterned quilt. Theo led her over and they lay down facing one another.

'I didn't honestly think you would want to come,' he said, wiping her damp cheeks with his thumbs. 'I worried about you taking the train and the *moffen* demanding to see your ID and not believing you. And that you'd end up in the camp as well.' His heart raced as his thoughts ran away with him.

'Shh... I was fine. They did ask to see my papers, but they were more interested in some other passengers who seemed to be travelling without a ticket.' She nuzzled her head into the crook of his neck, the way she always used to, making him remember how much he loved her. They lay like that till Theo felt his breathing calm.

'We don't have much time. Tell me how you've been. Are you coping?'

Annelise didn't answer straight away. With a sinking feeling, Theo regretted his question. He didn't want to cause her distress.

'I'm now living with my parents in Hooglanderveen,' she said, shifting her body so she could look into his eyes. 'Papa hasn't been at all well with the stress and I worry about him. We haven't been raided, but it's the anticipation that's made him so nervy. And of course, we aren't allowed out after curfew, though we sometimes have the neighbours in for a game of cards if the coast is clear. That must sound trivial compared to what you must have been through.'

She sat up and reached for her cloth bag on the floor. 'Here, I've brought you some things I've saved up for with my coupons.' She pulled out a small parcel containing a tin of meat, a tiny square of hard cheese and a packet of biscuits. 'It's not much, but you look as if you need them,' she said with a sad smile.

'This is too much,' he said, propping himself on one elbow. 'Shouldn't you be thinking of your family?'

'You're the one who needs help. We can get by, honestly.' She took a deep breath and went on, 'Theo, I've never seen you so thin.'

He turned his face from her, embarrassed by his appearance. He attempted to make light of it. 'You should have seen me a month ago. At least now I'm getting three meals a day, however bad the food.'

'Please, take this,' she said, before bringing another small package out of her bag and handing it to him. 'I thought you might like it,' she said hopefully.

A smooth oval soap fell into the palm of his hand and he pressed it to his nose, breathing in the familiar scent that reminded him of past summers. 'It's what you use, isn't it?'

'It was the last piece of soap in the shop before it was forced to close its doors. I kept it as a reminder of the good times.'

Theo wanted to refuse, knowing she and her family were going short, but how could he reject such a generous gesture? He took her hand and kissed each finger in turn, listening as she began to talk about Saskia, telling him about her work as a courier, which often brought her to Hooglanderveen.

'She makes a point of visiting me and we always have so much to talk about – it's as if we've always been friends.'

'When did you last see her?' said Theo, becoming still.

'I think it was last week. No, it may have been longer. Why do you ask?'

Theo shook his head. 'It's odd... Frans hasn't seen her either. He's worried something may have happened to her. Did she say anything about not being able to come the last time you saw her?'

'No, but sometimes I don't see her for a couple of weeks. But you're right, it is strange I haven't seen her. She gave me her parents' telephone number in case I ever needed to get in touch with her. I'll see what I can find out.'

Their intense conversation was cut short by Mevrouw Koop-mans' voice calling to them to come down. No more than fifteen minutes could have passed; it wasn't enough – it would never be enough. But the conversation about Saskia had unsettled him and he felt a wave of panic that the guards were about to discover them, arrest Annelies and send her to the camp. He wiped away the sweat forming on his brow. His appearance had changed, and so had his mind – every sudden sound and movement made him nervous, and he was painfully aware that she must have noticed.

'Theo, are you all right?' said Annelies, gripping his forearms.

'I don't know. But I want you to go before they find you here,' he said, his voice now panicky.

'It's fine. Mevrouw Koopmans is keeping a lookout. She has it all under control,' Annelies said, looking deep into his eyes.

Taking a breath to steady himself, he allowed himself one last embrace. 'Please wait for me,' he whispered desperately.

With tears in her eyes, she nodded. 'Now go.'

Chapter Forty-Six

Frans

When Saskia hadn't visited again the following day, Frans was sick with worry. It just wasn't like her. He kept turning over what they'd said to one another the last time she'd come, wondering if he'd upset her in some way. But he'd been scared for himself and most of all for her, and convinced she was in danger. There she was out on her bike, riding between the villages or into town, knocking on doors and going in and out of people's houses collecting and delivering letters of the camp. How could she be sure she wasn't being watched?

And now he knew for certain. Ma had taken the telephone call when Frans was in the fields. It was Annelies on the line. She had spoken to Saskia's father. Saskia was missing.

His bike, untouched for weeks, was leaning against the wall inside one of the outbuildings. He'd forgotten about the state of the tyres, now completely flat and so patched up that he had no choice other than to rip them off the wooden rims.

Cas turned up, wondering what all the noise was about, and stood in the doorway.

'What are you doing?' he said nervously.

Frans stopped what he was doing and went over to him. 'I'm trying to get my bike so I can use it again.' He felt guilty he hadn't been paying as much attention to his brother as perhaps he should.

'Would you like to help?' said Frans, lifting Cas's chin.

'Can I?' Cas's face lit up at being asked. Eagerly, he began removing the tattered rubber and dumping it in a corner of the barn.

Frans straightened up and surveyed the bare wheels of his bike. It was too late to go back. 'If Pa or Mama ask where I am, say I'm over by the boundary fence making sure it's secure.'

Cas glanced from his brother to the bike and back again. 'That's not where you're really going, is it?'

'No, but you'll keep the secret for me, won't you?'

Cas nodded eagerly, forcing Frans to smile. After all they'd been through, Frans knew Cas wouldn't let him down.

'I'm going to find Saskia,' he whispered, 'and they won't be too pleased if they find out I've gone. I won't be long, if this old thing holds up.' Frans mounted his bike and swerved out of the yard with a backwards wave.

Without tyres, the going was so much slower and every bump and rut made his body jolt painfully. Once he reached the road, he forced himself to pedal faster, but the rattling and grinding got so bad he worried that the bike would give up altogether. All he could think of was that Saskia was missing. There was no other news, but he refused to believe it. *Please let her be there*, he kept repeating to himself in time to the clunk of the wheels as they turned.

When he finally reached the turning to her house, he jumped off and half ran along the potholed track, hoping for a sign she'd returned home. His heart gave a dull lurch when he saw her bike wasn't in its usual spot leaning against the house. Throwing down his bike, he rushed up the path and rapped on the door. Seconds later it flew open and there stood Saskia's mother, looking greyer and smaller than he remembered. Her eyes were red-rimmed and she held a handkerchief to her mouth. From inside he heard Saskia's father call, 'Is it Frans?' before joining his wife in the hallway to put an arm around her shoulders. Frans was struck by the resemblance between him and Saskia: the dark wavy hair – though his was streaked with grey – and the soulful dark eyes.

'When I got your message, I came straight over,' Frans said in a halting voice.

Saskia's mother made a small noise into her handkerchief and her husband gave her a gentle squeeze.

'Frans, do come in and we'll tell you what we know,' he said, moving aside.

They went into the big room with its enormous picture window overlooking the garden. Frans felt his chest tighten at the sight of the bench under the apple tree where he used to sit with Saskia.

He took a seat with his back to the window opposite Saskia's parents, who sat down in matching armchairs upholstered in dark red velvet. The spacious room was packed with antique furniture: a tall dark oak cabinet, two bureaus with elaborate carvings, a walnut card table and several other small tables, each placed close to an armchair. A tall antique clock with brass figurines adorning the top ticked loudly in one corner. Frans wanted to compliment them on how *gezelllig* it was, but thought better of it.

'Paul, will you tell Frans?' said Saskia's mother in a small high voice from the depths of her armchair. Her husband reached over to touch her hand.

'She's very upset, you understand,' said Paul in a whisper to Frans. 'When we were raided it was only thanks to Saskia's quick thinking that I wasn't arrested. And now this.' He glanced at his wife, who was sniffing into her handkerchief and didn't appear to have heard him.

Frans gestured for him to continue.

'We don't know a great deal yet, but we received a telephone call yesterday from a friend of Saskia's. When she hadn't heard from Saskia she contacted Mevrouw Jansen, who Saskia has been visiting. Mevrouw Jansen was very distressed. Not long after Saskia arrived to pick up letters for the camp, she was raided by Nazi soldiers. You know all about what Saskia was doing, of course.'

Frans gave a small nod, feeling in some way responsible for her disappearance.

'They were all standing in the sitting room when the door burst open and the *moffen* proceeded to turn the place upside down. It was fortunate they didn't find any letters. Mevrouw Jansen just had time to conceal them under the floorboards. But that didn't stop them from arresting Saskia and the other man. Darling, what did she say his name was?'

'Stengel,' she said with a sob. 'But what does that matter now? I just want my daughter back…' She wept into her crumpled handkerchief.

Frans gave Paul Dekker an anxious look, before saying quietly, 'I kept telling her that Stengel fellow was up to no good. You do know he's the German officer who's been smuggling letters from the camp?'

'Saskia never mentioned anything to us,' said her mother, emerging from behind her handkerchief. 'She only ever said she helped out with the occasional letter, but it seems like it was a lot more serious. I had no idea that she was meeting… one of *them*.'

Saskia's father frowned. 'Frans, are you sure he's German? Mevrouw Jansen didn't pronounce it "Schtengel", so I assumed he must be Dutch.'

'He's German all right.' Frans shook his head in disbelief. More than ever he was convinced that Stengel was behind the raid and Saskia's arrest. He had never trusted him.

'Apparently he was arrested as well,' said Saskia's father. 'They were both taken to the police station for questioning. I rang the police station just before you came, but no one will tell us anything about Saskia. You understand, I must go and find her—'

'Paul – you can't,' Saskia's mother butted in and gripped his sleeve. 'They'll arrest you too.' Turning to Frans, her face was contorted with fear as she said, 'My husband had all that trouble from the *moffen* before he shut his shop. And then there was the raid…'

Frans was on his feet. 'Mr and Mrs Dekker, let me go to the police station. It can't be any more dangerous for me. And I owe it to your daughter.'

Chapter Forty-Seven

Frans was made to wait two hours on a hard seat while people streamed in, sat down, waited and were all called in before him. Increasingly agitated, he watched as an elderly man with a walking stick and being helped in by his son, a woman in a red headscarf carrying a crying child, two middle-aged women, also crying, and whispering softly to one another, all disappeared through the black-painted door to the side of the reception desk, leaving Frans to wonder if they'd forgotten he was there. Several times he went up to the counter to ask when it would be his turn, but the stony-faced receptionist refused to volunteer any information.

When the clock struck three, a short man in uniform with a bald head called Frans's name and led him into a small stuffy room with two chairs on either side of a wooden table. The man opened his file, shuffled some papers and extracted a form. Without looking at Frans, he began to ask questions, notating his answers laboriously in small black handwriting. Frans waited anxiously. He wanted to ask why this was necessary, but he didn't want to arouse the man's suspicions in case he thought he had done something wrong. This was about Saskia, he kept telling himself.

'Your name.'

'Frans Koopman.'

'Age.'

'I'm sixteen,' Frans said warily.

'Your ID.'

Frans pushed his papers across the table for the man to examine.

'Do you have an exemption?' The man finally looked across at Frans and gave him a hard stare.

'Yes, I work at the family farm a couple of miles from Amersfoort. You'll see my exemption papers are in order.' Frans leaned forward, eager to steer the conversation towards Saskia. 'I've come about a friend who was arrested and brought here some days ago. I can't be sure when. Can you tell me if she's still here?'

The man didn't answer, but extracted a fresh form and wrote something across the top. 'What is her name?'

Frans was so frustrated he was close to tears, but he tried his best to cooperate, as the man began questioning him about Saskia – her name, age, his relationship to her, why she had been arrested... Just when Frans thought he could bear it no longer, the man suddenly got up and left the room. Frans had no idea if he was expected to follow him, but thought it best to stay put. His heart raced as he waited, watching the minutes tick by on the clock above the door. Where could the man have got to? Would he bring back another police officer to arrest him?

After ten minutes, the door clicked open and the man came back into the room by himself. He was carrying another folder, which he leafed through until he found what he was looking for.

'Saskia Dekker. She is no longer in our custody,' he said curtly.

Fleetingly, Frans's hopes soared. She'd been released... she was on her way home... oh, the joy on her parents' faces when she walked through the door—

'Saskia Dekker,' the man repeated, 'has been deported to Kamp Amersfoort.'

Outside on the pavement, Frans steadied himself by taking several lungfuls of air. His mind was in turmoil. He simply couldn't believe that she was in Kamp Amersfoort – it just didn't seem possible. She'd always been so careful to cover her tracks and to keep her ID papers in a small leather pouch under her clothes. Didn't Paul Dekker say that the Germans had found nothing during their raid?

So why arrest her? *Stengel had to be involved.* And Saskia was now wrongfully locked up, alone and frightened.

There and then Frans made up his mind to cycle to the camp. He retrieved his decrepit bike, which he'd hidden in a nearby alley, and wasted no time in covering the distance. It was hard going, but he no longer cared about the state of his bike – at least the wheels were still turning.

But it was only when he was under way that it dawned on him how pointless it was. How could he even imagine he could just march in and expect to find her? The camp was teeming with guards and he no longer had the protection of the horse and cart, which had served him so well in the past. If he did manage to get past the guards he'd be surrounded in no time and in all probability shot. But he had to find a way to reach her. Maybe he could find someone he could convince that Saskia had done nothing wrong. Briefly he thought of the commandant, who knew him from the farm and was on reasonable terms with his father. Surely he'd be sympathetic? But as Frans approached the camp, at the point where the high wire fence began and the all-seeing watchtowers loomed menacingly over the top, his nerve failed him. Of course the guard on the gate wouldn't let him in without an appointment.

He came to a halt and deposited his bike behind the spreading beech tree. Walking nervously over to the front gate, he was relieved to see Roel on duty, in conversation with another guard Frans didn't know.

'Hello, Roel. I need to speak to you,' he said, his breath coming fast as fear washed over him.

Roel muttered a perfunctory *Heil* Hitler and, unsmiling, whispered a few words to the other guard, who eyed Frans suspiciously. It took a few more moments of discussion between the two of them before he left.

Roel looked nervous. 'It's not a good time for you to be seen here. I'm expecting officers from the high command to arrive at any moment.' As he spoke, he kept glancing down the road. 'I shouldn't be telling you this, but there's trouble inside the camp. Two prisoners have successfully escaped. Several others failed. They were brought back early this morning to face the firing squad. It keeps happening and the prisoners are growing restless. There's talk of increasing security and that's why the bosses are coming. You'd better go.'

But Frans was barely listening. He'd forgotten about the danger to himself; his only thought was to get to Saskia, however impossible it might seem. 'Wait. My girlfriend has been brought here. I have to find her, but the only person I can think who can help me is the commandant. Will you let me in?'

'No, it's not possible,' said Roel in a low voice. 'The commandant hasn't been seen since the first prisoners escaped. No one knows where he's gone. But there are rumours he's fled the camp and left Oberle in charge. And *he* would never agree to talk to you. Listen, Frans, I'm speaking to you as a friend. I strongly advise that you go home. It'll do you no good if you're seen here.'

They both swung round at the distant rumble of vehicles.

'Go!' hissed Roel.

Frans turned away, anger and frustration balling up his stomach. Saskia was caught up in something terrible just yards from where he was standing and there was nothing he could do to prevent it.

Chapter Forty-Eight

Frans

The ride back home was heavy going. Not only did Frans have to contend with the lack of tyres on his bike, but there was no shelter from the strong cold wind blowing straight off the flat fields. He was buffeted head on and the stretch from the camp to the turning of the farm seemed interminable. At least there was no one about, apart from the occasional tractor trundling past, and he was able to reach the turning without being seen. It was small compensation for what he'd endured since leaving with high hopes of a reunion with Saskia. He'd let her down, and her parents too, who must still be beside themselves with worry, waiting and hoping for Frans to return with positive news. If only he'd acted sooner, he thought angrily, he might have reached her in time, before she'd been moved to the camp.

It was late afternoon by the time he wheeled his bike back into the yard. Cas was briskly rubbing down the horse. 'You're back!' he said, his face lighting up. 'No one noticed you'd gone so I didn't have to say anything. Did you see Saskia?'

Frans slowly shook his head. 'I'm afraid it didn't work out.' He didn't want to burden his brother by telling him how dejected he felt, so he took his bike inside the barn and leaned it back in place against one wall. He walked back out and surveyed the field which was swarming with workers and guards.

'Don't be sad. Look, I've finished grooming the horse. Why don't you take him for a walk round the field?' Cas pulled him by the hand, but Frans wasn't listening.

'What? No, not today.' He glanced guiltily at Cas, who was looking at him expectantly.

His little brother fished a carrot from his pocket and handed it to Frans for the horse. 'You give it. Go on,' he said.

Frans was grateful for this small gesture, though his heart was heavy with foreboding. Then out of the corner of his eye he caught sight of Theo supervising a group of workers at the far end of the field.

'Take the horse back to the stable. Maybe we can both take him out tomorrow.' He thrust the carrot back at Cas and ran out of the yard and onto the field, stumbling over the uneven ground in his haste to reach Theo, the one person who would know how to help.

Several workers looked up in surprise from their digging and a guard swore loudly as Frans almost lost his balance and had to stop himself from lurching into him.

Theo was supervising a group of men who were clearing a ditch, and hadn't noticed Frans approach him from behind.

'Theo!' cried Frans. 'Something terrible has happened. You've got to help me.' He tried to grab hold of Theo's sleeve, but Theo caught his hand and spoke to him in a fierce whisper.

'Not here. Not in front of everyone. Go back to the house and I'll come as soon as I can.'

Frans opened his mouth to protest, but Theo gave him such a warning look that he fell silent.

Some minutes later, Theo came striding over. Frans was pacing up and down in the yard. 'What kept you?' he said, swinging round to face him.

'I came as quickly as I could, but I can't just walk away with all the guards watching. Tell me what's happened.'

'I've come straight from the police station in Amersfoort,' Frans said. 'Saskia was arrested, but I was too late. She's been sent to the camp.'

'Saskia? Was it because of the letters?' Theo was clearly shocked.

'No… I don't know. But I'm convinced that Stengel fellow is behind it,' said Frans, with a fresh wave of despair. 'You know what it's like in there. She'll be terrified and if they punish her like they did you… I've got to get her out.' He looked wildly at Theo, frantic for him to come up with a solution.

'We must try to be patient. In a few days everything might have changed and—'

'And in a few days it'll be too late,' Frans retorted before Theo could finish. 'I don't think you understand… I have to get her out.'

'I do understand. But listen to what I have to say. It could be over before we know it. I overheard a couple of SSers talking this morning. Berg's gone and Oberle's now in charge. They're saying the Allies are about to drive out the Germans – this is more than the usual rumours that have been going round. Red Cross trucks have started to arrive, bringing in food and medicines—'

'Red Cross trucks?' Frans interrupted, surprised.

Theo nodded. 'I've seen they're using an office at the administration building and heard they're helping with registrations. They might know something about Saskia. It's made me think the war is near its end…'

'If they're doing all that, do you think you can help get her out?' implored Frans.

'I can't promise anything. Leave it with me. It may take me a few days to find out. Frans… please don't give up.'

Chapter Forty-Nine

Theo

As soon as he arrived back in the camp, Theo headed straight for the administration building to find out what he could about Saskia, though he didn't hold out much hope of getting her released. Frans had been so upset and Theo was worried too. Even though he had never met her, she had done so much for him and Annelies, providing hope in the darkest of times. And though the Red Cross trucks were a constant presence about the camp, the guards had become far more brutal, and he had no idea what atrocities the women were enduring. No idea if the arrival of Red Cross personnel at the camp meant the end of the war. Or an end to this brutality.

The administration building was thronging with camp staff shouting orders and rushing in and out of the rooms that led off the main corridor. The woman on the desk also seemed harassed, as she sat sifting through a mountain of paperwork. She looked up irritably when Theo asked where he could find someone to speak to from the Red Cross.

'You'll find they've taken over the room at the end,' she said, and Theo surmised from her tone that she wasn't too pleased about the situation.

Head down, he strode down to the room she'd indicated and rapped on the door. When there was no answer, he stepped tentatively inside and clicked the door shut. A table stood in the middle of the room, piled high with boxes. More boxes, some labelled with the names of medicines, covered the floor.

A small middle-aged woman with uncombed wavy hair and flushed cheeks stood up suddenly from behind the boxes. 'Hello,' she said in surprise. 'Did you want to see me? I'm the only one on today and these deliveries are getting the better of me. I'm Truus van Houten… with the Red Cross.'

'Theo de Groot. I'm pleased to meet you,' he said, stretching out his hand. She took it with a broad smile, showing off a gap between her top front teeth. She seemed friendly enough and certainly more approachable than anyone else he'd come across during his time inside the camp. But he thought better of launching into his request regarding Saskia until he'd found out what role the Red Cross had in all this chaos and whether she could be trusted. 'I can give you a hand. You look as if you could do with it,' he found himself saying.

For the next half an hour, he helped her shift boxes while she told him about her work at the camp. She was part of the Red Cross contingent who brought in extra food twice a week. Kamp Amersfoort had been brought to their attention following reports of overcrowding and the maltreatment of prisoners, and growing concern over its organisation after the sudden departure of the commandant. Truus and her colleagues had been appalled at the state of the kitchens and the lack of nutritious food for prisoners, so had arranged for the immediate distribution of food parcels consisting of bread spread thickly with margarine and topped with ham or cheese, slices of spice cake, sugar for tea and tobacco. Mothers were provided with milk and cloth nappies for their babies. The sick received extra rations in the form of oatmeal and apple sauce against dysentery, along with essential medicines. It was a huge organisational effort, but far from perfect, she explained. Despite their best efforts to ensure everyone was treated fairly, Jewish prisoners often missed out and had their rations confiscated by spiteful guards. It seemed the Red Cross were here to keep an eye on conditions, but had no control over the prisoners being here in the first place. Were they sympathetic to the Nazis? Theo had no idea.

She straightened up and tried patting her springy hair back in place. 'I'm sorry, I'm probably babbling on too much when I don't even know you, but it was hearing you speak Dutch that did it. What's your work here?'

Theo wasn't inclined to tell this stranger, however friendly she seemed. Months of ill-treatment at the hands of the Nazis had made him innately wary of anyone new. He decided to omit telling her that it was because of the commandant he now worked for the Germans. 'I was taken on to supervise prisoners working at the farm down the road. I've been noticing the Red Cross vans and personnel around the camp. Is it a sign that the war might be over soon?'

Truus held the back of a chair as she replied. 'The Red Cross have been going into the camps for some time now and we were only granted access to Kamp Amersfoort a short while ago. It's true, the Allies are getting closer to liberating us, but we mustn't get our hopes up till it actually happens. In the meantime, our role is to do all we can to alleviate prisoners' misery.'

'Then maybe you can help me,' said Theo, seizing his opportunity. Truus had spoken of Allies, liberation and hope. Maybe she *was* on his side. 'Do the Red Cross keep records of prisoners when they arrive in the camp?'

Truus nodded. 'The Germans don't like it, but we make sure we have a record of everyone who comes here, yes.'

'I want to trace a female prisoner who was brought here recently. She's the girlfriend of my friend Frans. He's frantic with worry she's been wrongly arrested.'

Truus let out a deep sigh. 'Just like every other person who's ended up here, I imagine. It's so sad to see innocent people mistreated. But let me see what I can do.' She went over to a cupboard and brought out a ledger, which she placed on the newly cleared table. 'What's her name?'

'Saskia Dekker.'

She turned the pages to the most recent entries. 'Here she is.' She pointed to the record with a finger. 'She was processed for entry into the women's camp last week. But that's all I can tell you.' She looked up at Theo.

He ran a hand over his brow as he felt his anxiety mount. 'There are so many women and children crammed in there. You can see them through the wire fence. It's appalling to see women with such young children and babies kept in those conditions.'

'I know – I'm all too aware of the hardship and we're doing all we can to help. I go into the women's section daily with food and essentials and to give extra care to those with children. In fact, I'm going there now. If you give me a description of Saskia, I'll look for her. Come back in an hour.'

As Theo waited for the hour to tick past, he became increasingly jumpy, so decided to distract himself by going to the canteen. Normally by six thirty he was desperate to get some food inside him, but today he had no appetite for the uninteresting bean and pork stew, which he pushed around his plate, knowing that Saskia was just yards away.

Theo gave a start when he felt a hand on his shoulder and turned to see Peter standing next to him. 'Can I join you?' he said, placing his plate next to Theo's.

Theo nodded and shifted to make room, though the last thing he wanted was to engage in conversation with this man. Peter always ended up speaking in empty boasts about the latest successes of the Nazis, even though it was clear to everyone they were losing.

'I haven't seen much of you recently. Where've you been?' said Peter, flattening the food on his plate into an unappetising mush, before shovelling it in his mouth in big spoonfuls.

'I'm working on the Koopmans' farm these days. You knew that, didn't you?'

Peter shrugged. 'It's nothing to do with me. Another of Berg's pet projects, no doubt. Or should I say Oberle, now that the bird has flown.' He gave Theo a sly wink, but Theo refused to be drawn. He had no time for any of them, never had; nor did he trust Peter's motives, whatever they might be. Her returned to his own plate of food, taking a half-hearted mouthful as Peter moved on to his favourite topic.

'You must have seen all the new arrivals? Well, I have my hands full finding jobs for all those layabouts. Frankly, most of them aren't up to a bit of hard graft. Believe me when I say it's a shame they need getting rid of, but what else am I to do when another truckload turns up?' He let out a harsh laugh that sent a chill through Theo. He'd always suspected Peter of being ruthless, but was he now actually involved in sending prisoners to their deaths?

Theo kept his eyes on his plate as Peter carried on, oblivious to the fact that Theo wasn't engaging in conversation. All at once, Peter said, 'Are you coming to the party tomorrow night? It's going to be quite a do. They'll be music and plenty of local girls. I know I could do with a bit of distraction.' He let out a guffaw and made a lewd gesture, followed by another burst of raucous laughter.

Theo was shocked as he tried to process this information. While he knew what the guards got up to, with their celebration of everything that happened in the camp, how they ate, drank and enjoyed themselves and their positions of authority, something about this invitation felt different. With the Red Cross here, shouldn't they be worried about the end of the war? If the Nazis were defeated, did they expect everything in the camp to carry on as before? Theo wondered if they believed that Amersfoort was far enough away from the towns in the south freed from German control that it wouldn't change anything for them.

Peter had finished his meal and was on his feet. 'I'll see you tomorrow night,' he said, giving Theo a conspiratorial wink, before joining another table of SSers, who were laughing loudly at a joke one of them had just made.

On his way to the administration office it was all that Theo could think about. He was beginning to realise that these brutal men in their positions of power were carrying on in this way because they thought they were invincible. They'd got away with it before and they'd convinced themselves they would do so again.

He arrived as Truus, dressed in a pale blue uniform with the red cross stitched onto her left breast pocket, came through the door carrying a large black bag, which she dumped on the table.

'Well, I found her,' she said, heaving a sigh. 'It took me a while as I had to avoid Frau Koch, who lords it over the women's section. She's someone you wouldn't want to cross swords with.' Truus frowned. 'It's hard to tell the women apart after they've had their hair shorn, and they're dressed all the same in those awful grey shifts and colourless head coverings. But I found her standing by herself over by the fence. She looked so hopeful when I called her name. I gave her a packet of bread and cheese and told her that I would do all I could to make her comfortable. We're getting a consignment of blankets tomorrow and I'll make sure she gets one. I only wish I could have done more. I'm sorry I can't say anything more positive.'

Theo nodded. He hadn't expected her to, but was still disappointed that she hadn't come up with a solution to getting Saskia released. 'How was she in herself?' he said, though he could guess the answer.

'She seemed depressed, which isn't surprising. She didn't say much, just kept moving her head side to side as if in disbelief. But she did brighten a little when I told her that her Frans was looking out for her.'

Theo nodded and suddenly found his eyes starting to prick with tears. It had been a long time since he'd seen someone in authority show such kindness. 'I'm so grateful for everything you're doing,' he said quietly.

Truus gently laid a hand on his arm. 'I can't bear to see this suffering either. We're doing all we can. It can't be long now.'

Chapter Fifty

Frans

It was late the following evening and Mama was dampening down the stove before preparing to go to bed when there was a soft knock on the door. Pa looked up from the newspaper he was reading. Frans caught his breath as the sudden thought came to him that Theo had helped Saskia escape the camp and was bringing her straight over to him. He started as another, more insistent knock broke the silence. 'Let me go,' he told his father.

Relief was already surging through his body when he threw open the door, only to find two young men in German uniform shivering in the half light, eyes wide with fright.

'Please, can we come in? There are men chasing us,' one of them said in a rush.

'Who is it?' said Pa, striding over at the precise moment there was a crack of gunfire close by. Pa made to close the door, but one of the men blocked it with his foot. Another volley of gunfire decided the matter and the two men pushed into the narrow corridor and leaned with their backs against the door.

Frans's head was still reeling at the disappointment of it not being Saskia when the other of the two men spoke rapidly in broken Dutch, saying they'd fled from their unit after being ambushed by American soldiers. 'We ran across the fields and thought we'd lost them and then saw the farmhouse.'

'Are there any others with you?' asked Pa suspiciously.

Both men shook their heads, looking so scared that it had to be true.

Frans listened, hardly daring to believe that the Allies had finally reached Amersfoort after so many setbacks and so much speculation. Their hopes had been raised almost nightly: every evening, just before nine, his father brought the wireless set out from under the floorboards, so they could gather round to listen to the crackly Radio Oranje news broadcast from London. That evening, the airwaves had been full of reports of heavy fighting across the country. Canadian vehicles were sweeping north and reclaiming towns, villages and countryside from the Germans. Liberation was finally within the country's grasp.

Frans stared into the imploring faces of these two young men who were petrified for their lives. Despite them being in the uniform of the enemy, he couldn't believe they were here to cause harm. He thought of Theo in his SS uniform. Suddenly, it didn't matter that they were on the opposing side. He shot a questioning look at Pa, who nodded. 'Come quickly where I can hide you,' said Frans, shooing them into the scullery, where he cleared a space for them to crouch behind the big old mangle that took up most of the floor space.

Frans and Pa went to the back door to investigate, but all around there was silence. They waited a few minutes. The firing started up again, but this time it came from further away. The danger appeared to have passed.

They allowed the fugitive Germans to hide overnight in the barn among the hay bales, but told them they must leave at first light for their own safety.

Frans had a restless night's sleep, broken by the sound of far-off sirens, distant gunfire and a repetitive dream that Saskia was running frantically from the Germans and banging on his door. The sound of her voice, the feel of her soft curls tumbling gently against his face as he kissed her – she seemed so real to him. In the darkness before dawn, Frans resolved to save her, whatever it took. But when he woke in the morning, he realised how impossible a task this would be. The watchtowers were a constant menacing presence, preventing anyone from escaping – or entering – the camp. How would he ever gain access, let alone into the women's section, without being detected? His only hope was Theo, though he knew deep down that even his friend's chances of reaching Saskia were slight.

Tired and despondent, Frans dressed and went outside, to find the barn door open and the men gone. Fastening the door to, he let out a small sigh that they at least had got away.

The sun was beginning to creep above the horizon when a small movement crossed his line of vision, a shadow travelling silently in the direction of the farm. The workers were not expected today as it was Sunday. *Who could it be this early?* thought Frans. He couldn't allow himself to imagine it was Saskia, as he watched a figure on a bike emerging through the mist, revealing a woman dressed in a dark grey uniform with a red cross stitched on to her jacket.

'I hope you don't mind the intrusion so early in the morning,' she said, her voice faltering as she caught her breath. She adjusted her bike onto its stand. She looked anxiously about her, checking that there was no one eavesdropping on their conversation. 'I have a favour to ask. It's rather important. I'm from the Red Cross,' she went on in a whisper.

'You'd better come in,' said Frans, hoping against all hope that she had come with news from the camp.

The kitchen was filled with the warm smell of porridge bubbling away on the stove. Mama was leaning over the large pot and stirring it with her long wooden spoon. Pa was seated at the table, poring over a ledger.

'Mama, Pa, we have a visitor.' Frans pulled back a chair for the woman to sit on, but she remained standing.

'Thank you, but I can't stay long,' she said.

Mama put down her spoon. 'I'm sorry, do we know you?'

'I should have introduced myself,' said the woman. 'I'm Ineke de Vries, from the Red Cross. I've been volunteering at the detention camp at Leusderheide. She looked flustered. 'I wouldn't normally ask,' she went on, 'but we've had a huge influx of inmates following the big raid over in Hilversum. Did you hear about it?'

Frans and his mother exchanged glances and shook their heads. Reports of raids came through almost daily, but this one must have been serious for someone to have come all this way.

'It was terrible. Thousands of men were arrested and they've been sending them to all the camps, including ours, until the Germans decide what to do with them and where to send them next. The Red Cross are providing the basics, but there's only so much we can do. I was wondering… would you be prepared to give up one of your cows?'

'One of our cows?' said Pa incredulously.

The woman flushed and examined her hands. 'One cow can feed several hundred people. I can understand if it's not possible.'

'We can spare one, can't we?' said Frans to his father with a pleading look. 'Didn't we always say we must do everything we can to help?' It wasn't the first time the subject of donating one of their precious animals had come up. Pa had argued that if they gave a cow away, word would reach the Germans, who would be at the door demanding he hand over the food he'd worked so hard to produce. And it was already becoming such a struggle to make ends meet. But these were desperate times, thought Frans. They couldn't just look the other way.

'A cow?' Pa repeated, and seemed to be mulling over the possibility. 'It will need to be slaughtered and butchered. I no longer have the manpower to do that on the farm.'

The woman's face brightened. 'We've already thought of that. I have six men who are willing to undertake the task. They're not butchers, but they are prepared to do the job. Would that be acceptable?'

'Of course we will help. Send over the men and we'll get the job done,' Pa said.

*

As dawn was breaking the following morning, Frans went into the shed to milk the cows. The six men had arrived late yesterday afternoon with a uniformed guard. Frans had led them round the back and worked alongside them as the prison guard had stood by, disinterested, smoking cigarette after cigarette while they got on with the job. The men had been so happy just to be out in the fresh air. Even Frans had been distracted from his incessant thinking about Saskia.

And now Ineke de Vries was back, wheeling her bike into the yard.

'Is everything all right?' said Frans, as he came out of the cowshed.

'I'm so sorry. I had to come at once,' she said, clearly agitated. 'The detention camp was evacuated last night and the men have all gone, most deported to labour camps in Germany.'

'Including the men who came yesterday?' said Frans incredulously.

'No. Some were transferred to the main camp, even though there's no space. The authorities must have been planning to close the detention centre for ages and didn't tell us a thing.' She took in a deep breath. 'When I heard the news, I came over straight away to apologise for wasting your time,' she went on, wringing her hands as she spoke. 'And for needlessly sacrificing your cow. The meat has already been taken to the staff kitchens. No doubt to be used in a feast to fatten up the officers. What do they care about all those men forced to go without?' She appeared close to tears, but quickly apologised. 'It's not my place to speak like that, but sometimes it all gets a bit much.' Her face crumpled and she quickly wiped a handkerchief across her eyes before regaining her composure.

'Come inside and sit down,' said Frans, uneasy at what this turn of events might mean. He was already on edge as he waited for Theo's arrival and any news he might have about Saskia.

Ineke smiled weakly and followed him inside. Mama was at the stove and brought over the pot of coffee and poured a cup for Ineke and Pa. Frans took a seat, declining the offer of a cup.

'It's *ersatz*,' Mama said apologetically, 'but at least it's hot.'

'Thank you for your kindness. I haven't stopped for a break in weeks.' With a trembling hand, Ineke lifted the cup to her lips. After swallowing some of the coffee, she said, 'This war… I joined believing it would be for just a few weeks. But however hard we try, it's never enough as long as those brutes are in charge.'

Frans's father replied in a quiet but firm voice. 'The war isn't going well for them. The Allies are pushing back all over the country. The *moffen* can't hold out for ever.'

'That may be so, but until that happens it seems they're bent on revenge. They're becoming angrier and more brutal in their arrests, and dumping people in camps before shooting them. It's what the Red Cross are seeing on a daily basis when we go into the camps. I'm afraid it's not looking good for anyone who's locked up.' She drained her cup and got up to go. 'I'm sorry to bring you bad news, but it's best we all know.'

Frans needed to know more. He got to his feet when she did, and accompanied her outside. 'What will you do now the detention camp has closed?'

'Red Cross volunteers are being transferred to Kamp Amersfoort. We'll provide reinforcements – they need all the help they can get. We'll keep providing it as long as we can,' she said with a sigh.

She released her bike stand with a kick and turned to go.

'Wait a minute. You said volunteers. I have friends locked up in the camp. Is there anything I can do to help?'

She scrutinised Frans for a moment. 'We always need van drivers to bring in supplies. Can you drive?'

'I can drive a tractor. It can't be that different, can it?'

'Anything's possible,' she said, smiling for the first time since she'd arrived.

He watched her cycle away, pondering on whether driving into the camp under the protection of the Red Cross would give him immunity and gain him access to the women's camp. His heart beat faster as he turned over the possibilities that would bring him one step closer to saving Saskia. He didn't know it then, but it was the imminent arrival of Theo that would provide the answer.

Chapter Fifty-One

The earlier rain had moved away, leaving a clear night. Frans glanced up at the moon, still shrouded in a ghostly haze, as he set off across the rutted field, keeping his body low and his gaze fixed on the thicket. Every so often, he flicked his torch on and off. The only discernible sound, apart from his breath, was the distant hoot of an owl slicing through the still night air.

From the safety of the thicket, Frans took stock of his surroundings, listening for any unusual sounds. Spring had come late after the long cold winter and the woodland was gradually coming to life. He started at the rustle of leaves and caught sight of a small dark shape – a nocturnal rodent – scuttling away. He took several deep breaths in preparation for what was to come. Looking quickly left and right, he stepped onto the almost pitch black avenue where the tall beech trees formed a dark canopy with their branches. But he wasn't perturbed by the thick darkness – he'd navigated the bumps and potholes so often with the horse and cart that he knew this avenue like the back of his hand.

From far off, he heard a church clock strike the hour. Counting eleven strokes, Frans knew he must get a move on. His mouth turned dry and he swallowed painfully. If everything went according to plan, Roel would be waiting with the key at the back gate. *And if he wasn't?* Frans refused even to countenance the idea.

He was just close enough to make out the outline of the high wire fence when several vehicles appeared up ahead, their headlights bobbing and dipping as they bumped along the road. Frans shrank behind a tree, thankful for its cover, as they came thundering past. They weren't German – he could see that much – but had gone before he was able to make out if they were American or Canadian. He sucked in a deep breath, wanting this to be a good omen.

Half crouching, he set off at a run along the path that skirted the perimeter fence. He was almost at the gate when a searchlight swooped across his path, missed him, and carried on lifting and dipping in what seemed to be large figures of eight. Frans fell to the ground and stayed very still, his heart pounding wildly. As minutes passed, the beam kept plunging tantalisingly close to where he lay, but failed to reach its target. *This isn't going to work*, Frans told himself despairingly, remembering how confident Theo had been when he'd outlined the plan.

As dramatically as it had appeared, the searchlight switched off. Frans took shallow breaths, not quite trusting that it wouldn't start up again. *I need to find Roel.* His mind raced as he pushed himself to his feet. Keeping his head dipped, he took tentative crouching steps towards where he knew the metal gate to be. The tiny crack of a twig stopped him in his tracks. A shadowy figure stepped forward, tall and in uniform. For a split second, Frans was convinced it was all over. Then he saw who it was.

'Roel!' Frans whispered hoarsely. 'You came,' he went on, almost sobbing with relief. He was unable to make out Roel's features, but he could tell from the way he answered that he was petrified about being caught.

'I thought you weren't coming… but we've no time to lose. I've got the key, but I have to get it back before anyone notices.'

'Meiss?' gasped Frans.

'No, not Meiss. All the same—' Roel broke off with a sharp exhale and went to unlock the steel padlock.

Frans watched, his insides in turmoil. This was it. There was no turning back now.

'I'll wait here to lock up after you and the girl have gone.' Roel hesitated, before going on, 'But understand I can't hang around if it looks like it's not going to work out.' He opened the gate very slowly to avoid any unnecessary noise.

'Thanks for doing this,' said Frans, not wanting to confront the possibility of failure. He slipped through the gate and heard it close softly behind him as he looked around him for any signs of danger. From across the fence dividing the prison yard from the SS compound he could hear the muffled sounds of a party in full swing. The words Theo had spoken to him the day before came into his head: *They'll be too tied up with drinking and singing for anyone to notice you. Keep low and you won't be seen. Then make a run for it.*

Frans's eyes kept darting around for any danger as he tried to remember Theo's other instructions. The sudden crunch of footsteps had him pressing hard against a wall, then they faded away. He checked the watchtower but it was too dark to discern whether anyone was up there. If he could just get past and reach the buildings in the far corner. Not allowing himself to hesitate a moment longer, he burst forward and dashed along the fence till he was level with the officers' mess, where the party was being held. The sound of loud piano music erupted from within, accompanied by raucous male voices singing drunkenly along to the strains of a German song.

Frans dropped to his knees and crawled along the ground, trying to keep his eyes fixed on where the music was coming from. Then the door was flung open, letting forth a deafening roar of voices singing the unmistakeable words of the Nazi anthem: *'Der Nationalesozialismus/Wird Deutschlands Zukunft sein.'*

'National socialists… Germany's future…' Words Saskia had once read out to him in disgust from *Het Parool*.

Frans remained crouching as he observed several Germans come staggering out into the night air, their arms grasping the waists of young women dressed in low-cut dirndl dresses that left little to the imagination. The men were laughing raucously, and passing round bottles of something, schnapps probably, before swooping in to kiss the women, their giggles reverberating across the compound.

Taking advantage of the distraction, Frans stood up, and was preparing to run when a voice rang out from across the fence.

'Who's there? *Halt!*' It was one of the Germans from the group. He must have spotted Frans. He started to walk unsteadily towards the fence. Frans was unable to move.

'What's going on out here?' another deeper voice bellowed. 'Is there trouble?'

And then Frans saw Theo coming out of the door of the officers' mess, followed by a young girl in a dirndl dress. Behind him more people came spilling out into the night air.

'Peter!' shouted Theo at the German, who was having difficulty focusing as he tried to make out who had caught his attention.

'Come here!' Theo spoke loudly and urgently. 'I have someone with me I think you know. Her name's Lieke.'

The German turned immediately at the mention of the girl's name and staggered drunkenly over to Theo. Theo looked directly at Frans, frantically mouthing, 'Go!'

As Frans began to run for cover, the searchlight snapped back on, swivelling back and forth across the wide expanse of the compound. From behind him, he could hear the sound of the party revellers running and shouting, but it didn't sound as if they were enjoying themselves. And then the shooting began. Deafening cracks of gunfire seemed to come from all around him. A roar of pain as someone was hit, followed by another and another.

His instincts told him that Theo had been shot, but if he turned back now he would be running straight into the line of fire. He heaved in great lungfuls of air; his chest hurt so badly, but he didn't stop. Somehow he managed to dodge the bright beam and the bullets and made it over to the kitchen unit, which stood in total darkness. He cowered out of sight by a large metal bin, and stared back fearfully at the pandemonium that had broken loose. Making out bodies lying motionless on the ground, he prayed that Theo was not among them.

But he knew he didn't have much time before they found him, and if Roel got wind of what was happening, he wouldn't hang around either.

Go inside the hospital block to the doctor's office. She will be waiting for you.

When Theo had explained how he had arranged this part of the plan, Frans had been dubious it would work. Theo had arranged with Truus that she would visit the women's camp, pretend to find that Saskia was ill, and insist she needed urgent medical attention, before personally escorting her to the hospital block and to safety.

Frans pushed open the door and crept along the empty corridor. He was just moments away from being reunited with Saskia. But as he approached the door, he hesitated, afraid at how he would find her. After everything she'd been subjected to, would she be OK? *Please let her be there...*

He reached the door Theo had indicated and opened it a crack. The room was in darkness and all his hopes came crashing down. *She hadn't made it.*

But then he heard a small sound like a child's cry, a whimper from one corner, and all at once Saskia was in his arms, crying against his face. He knew it was her from the feel and smell of her, but when he clasped her head to·him he took in a sharp breath. Her shaven head, shorn of her beautiful hair. And then, in the half light, he saw it. It was unmistakeable. A yellow star was stitched to her prison dress. *What had they done to her?*

'There's no time to lose. We must go now,' he whispered urgently.

There was that cry again, from the corner. There was someone else in the room with them.

He heard Saskia take a breath and speak in a soft pleading voice. 'Lily and her child. Please, they have to come too. They've been through so much.'

There was no time to reflect on the danger this would pose to them all. Of course they must come. Frans explained how they would escape and that they needed to keep close together, though he was concerned for the woman and her child. She was so thin, she hardly seemed capable of standing, let alone running with a child in her arms.

'Let me carry him. What's your name, little one?' he said, crouching down.

The child gazed at him with large frightened eyes.

'Robbie, now be a good boy. The nice man is going to help us. I'll be right there with you,' said Lily in a shaky voice.

When Frans lifted the boy up in his arms, he was relieved at how light the boy felt, as they would need to move as fast as possible to get to safety.

They left the building without being seen and hurriedly followed it round to the back and well away from the centre of the camp, where chaos was still reigning. Saskia supported Lily, who was very weak, but carried on with grim determination. At one point, a searchlight swooped close by and Frans ordered everyone to their knees. With Robbie clinging onto his back, the three of them crawled forward. When they finally reached the gate, Frans realised to his horror that Roel wasn't there.

'Here, can you take Robbie?' he said to Lily, who had collapsed exhausted on the ground. 'I'll be back in a moment.'

'Frans, no, don't leave us!' cried Saskia, clinging onto his arm.

He stooped briefly to kiss her face, which was wet with tears. 'I have to find Roel. He has the key.' After all they'd been through, it seemed like a betrayal leaving them, but he had no choice.

He hurried along the fence, peering through to the other side for any sign of Roel, hoping fervently he'd only recently left his post.

'Roel,' he called out in a fierce whisper, as loudly as he dared.

At the third call, Roel swung round. He was about to turn onto the avenue that led back to the main entrance.

'You left without us,' said Frans in a sudden burst of anger, but also immense relief to have found him.

'I told you I wouldn't wait, and when I heard all that gunfire I had to go. What's going on?' said Roel, clearly in a heightened state of nerves.

'Never mind that now. Can you please let us out?'

Frans's relief at escaping the camp was rapidly replaced with a new fear that he would be unable to bring them all to safety. They encountered no one as they emerged from the path onto the avenue, keeping close to the edge and under the trees. But Lily and Saskia were rapidly losing the will to carry on. They clutched onto one another, taking faltering steps, and frequently stopped for breath, making progress well-nigh impossible. Frans wished he'd had the foresight to bring along something to eat; he hadn't realised just how weak the women were, both from lack of food and from living in constant fear for their lives.

'It's not far now. Just a bit further, then we can take a proper rest,' Frans kept repeating encouragingly, while holding onto a whimpering Robbie, who kept reaching out to his mother for comfort.

At one point, Lily slumped to her knees and lay down on the hard ground, taking shallow breaths.

'What are we to do?' Saskia said imploringly to Frans, before dropping down to comfort her friend.

'We'll stop and wait here a while,' said Frans, tilting his head to listen for danger. It was quiet now, the only sound the rustling of leaves high up in the trees above them.

He laid Robbie beside his mother, who instinctively pulled him in close. Frans sat beside Saskia and did the same. Within seconds, he felt her slump against him as she fell asleep.

He had no idea how long he'd been dozing when a noise brought him to his senses. Carefully, he laid Saskia down, and climbed out of the undergrowth to investigate.

Two small pricks of light were visible far off down the long straight avenue, accompanied by the low rumble of a vehicle.

Later, when Frans thought back on the events of that night, he wasn't sure what had made him act so impetuously. Had it been fear that he would never manage to escort the group safely in their current state? Or that they would be discovered so soon after escaping the camp?

Frans hurried to the side of the road, waving frantically. For what seemed like the longest, most terrifying moment, he thought the vehicle wasn't going to stop as it came closer and closer. But it pulled up just feet from where he stood. Relief flooded through him when he saw the distinctive cross painted above the windshield.

'What's going on? Are you hurt?' The driver, a woman in uniform, looked visibly shaken as she leaned out of the window while simultaneously engaging the handbrake.

'No, no one is hurt,' said Frans, frantically looking over his shoulder to see if the noise of the vehicle had woken the three fugitives. 'There are two women and a child over there, and they're very weak. I've hidden them as best I can, but they need help,' he pleaded.

The woman turned to speak to her passenger. Both women jumped down with their black bags, and Frans took them over to where Saskia was now sitting, wide-eyed, with her hands clasped round her knees. Lily stirred, and, on opening her eyes, grasped her son to her in a swift protective movement. One of the Red Cross women fell to her knees and spoke soothingly in a quiet voice.

'They've come from the camp, haven't they?' said the other one, looking to Frans for confirmation. 'And you got them out?'

Frans gave her a weary nod.

She shook her head, but she was smiling. 'What a brave thing to do. That must have been quite something,' she said, taking a long look at him.

But Frans was distracted. He was stealing a glance at Saskia, the girl he loved. He couldn't quite believe he'd found her. Yet here she was, and, true to her character, she hadn't thought of herself when she'd put herself in danger one last time so she could save the lives of others. It was Saskia who was really deserving of praise.

'We'll take over now,' said the woman, touching his arm. 'We'll give them medical care and find a safe place until they recover.'

'What will happen to them then?' said Frans in a tremulous voice.

'By then, it should be safe for them to return home.' She glanced over at Saskia, who was staring at Frans. 'She's special to you, isn't she?'

Frans nodded. 'I'm scared of losing her again.'

'Trust us. We'll look after her. It's what we do.'

She went off to attend to Lily and Robbie and Frans went to sit beside Saskia.

'Must I go too?' she said, and Frans realised she had been listening to the conversation.

He hugged her frail body tight. 'I don't want to leave you, but it's best you go with them. They'll take care of you till it's safe for us to be together.'

Frans watched as Lily, Robbie and Saskia were helped into the truck, made comfortable with blankets and given water to drink. With a small wave, he stood aside as the driver started up the engine and pulled away. Frans walked into the middle of the road and watched till it was out of sight.

Chapter Fifty-Two

Theo

'What's going on? I've never seen so many Red Cross trucks,' said Michiel, the guard in charge of the unit returning from the Koopmans' farm. He held up his hand to halt the group and everyone stared at the spectacle.

'That's not Red Cross,' said Theo, standing aside for a convoy of unmarked lorries belching out black smoke.

With a deafening squeal of brakes, the lorries stopped short of the front entrance and a swarm of uniformed men jumped out and opened up the backs of the vehicles, before heading briskly into the camp. The group watched transfixed as, moments later, a phalanx of prisoners appeared, accompanied by dozens of SSers, among them Oberle and Meiss, the vile guard from the front gate who terrorised everyone. But now they weren't the ones giving the orders. The prisoners pressed close together in a terrified huddle as the men from the trucks barked out orders for them to get into the back. One by one they clambered in, but obviously not fast enough. They were pushed and pummelled until they were all inside. The last ones to join them were Oberle, grim-faced, and Meiss, who looked about ready to explode in anger. The doors banged shut and the lorries rolled away.

Horrified, Theo stared at the departing vehicles, trying to make sense of what he had just seen. He had noticed that many of the prisoners wore yellow stars, which could surely mean only one thing: they were being taken to another Nazi camp to face certain death.

But why Oberle and Meiss? With Kamp Amersfoort's two most senior men gone, surely that meant that the SS were no longer in charge?

Theo had no time to ponder on the significance of this turn in events; a car came driving past with Red Cross flags pasted to the sides and back. Theo glimpsed the driver, a determined-looking woman dressed in a red uniform. He stayed very still, sensing something momentous was about to happen. Without stopping, the car swung through the open gates.

Truus would know what was going on, thought Theo, as he hurried along behind a convoy of Red Cross trucks rumbling across the compound towards the administration block. They had become a common sight in the camp over the past week and Truus and her team of volunteers had worked tirelessly, receiving and sorting hundreds of boxes and crates crammed with food, medicines and other essentials. It was a huge task that relied on efficient systems to ensure that the right items reached the prisoners in order of need.

Theo found Truus standing at the window of her office, wringing her hands. His heart gave a lurch when she swung round and he realised she was crying.

'What's happened?' He rushed over and grabbed her hands, squeezing them tight.

'I can't believe it's over,' she said in between sobs. 'The commandant, his cronies, they've all gone. I saw them leave with my own eyes.'

'I did too. But did you see all those prisoners with them? Where are they being taken?'

'I can only hope to safety,' said Truus, mopping her eyes. 'It's the first time I've seen the Canadians take such decisive action. You know what that means, don't you?'

Theo couldn't bring himself to utter the words. He wanted to hear them from Truus, whom he had grown to trust and rely on as he witnessed first-hand the solace and comfort she selflessly provided to others. But Truus was staring out of the window at the prison yard, which was filling up. Little by little, the din of raised voices increased like nothing Theo had ever heard in this godforsaken place. Truus wiped her eyes again and said, 'There's going to be an announcement. We must hear this.'

Theo's scalp prickled with anticipation as she grabbed hold of his hand and pulled him out of the office, along the corridor and into the yard. He felt conspicuous in his German uniform alongside a member of the Red Cross, but Truus clearly had no such qualms and carried on walking, holding him firmly by the hand.

The prison compound was now completely full. Truus urged Theo to stay close to her as she marched to the front, where dozens of other Red Cross volunteers were waiting.

There was an audible hush as the driver of the car, a short middle-aged woman dressed in a smart red fitted jacket and skirt and charcoal grey cap bearing an enamel Red Cross insignia, stepped onto a low wooden chair. She paused to gaze at the assembled throng, who looked up at her expectantly.

Her clear firm voice rose up into the air. Announcing herself as Loes van Overeem, she told them she was the new leader of the camp. Theo felt his chest tighten as he listened to the words he had thought he would never hear. Every one of the prisoners was now free. From that day, the Dutch Red Cross would be in charge of the camp. A cheer erupted from a few brave souls, then more and more joined in, until van Overeem lifted her hands up for quiet. Now wasn't the time for celebration, she warned, for the country was still under occupation. Things would improve but they must remain patient.

A murmur rippled through the crowd as they tried to absorb the weight of her words. Their new leader looked to her left and nodded. A voice rang out, daring to sing the first line of the 'Wilhelmus', which had been banned by the Germans during their five years of occupation. The first ones joined in, singing in wavering voices, then more, until everyone was singing at the tops of their voices, many with tears streaming down their faces. Then, as if this wasn't enough, a frayed Netherlands flag was slowly hoisted up a pole someone must have hastily erected. As it reached the top, a gust lifted the red, white and blue horizontal stripes and the flag flapped strongly in the breeze. It was a sight that no Dutch person had witnessed in five whole years.

As the last words of the Dutch anthem died away, Loes van Overeem asked everyone to stand for a minute's silence in memory of the many who had lost their lives during the long years of occupation. Fighting back his own tears of joy and grief, Theo blinked as he viewed the multitude, many barefoot and wearing filthy tattered clothes that hung off their frail bodies. Most looked broken, but a few wore grim expressions of determination. They were all survivors, the ones who would never give in. He thought of Lily and Saskia, two brave young women caught up in the horror, but who had made it thanks to Truus's courage, and the unflinching resolve and bravery of his dear friend Frans. Not least, he dared to picture a proper reunion with Annelies after their few snatched precious moments together in the secrecy of the farmhouse, regretting how Annelies had sacrificed so much on his behalf, never knowing if he would survive.

By his side, Truus must have sensed his emotion; she gently squeezed his hand. 'Come with me,' she whispered, and they slipped back to the other side of the fence.

Truus shut the door of the office and looked at Theo with concern. He slumped onto a chair, unable to control his shaking. His euphoria at witnessing the end of the brutality had been short-lived. Just like all the other prisoners, he knew he was not free to leave.

'I can't keep up this pretence any longer. What am I to do?' he said desperately. 'In this uniform, I'm one of them. You see that, don't you? Berg gave me no choice but to work for him. Now the whole lot of them have gone, I have to get out.'

Truus laid a reassuring hand on his. 'You've nothing to fear. There are only a handful of Dutch SSers left. If there is a prisoner number against your name you are going home. But I need your help...'

She told Theo her plan was to move prisoners out of the camp to safe houses in nearby Amersfoort and further afield. Those too sick to leave would be looked after by the Red Cross in the hospital block. The prisoners would need clothes, health certificates and ID, which Truus would organise. She wanted Theo to be in charge of distributing them. By the time she had finished, Theo was nodding in agreement, with a renewed vigour. And as he left her in her office he felt a sense of power that he hadn't in a long time.

'Theo, where are you going?'

The familiar voice rang out across the yard and stopped him in his tracks.

Peter approached, looking decidedly dishevelled. His uniform jacket was crumpled and the edge of his collar had a dark stain that looked suspiciously like sweat. Even the buttons had lost their usual gleam. For a split second, Theo felt pity, but quickly dismissed the thought, remembering it had been Peter's choice to join the Dutch SS.

'I'm walking over to Block IV,' Theo said, moving off. 'Would you care to join me?'

Peter visibly shrank back. 'Whatever for? It's full of people with diseases. You can't seriously want to go in there.'

Theo shrugged. 'It doesn't bother me. I've been helping out ever since the Red Cross took over.'

'Well, good luck to you but you won't catch me mixing with sick people.' Peter spoke fearfully, then all at once the expression on his face changed. He took a deep breath. It seemed as if he was on the verge of a confession. But Theo didn't want to hear it and carried on walking. Peter hurried to catch him up. 'I want you to know, all that stuff about allegiance to the Fatherland, I didn't really believe in it.' The words tumbled out in a hurry. 'I had no choice – really

I didn't. It was either sign up or go and work in one of their bomb factories. I only got the job here because of Paul Westerveld. He told my father Berg was looking for Dutch recruits and made it sound so attractive, the uniform, the job prospects… Now I know I made a mistake and when I get out, I'm going to America where my uncle lives. To start a new life and put all this behind me.' He stopped to catch his breath. Reluctantly, Theo stopped too.

'You're different. I wish I could've been more like you.' Peter stared at Theo but didn't elaborate. 'I've always liked you,' he went on. 'And that party was a bit of fun, wasn't it? That Lieke, she's quite something.' Already forgetting his contriteness, he laughed unpleasantly and rubbed his hands together.

Theo wanted to walk away. He couldn't meet Peter's eye. He felt total disbelief. Did the events of that fateful night, descending into an affray that had left four innocent prisoners dead, mean nothing to him? His disbelief turned to disgust as he recalled how the SSer officers, including Peter, had all stood by and let it happen.

'We'll keep in touch, won't we?' Peter said, his voice now pleading. He tried to grab hold of Theo's sleeve, but Theo jerked it away.

'Stay in touch? I don't think so,' Theo said. 'You're not innocent in this.'

This time Theo did walk away – and didn't stop.

Chapter Fifty-Three

Frans

In the days following Saskia's escape and the liberation of Kamp Amersfoort, Frans was gripped by a renewed desire to aid the prisoners left behind. Ineke de Vries was only too pleased to have a driver for the Red Cross van to make the frequent trips to the camp that were needed, so she could get on with the pressing business of organising things so that essential food, medicines and clothing reached those most in need.

But as he got into the driver's seat for the first time, Frans's nerves almost got the better of him. He tried to familiarise himself with the gearstick and clutch, while Ineke busied herself with the checklist of things they needed to do once inside the camp.

Starting up slowly, Frans managed to control the clutch and move off carefully. He glanced in his mirror, unsure whether Pa's expression was concern for his driving or because he was back visiting the camp. Since the Red Cross had taken over, his father had remained distrustful, thinking that the situation could still backfire. Pa knew nothing about the details of his son's dramatic rescue of Saskia, Lily and Robbie, and Frans didn't want to give him another reason to worry. After returning home in the early hours of that morning to a slumbering household, Frans had crept up to bed without disturbing anyone. The news of what had occurred that night didn't reach the Koopmans till a few days later, by which time Frans thought it was safe to keep quiet.

It had been months since Frans last travelled along the empty road with the horse and cart, and as he turned onto the avenue he was surprised at how busy it was. Army vehicles drove nose to tail and there were streams of official-looking cars and lorries carrying soldiers and equipment, many Red Cross vans, all heading to and from the camp.

'Follow the one in front and straight through the gates,' said Ineke, leaning forward in her seat.

'Won't there be any checks?' Frans nervously eyed the controls, wondering if he'd be able to change into a lower gear.

Ineke had her eyes glued to the road and didn't answer until they reached the edge of the camp and the high perimeter fence. She told him to indicate right. Gritting his teeth, Frans shifted the gear with a loud grating noise, but at least it didn't stall. A Red Cross official stood at ease by the open gates, waving vehicles through with a smile. No officious guards, unpleasant interrogations or inspections. Frans couldn't believe how much had changed.

He hardly recognised the inside of the camp. Prisoners were strolling freely in groups of two or three, something that would never have been allowed under the previous regime. There were also dozens of women in uniform, hurrying along with piles of bedding, clothing and boxes of food and medicines between the administration area and the rest of the camp. It was the absence of fear that struck Frans the most.

'Take us over to the hospital building. Over there,' said Ineke, pointing, though Frans didn't need to be shown. He took it slowly past the group of men peeling potatoes, noticing that now there were also carrots, turnips and parsnips piled up in the middle of the work bench. One or two looked up from their work and waved. Frans waved back.

'Vegetables. Good nutritious food at long last. That'll be our next delivery,' said Ineke. 'Carry on and park round the back.'

They spent the next hour unpacking boxes from the back of the van and taking them into Herr Doktor's office, now a storeroom for medical supplies. They were finishing up when the doctor himself came past and popped his head in. He blinked myopically through his glasses before recognising Frans. When he did, his face became rounder as he broke into a grin. 'I might have guessed I'd find you in here doing your bit. When you've finished, can you sort through the letters? I would do it, but I'm needed back on the wards getting patients well enough so they can leave.'

'Of course I will. That is, if I'm allowed,' said Frans, glancing at Ineke for approval.

'Go on,' she said. 'Letters home should always take priority.'

The following day, they began the process of transferring women, children and babies out of the camp to safe houses. It was a delicate operation as many were extremely frail after months of starvation and deprivation. Ineke provided piles of blankets and pillows to make their journey in the back of the van more comfortable.

Frans drove to the women's section, where Theo was waiting with the documentation for the women's release. He jumped down from the driver's seat and they fell into an embrace. It was the first time they'd met since Theo had been stationed back at the camp.

'Any news from Annelies?' said Frans.

Theo broke into a smile. 'She's helping at the reception centre, feeding and looking after the babies and young children until their mothers are strong enough to move to safe houses. But what about Saskia? How is she coping?'

'Still shocked by what happened, but she's safe. They found her a place to stay with an elderly couple in a remote village in Friesland. It's a long way away, but her parents have agreed for her to remain there till it's completely safe for her to return home. I haven't heard any more from Lily and Robbie, but the Red Cross have assured me they're also in safe hands.'

Theo sighed. 'I owe you a huge thanks for helping them escape too.'

'What do you mean? It was Saskia who wanted to help them, wasn't it?'

'I knew about Lily. I once tried to pass food through the fence, before she disappeared. Truus mentioned her name to me after one of her mercy visits to the women's camp, and told me Lily often sat next to Saskia. When we worked out the plan for Saskia's escape, I simply couldn't allow her and her child to be left behind.'

'I'm glad you did. I would have done the same,' said Frans, touching Theo's arm. 'I'm also glad you're still here. I was so sure you'd been hit in the gunfire.'

Theo briefly closed his eyes. 'As soon as it broke out, I ran for cover and hid. I'm not proud of standing by and watching four fellow prisoners gunned down.'

Frans shook his head sadly. 'No, but if it hadn't been for you, three others wouldn't have escaped.'

Frans lost count of the number of trips they made that day and the next, though Ineke was excellent at keeping track. She checked everyone on her list against Theo's, ensuring that no one could leave without their rightful identification papers and a signed certificate giving them a clean bill of health.

The women showed little enthusiasm at their impending release. It was hot and airless in the back of the van, even with the side windows open. Tempers were frayed as babies whined and toddlers bickered. One mother was so distressed that she spent the whole journey sobbing, only to break down again on discovering that her husband wouldn't be at the reception centre to meet her.

A week later, Frans made his last trip into the camp. The nerves he'd felt the first time, all those months ago, were back, intensified by the sharp memory of that long-ago conversation with Theo by the bins that had precipitated the devastating chain of events that neither could have predicted. Together, they had first helped a prisoner flee the camp and certain death. As far as he knew, Jozef hadn't been recaptured, and it cheered him to hope that he was back home in Poland, safe from the murderous intent of the Nazis due to Theo's swift actions. Frans also remembered Theo's own unspoken request for help to get him out of the camp. But that was before Theo had endured more punishment in the rose garden, incarceration in the cells and enforced labour.

He switched the engine off and looked at Ineke.

'Don't forget these,' she said, passing him a bundle of clothes that she had been holding in her lap. 'I'll wait here.' She spoke with a kind smile.

He walked towards the door of Block IV and pushed it open. Theo was at the end of the long corridor, in conversation with a woman in nurse's uniform. She looked up as Frans approached. 'Your friend is here,' she said, then, turning to Frans, 'Truus van Houten. And you must be Frans. Theo's been telling me all about your smuggling operation together. How incredibly courageous. I'm sure it will have helped a lot of prisoners through dark times.'

'I hope so,' said Frans with an embarrassed shrug. 'It was the least we could do. I'm sure you understand that.'

Frans handed over the clothes to Theo. 'Thought you'd prefer to wear these.'

'Well, I suppose this is goodbye,' said Theo to Truus. 'You'll also be leaving soon, I hope.'

'We have a few more things to sort out here, before handing over to the Canadians. I hope to go home and see my family. It's been a long six months.'

The three of them faced one another awkwardly. Theo was the first to speak.

'Damn it, I don't know why this should be so hard. It's not as if I want to stay. All I wanted from the first day was to get out,' he said with a shaky laugh. 'You two... not many have put themselves through what you have to give people in such dire need a second chance.' He spoke haltingly and, when he'd finished, embraced Truus in a clumsy hug.

'You'll have to wait,' he said to Frans. 'I need to get out of this wretched uniform.'

Five minutes later he appeared at the front entrance in a pair of dark grey trousers, blue shirt and jacket. He was holding a buff envelope containing his release documents.

Frans and Ineke were waiting by the van and Theo climbed up so he could sit between them.

'Ready?' said Frans when they were all in place.

He started the engine, this time without a hitch, executed a perfect turn and drove out of the front gates of Amersfoort's concentration camp for the very last time.

In the weeks after Saskia's return home, Frans often rode over on his ancient bike, which he'd finally managed to repair. They would sit together on the bench under the apple tree, Saskia huddled under a thick blanket as she was always cold. At first, she said little about what had happened to her following her arrest, but as she gained in strength, Frans gently probed till she was able to talk about the series of events that led to her ending up in Kamp Amersfoort.

'I should have known I was being followed, but I was so distraught when that German stole my bike, that I ran all the way to Mevrouw Jansen's house without thinking. I just wanted to get away. I was so relieved to shut the door behind me. And then...' Saskia stopped speaking as her emotions got the better of her. Frans waited patiently for her to continue.

'I don't remember anything till I woke to hear a man in uniform screaming at me to move. I was so scared that I barely registered where I was. The next thing I knew I was being bundled into a van and driven to the camp. I was in such a state of shock, when the woman guard handed over my uniform I didn't notice it had

a star on it. I had to put it on. They took my other clothes away.'
Tears leaked from Saskia's eyes as she tried to compose herself. 'I
couldn't prove I wasn't Jewish as they'd taken everything from me,
and I learned quickly there was no point arguing. Poor Lily ended
up in the rose garden after she begged for food for her Robbie – and
all because she was Jewish.'

Frans didn't want to distress her any more, so distracted her
by reading letters he'd received from prisoners after their release.
Saskia listened to their stories with a gentle smile on her face. Lars
had returned to Eindhoven, where he now worked at the Philips
factory as an engineer. His wife was expecting their second child
and they were hoping for a boy. And Joost, the first prisoner to
meet his girlfriend on the farm, told Frans that he and Toesje were
getting married and moving to Elburg to be near her mother and
sister. All wanted to express their gratitude for everything Frans
and his family had done to provide a lifeline to the outside world
during their darkest times.

Most of all, Saskia enjoyed Theo's letters. After the postmaster
in the village where he now lived had retired, Theo had taken the
position, describing it as 'the perfect job'; it enabled him to carry
on the work he'd started in the camp.

One day, a letter came from Theo with the news that Berg,
Oberle and Stengel had all been prosecuted and sentenced to life
imprisonment for their participation in the SS and plans to subvert
the peace. Frans had been sure this would stir Saskia from her dark
thoughts, but she said wearily, 'What's the point in going over it
all again? It's in the past. I want to forget about it now.'

But Frans was unable to forget the war. His family had survived
relatively unscathed, and were now doing all they could to help
the local community get back on its feet. The horse and cart,
driven by Frans with Cas by his side, became a familiar sight
in the surrounding villages, delivering milk, eggs, butter, bread,
meat and vegetables to those most in need. The camp was now

an accommodation centre for Dutch soldiers, but every time he entered the gates, Frans still felt himself tense up. Memories like these would never fade.

One afternoon, Frans arrived at Saskia's to find Aart sitting in his place under the apple tree. Saskia stretched out her hand to him. 'Look who's here. Isn't it wonderful?'

'Well, this is a surprise,' said Frans, pleased to see his friend, but also feeling guilty that he'd been unable to do anything for him during his long months in hiding. It had been six months since they'd last seen each other. He walked over and embraced Aart, shocked to see how thin and drawn he looked. 'How are you?'

'I'm better than when I first came home. I was grateful to have a safe place to hide, but my uncle's attic was so cramped that after five months I could barely walk.' Aart's voice tailed off as he broke into a coughing fit. When he'd regained his composure, he said, 'What about you, Frans? It's been such a long time.'

'It has,' said Frans, with a sudden surge of nostalgia for the carefree days they all used to spend together. 'I'm working at the farm. Pa has given me more responsibility and wants me to take over when he retires. What do you think you'll do now?'

'Finish my studies. I hope to get into Leiden and study Law if they'll have me.' His smile was wistful, and Frans knew he would never fully understand everything his friend had endured.

Epilogue

Spring 1946

Across the street, the gold lettering above the door of the newly painted drapers' shop glinted in the afternoon sunshine. Frans watched as a customer came out of the shop carrying two boxes embossed with the words 'P. Dekker, High Quality Drapers', and greeted another who was on her way in. With a smile on his face, Frans crossed over so he could take a closer look at the window display. Two tailor's dummies were attired in dresses with cinched-in waists, next to a spread of fabrics artfully fanned out to show their quality and eye-catching patterns.

The bell tinkled as he pushed open the door. Saskia looked up and smiled at him from behind the counter. She rolled her eyes at him before going back to serve her customer, a woman in a smart crimson coat and matching hat.

'I can't make up my mind which one I should take. Do you think this would be too thick for a summer blouse?' the woman was saying as she fingered one of the materials laid out for her. Saskia advised her on which would be suitable and reached under the counter for the large wooden box containing buttons, neatly displayed by shape, size and colour. 'How lovely,' said the woman, coming in for a closer look. 'Can you help me choose which one works with this material?'

Saskia picked out several buttons and placed them down in a row. 'I think the turquoise works best as a contrast, but you may prefer the cornflower blue if you want it to blend in.'

Frans went over to the glass display cabinet and pretended to show an interest in the men's hats and shirts while discreetly admiring Saskia, confident and perfectly at ease in her work environment. Her short hairstyle suited her, he thought, though she'd told him she couldn't wait for it to grow out as she preferred her curls longer. Working in her father's shop did her the world of good and it made him happy to see her so settled after all she'd been through.

Bored with looking at the hats and shirts, Frans turned to listen to the conversation between Saskia and her customer.

'I remember when you were a little girl and your papa let you sit at the counter. Do you remember?' said the woman as Paul Dekker came over and joined his daughter.

'She was as good as gold as long as she had her button box to play with,' he said fondly as he rolled out a length of the woman's chosen fabric along the counter. He measured it with the tape measure that hung round his neck and proceeded to cut it in one swift motion with a large pair of scissors, before folding it into a neat square. 'Would you like six of the small turquoise buttons?' he asked.

The woman was still undecided and continued to examine the buttons while she kept up her conversation. 'I'm pleased you decided to open the shop again. There was nowhere else that sold any haberdashery goods. And we all missed you so much. It must have been a trying time for you and your family having to close for so long.' She waited for Mr Dekker to answer.

He calmly replaced the bolt of material back on its shelf. 'Thank you for your kind words, but as you can see, things are getting back to normal now, thanks in no small part to the efforts of my daughter. She has quite a talent. Did you see the window display?'

'Yes, and I was most taken with it. You have a natural flair.' The woman beamed, turning to Saskia.

'Thank you, though it was my mother who made the dresses. I had the idea of displaying the material to inspire customers to come up with their own ideas.' Saskia's cheeks had grown pink with the compliment. Frans's heart swelled with pride at how much she'd achieved since her father had invited her to manage the shop.

At last the woman was satisfied with her purchases, which she asked Mr Dekker to put on her account. She left with a cheery goodbye.

'She was one of the first through the door when we opened up again,' he said to Frans, as if he needed to explain the woman's manner. 'A gossip too, but I'm sure it's because of her that all my old customers have come back.'

'I hope I haven't made us late,' said Saskia, after they had left the shop and were hurrying back to the car parked in the square. They were on their way to visit Theo and Annelies, who lived half an hour's drive away.

In her lap, Saskia held a rag doll she'd made from scraps of left-over material and twists of wool for hair. It was a gift for the couple's new baby of two weeks. She was so excited; it would be the first time in months she had seen Annelies, although the two of them had kept in touch, Saskia telling Annelies about her new job and Annelies talking about her desire to keep working for a charity for war refugees after the baby was born.

'Do you think they'll like it?' she said, showing Frans her creation.

'They'll love it,' said Frans, starting the engine. He could never get enough of gazing into her soulful dark eyes and leaned over to give her a lingering kiss. 'I'm so pleased to have you back.'

'What do you mean? It's a whole year since I came home,' she said, looking puzzled.

'But today was the first time I've seen you look so radiant. What you've done in the shop is wonderful. And today, I saw the old you again. Now, the war is finally over.'

A Letter from Imogen

I want to say a huge thank you for choosing to read *The Girl Across the Wire Fence*. If you did enjoy it, and want to keep up to date with all my latest releases, just sign up at the following link. Your email address will never be shared and you can unsubscribe at any time.

www.bookouture.com/imogen-matthews

I have a lifelong love of Holland through my Dutch mother and the many cycling holidays my family and I spend in Nunspeet, a small town on the edge of the beautiful Veluwe woods.

My mother was a teenager when war broke out and survived near starvation during the well-documented Hunger Winter of 1944/45. It was only because of her determination to search for and dig up tulip bulbs from the frozen soil that she was able to put food on the table for herself and her parents. I grew up listening to her incredible stories of life as a young woman during five years of German occupation and I have no doubt that her experiences have deeply influenced my writing of Second World War novels.

I had never heard of the Nazi-run Kamp Amersfoort until 2018, when on one of my holidays in Holland I picked up a leaflet describing that it was one of the largest Dutch concentration camps during the Second World War. I had previously written about the settlement of Jews in the nearby Veluwe woods and was intrigued to discover more.

Today, there is little left to see of Kamp Amersfoort. A memorial centre and permanent exhibition stands on the original spot where 37,000 men, women and children were held prisoner by the Nazis between 1941 and 1945. All that remains is a forbidding watchtower at the entrance, a sombre reminder of the horrors that took place within.

At the end of my first visit, my guide (who spoke excellent English, as so many Dutch people do), recommended a book for me to read called *Bij de Beuk Linksaf* (At the Beech Tree, Turn Left) by José Huurdeman. Not only is it a gripping and astonishing story, but it is aimed at young readers, so I had a good chance of understanding it with my limited knowledge of Dutch. I was instantly gripped by the story of the farmer and his ten-year-old son, Jan, who drove their horse and cart into Kamp Amersfoort every day to collect potato peelings for their cattle. But the story was about much more – they began to smuggle letters tucked into Jan's knee-length socks in and out of the camp for the prisoners. And they went even further when they devised a plan to allow prisoners who were working on their farm to meet their wives and girlfriends in private inside the farmhouse, while Kamp Amersfoort guards were prowling in the fields just yards away.

What an incredibly brave and risky thing it must have been for them to do, and the fact they got away with it under the noses of the concentration camp guards was even more unbelievable.

I knew then that this was the story I wanted to tell, a story about ordinary people's courage and self sacrifice to help weak and infirm prisoners who were close to giving up hope of surviving at the hands of brutal Nazi guards.

In 2019, and a few months before the pandemic prevented any foreign travel, I visited Kamp Amersfoort again. I joined a guided tour in Dutch which gave me an even better understanding of what took place there. The guide, whose own father had suffered terribly in a Polish concentration camp, showed us the place of the infamous Rose Garden, where prisoners were punished and forced to stand in a barbed-wire cage for hours on end, the firing range which had been dug out by Jewish prisoners before many were executed there themselves, and the burial ground, also dug by prisoners who must have guessed their terrible fate. I came away, my head spinning, not just with all the intense detail I had gleaned, but because of the notes I had managed to scribble down in English as I attempted to simultaneously translate from the Dutch.

One of the most heartbreaking scenes I came to write was based on true events that happened right at the end of the war, when the Red Cross took control of the camp from the Nazis in April 1945. Their new leader, a formidable woman called Loes van Overeem, gave a speech, as she stood before thousands of assembled prisoners to inform them that the Red Cross had taken over and that they were safe. What was so heart-rending was that the Netherlands was still under German occupation, so they weren't at liberty to leave.

It was always my intention to include these true events in *The Girl Across the Wire Fence* to provide realism to what is essentially a fictional story. Many of the characters are based on real people that existed at the time and I have added others from my imagination.

I do hope you enjoyed reading *The Girl Across the Wire Fence* and if you did I would be very grateful if you could write a review. I'd love to hear what you think, and it makes such a difference helping new readers to discover one of my books for the first time.

It gives me great pleasure to hear from my readers – you can get in touch on my Facebook page, through Twitter, Goodreads or my website.

Many thanks,
Imogen

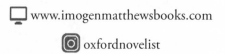

🖥 www.imogenmatthewsbooks.com

📷 oxfordnovelist

🐦 @ImogenMatthews3

📘 profile.php?id=100012815381780

Ⓖ 16870885.Imogen_Matthews

Acknowledgements

I'm so grateful to everyone who has helped me during the writing of my book: my husband Matthew Johnson, who listened patiently and successfully helped me unravel parts of the plot that were bothering me; my three writers groups: Headington Writers, The Summertown Literary and Banana Peel Pie Society, and Aynho Writers, who I'm hoping to meet up with in person rather than on Zoom very soon; my Dutch second cousin, Anita Poolman, who I never knew existed before an unbelievable and delightful discovery during lockdown.

I would like to extend a personal thanks to Anita:

Lieve Anita – thank you so much for your encouragement and for reading an early draft of my book to correct Dutch spellings and inject more authenticity from your (and of course my) family history.

I would also like to thank my editor at Bookouture, Jennifer Hunt, who has encouraged me with her excellent suggestions and great patience, to make my story the very best it can be.

Made in the USA
Columbia, SC
10 February 2022